Murder House

Phillip Strang

ALSO BY PHILLIP STRANG

MURDER IS A TRICKY BUSINESS

MURDER WITHOUT REASON

THE HABERMAN VIRUS

MALIKA'S REVENGE

HOSTAGE OF ISLAM

PRELUDE TO WAR

Copyright Page

Copyright © 2017 Phillip Strang

Cover Design by Phillip Strang

All rights reserved. No part of this book may be reproduced, stored in a retrieval system, or transmitted in any form or by any means (electronic, mechanical, photocopying, recording or otherwise) without the prior written permission of the publisher, except by a reviewer who may quote brief passages in a review to be printed by a newspaper, magazine, or journal.

All characters appearing in this work are fictitious. Any resemblance to actual events, locales, or persons, living or dead, is coincidental.

All Rights Reserved.

This work is registered with the UK Copyright Service
ISBN - 13: 978-1520950433
ISBN – 10: 1520950438

Dedication

For Elli and Tais who both had the perseverance to make me sit down and write.

Chapter 1

Number 54 Bellevue Street was a good address. At least, it was to Trevor and Sue Baxter. They had come down to London after a transfer from Trevor's company up north in Manchester. Trevor specialised in corporate taxation; his wife Sue, a qualified teacher, saw no problems in her finding another position in London.

They both knew it would not have been possible to purchase such a house in Manchester, but in London there was the salary and the company offer of a low-interest loan for five years while Trevor Baxter established himself. The house, three storeys, built during the reign of Queen Victoria, excited them enormously, even if it needed renovating. It had ornate ceilings, solid double brick construction, and a basement originally designed for coal which Trevor hoped to convert into a wine cellar. The burning of coal had been banned long ago, due to the pea-souper fogs that belching chimneys had caused in the city back in the fifties.

They saw it as a shame they could not use the open fireplaces in the house. At least they would be open to view once a local handyman had removed the cheap panelling that covered them.

'Always costly, home renovations,' Ted Hunter, the local handyman said. 'Everyone's the same; thinks it's easy, and it will come under budget. Mark my words, they never do.' In his fifties, Ted was as fit as any man could be after thirty-five years with the tools of his trade. He had done it all: bricklaying, painting, fitting new ceilings, patching up old ones.

'It's more than we budgeted for,' Trevor, the now more financially-encumbered mortgagor, said.

'I'm sorry, but that's how it is. You can get another quote, but they will hit you afterwards,' Ted said. He had seen it all before: enthusiastic homeowners embarking on the great challenge, assuming a couple of coats of paint, a little bit of tender love and care would transform a pig's ear into a silk purse.

Ted knew the costs would escalate once they attempted to deal with what could not be seen: dry rot, rising damp, even the foundations if the house had been built on swampy ground.

The first task in the house was to remove the encumbrance that covered the fireplace in the main room. Ted Hunter knew the house had been rented out in the past, each room converted into a depressing bedsit, with a toilet and a bathroom on the first floor, and money in a meter for hot water.

Sue Baxter had made a special effort to be present for the great unveiling of the centrepiece of the room, the fireplace. Ted had warned her that it would not be pleasant: twenty years of pigeons trapped inside the chimney as well as accumulated dust and decay. She could not be dissuaded and even wore a mask for the occasion. She was compiling a photographic history of the renovation, and she had a camera ready in her hand.

'Just ease it over to your side,' Ted said to Kyle Sanders, a thickset twenty-something of limited words and intelligence. A good worker, even if he was likely to get stroppy of a night time down the pub. He was known at the police station for putting a few smart-arses in hospital. Still, to Ted, he was trustworthy, always turned up to work on time: the ideal employee in his estimation.

'It's heavy,' Kyle said.

Jimmy Pickett stood to one side. A sullen man of forty-two, he had neither the love of work nor the strength of Kyle. Ted had only taken him on as a standby, and then only as a favour as he was married to his wife's sister. Jimmy's function, according to Sue Baxter, was to stand to one side and offer verbal encouragement liberally peppered with expletives. Not that Sue would have minded, but April, the eldest child, was upstairs after taking a day off from school, and she did not want her exposed to the foul language.

'It's coming free,' Kyle said. He was down on his knees with a lever inserted between the wall and the covering. Ted, standing up on the other side of the fireplace, was attempting a similar exercise. Both were blanketed with copious amounts of coal dust mixed with the occasional feather as they progressively freed the structure.

'Jimmy, secure the top, stop it falling over,' Ted shouted.

'I've got it,' Jimmy said. He had reluctantly been pressed into service and was coughing. Sue Baxter was unimpressed. She had spent too many years as a teacher not to know a faker when she saw one.

'It's an open fireplace,' Ted said. 'Looks to be in good condition.'

Excited, Sue pressed forward, camera in hand. Ted warned her to stand back. She could not be dissuaded.

'What's that at the bottom?' Sue asked.

'No idea,' Ted said. 'Wait till we get it free.'

Jimmy had relocated some distance away due to the coal dust exacerbating his asthma. Two minutes later, the old wooden structure was placed to one side, resting on the far wall.

April had come down to see what was happening, and Sue was taking photos. Ted had seen plenty of old fireplaces in his time, and this one, even though it was bigger than most, would need to be removed and renovated.

Down on his knees again, Kyle prodded at what appeared to be blankets in the bottom of the fireplace. There were some ropes wrapped around it.

Ted warned him to be careful on account of the dust. Jimmy had left the room. April and Sue were hovering close to Kyle.

Ted told them all to stand back. It did not look right to him. He slowly cut one of the ropes. A bone fell out.

'You'd better call the police,' he said to Sue.

Chapter 2

As the Senior Investigating Officer of the Murder Investigation Team, Isaac Cook could see that the chance of a few days off looked unlikely. There had been a couple of cases lately which had taxed his people, a well-crafted team of professionals. Everyone, not only Isaac, was looking for time off, or at least the chance to go home to the family at a reasonable hour, instead of close to midnight, as had been the case for weeks. They had just wrapped up the murder of a child, a crime that always depressed everyone in the office. It had proved hard to pinpoint the murderer until the elder brother, only eleven, admitted he was angry after the younger brother took his bike without asking. Isaac Cook knew the Youth Court would struggle with an appropriate sentence, as the child came from a good home with good parents.

The other murder, of a derelict down behind the railway station, was found to have been committed by four hooligans spaced out on crack cocaine.

'It's clearly murder,' Gordon Windsor said over the phone after a cursory inspection of the body wrapped in blankets. He and Isaac had worked together before, and if Windsor said it was murder, then it was. Isaac, as the senior officer in the department, knew it was time to bring the Murder Investigation Team back to full mobilisation, even though, after so many years, the death could be classified as a cold case.

'Your initial evaluation?' Isaac asked.

'The body's been here for thirty years, I'd say.'

'Did you say thirty years?'

'That's a guess at the present moment. We found some old newspapers under the body.' Gordon Windsor, the crime scene examiner, had been out to the scene within two hours of the body being discovered. The first person at the scene, a local detective inspector who had responded to a phone call from a distraught woman.

'What's the story?'

'Unusual. The owners are renovating the house. They removed an old wooden structure that had been built around the fireplace. That's when they found it.'

'Male or female?'

'Probably male, judging by the clothes.'

'Age?'

'Indeterminate. I'll hazard mid to late thirties.'

'Who's there at the present moment?'

'There's a uniform out the front of the house, plus a local detective inspector, Larry Hill. He says he knows you.'

'We've worked together,' Isaac replied.

'You'd better get down here before we remove the body.'

'Give me twenty minutes.'

***

'We only moved in six weeks ago, it's not what you expect to find,' Trevor Baxter, who had rushed home from work, said.

'Sorry about that, but now it's a murder investigation,' Isaac Cook said.

'Does that mean we'll have to move out?'

'For a few days.'

'I don't want to stay here,' Sue Baxter said. 'I never want to come back here again.'

'I can understand your sentiment,' Isaac Cook said. 'It's easier to deal with in time.'

'Are you sure it's murder?' Trevor Baxter asked.

'Wrapped up in a couple of blankets, tied with rope and thrust in a fireplace.'

'You're right. What else could it be?'

The husband was correct with his question, the DCI conceded. So far, there had been no cause of death, no weapon, no inspection of the body, other than of a leg bone which had fallen out when the tradesman had investigated the blankets in the fireplace. There were too many indicators to believe it could be anything but murder. Gordon Windsor would be working overtime to follow up on a definitive cause of death. If it was not murder, then the concealment of the body indicated foul play, and failing to report a death was still a crime.

The Baxter family checked into a hotel for the night, while a full investigating team went over the house with a fine-tooth comb. There was a lot of work to do before the house would be available for habitation again. The history of the house needed to be checked: who had lived there, who had owned it, and who may have had a motive for concealing a body. Bodies always give off an odour as the decaying process commences, so someone must have smelt something, or the house was empty, which seemed unlikely.

***

Forty years earlier, Bellevue Street, where the body had been found, had been no more than a seedy part of London, where the influx of immigrants from the Caribbean, Africa, and the Indian subcontinent had been deposited in slum dwellings. Isaac Cook's parents had lived in a ground floor room in a similar street when they first arrived in the country from Jamaica at that time. By the time Isaac had been born, their situation had improved, and they had secured a loan on a two-bedroom flat not far from Hyde Park. He remembered their conversations on how hard it had been on their arrival, with the aggressive landlords and their escalating rent demands. He was thankful that the protection of the tenant had improved dramatically since then, although he had had a difficult landlord before buying his flat in Willesden.

Isaac Cook had planned an early night, but that was clearly off the agenda now. He was hopeful that Jess would be sympathetic. They had met on a previous case, and she had moved in with him. He had been confident that the romance would last, but even now it was looking shaky. There had been a few arguments in the last couple of weeks, and every time, as he had expected, the name of Linda Harris had been brought up. 'You slept with her, and don't give me that nonsense that it was vital to the case. When does screwing form any part of a police investigation?'

He always knew it would cause a problem, even though they had not been an item then, merely a flirtation, but Jess never saw it as that.

***

Isaac summoned his team together. Detective Chief Superintendent Richard Goddard, their boss, attended as well. The addition of 'Chief' to his title had come about a few months previously, after a particularly trying case, where Isaac had met and bedded Linda Harris, and flirted with Jess O'Neill. Since that one night, Isaac had not heard from Linda except for a brief phone call, when she stated that she had not murdered anyone, but he was never sure as to the truth. Even though he wanted to settle down with Jess, he could see that the romance was heading to an inevitable conclusion.

Larry Hill was pleased when Isaac offered him the vacant detective inspector's position in his team. He would be transferred officially to Challis Street Police Station within the next week.

Farhan Ahmed, the previous detective inspector, had taken the opportunity of a transfer and a promotion up north. Isaac had wished him well, although the detective inspector's involvement with a former high-class escort, now a lawyer, was hampering further advancement opportunities.

Constable Wendy Gladstone was on board. He would see if she could be made up to sergeant, even though her abrasive nature had precluded this in the past, and exhaling cigarette smoke as she entered the office annoyed Isaac, and he had still not spoken to her about it. He knew that he should, but she had enough on her plate with a husband in a parlous state, even looked close to expiring due to a respiratory condition. Wendy did not speak about him much, only to say that dementia had set in, and he was too difficult for her to handle. Reluctantly, she had placed him in a nursing home, although she visited every day.

Bridget Halloran had been brought in closer to the team on Wendy's request. Previously the CCTV viewing officer, she had taken on extra responsibilities in collating all the documentation for the team. Wendy was pleased, as she was a good friend.

***

'DCI Cook, a summation please,' Detective Chief Superintendent Goddard asked, anxious to start the meeting. Isaac could do without his constant input, his need to be updated and to offer advice, but they went back a long time. Two people separated by age and rank, although each regarded the other as a friend, not just a work colleague. Richard Goddard had asked Isaac to call him Richard on social occasions, but it was too hard for him to acquiesce. It was either 'sir' or 'Detective Chief Superintendent'.

Larry Hill had arrived earlier, pleased that he was joining the team. He and Isaac had met on a previous case when the DI had been the investigating officer.

'This is the situation so far.' Isaac commenced his outline of the case. '54 Bellevue Street, Holland Park. Family of four, husband, wife, and two children, both under thirteen. They had recently moved in after the husband transferred down from Manchester. The house, judging by its condition, needs a lot of renovation. Would you agree, Larry?'

'A lot of work, a lot of money.'

Isaac continued. 'The house is over one hundred and thirty years old. It is a substantial three-storey construction that is showing the wear and tear of many years of neglect. No doubt one of the slum dwellings of the fifties and sixties, but the area is now gentrified and upmarket. However, it appears to have been rented out as single room bedsits during the nineties. After that, we believe that it has remained unoccupied up until the Baxters moved in, disputed property by all accounts. We'll need to investigate the history further.'

'Any name for the body?' Goddard asked.

'Not yet,' Larry Hill said.

'Gordon Windsor will let us know as soon as he can, but at this present time we are assuming the body to be male, aged in his thirties. No more at this time, as the body was wrapped in some blankets and tied with rope,' Isaac said.

'The cause of death?' Wendy Gladstone asked.

'We'll need to wait for confirmation.'

'It's not much to go on,' DCS Goddard said.

'Not much, sir. Bridget, can you check out the history of the house: who has lived there, who owned it? Wendy, follow up on any relevant names, go and visit.'

'Yes, sir,' they both answered.

'Larry, can you get back to the house, see how the investigating team is going? See what else they can find.'

'DCI, what about you?' Goddard asked.

'I'll stay here, put the team together, keep in contact with Gordon Windsor.'

***

Larry Hill quickly returned to the house. Trevor Baxter was there, upset that he was not allowed in until a thorough investigation was completed. The Baxters were not unreasonable people, just concerned that it was their house where the body had been found. Apparently, his wife was now talking about returning at some stage. Larry had to explain that it could be some weeks, possibly longer, before they would be given clear access. Trevor Baxter had been offered a serviced two-bedroom apartment by his company for a month, and they were moving in that day.

The crime scene investigation team did not have much to say, other than the house was in a reasonable if neglected state. Apart from the body, they did not expect to find much more of interest, and after thirty years, they were hardly likely to find any fingerprints or DNA. In fact, they assumed they would come up with nothing, other than where the wood that had concealed the body and the fireplace had come from, maybe some information on the screws used. They did not see themselves being on the premises for longer than a day.

Larry phoned Isaac with the news. It was not unexpected. With little to be achieved, he returned to Challis Street, passing by his old station to wish them well and to tidy his desk. Detective Chief Superintendent Goddard had pulled some strings, and the transfer to the Murder Investigation Team had been immediate.

Wendy and Bridget, glad to be working together, were looking into the history of the house. Bridget, a dab hand with a computer, quickly found out the salient facts regarding the house: built in 1872, and purchased by a wealthy businessman who had made his money with a few upmarket clothing stores. A local newspaper of the period attested to the fact. After that, a succession of owners: one who had committed suicide in the back bedroom in the twenties, as the economy went into a severe depression, another who had spent time in prison for living off the illegal earnings of prostitution. Even one who had run for Parliament, but failed to receive more than three hundred votes. The 1950s and 1960s showed a period as low-cost accommodation, housing immigrants flooding into the country. It was good their period of interest was later, as the records from that period were sketchy.

The key date: January 21, 1987, based on the newspaper found under the body; the assumption was that the body and the paper had been placed in the fireplace at the same time, but that was for Gordon Windsor to confirm. He had phoned Isaac five minutes earlier to say that identification should be possible. So far, he had not concluded his investigation, other than to confirm that the body was definitely male, Caucasian, and clothed. No papers had been found, but they had not checked all the pockets yet, as after so many years, with water ingression from the chimney, coupled with coal dust and pigeon feathers, every part of the body and the clothing was rotten and welded together. He indicated that it would be another twenty-four hours before an initial evaluation would be concluded, and then there would need to be a full autopsy.

Bridget, continuing her search with Wendy sitting close by, turned her attention to the relevant date. The records, easily obtained from the local council's database, showed ownership from the late 1980s up to the present time when the Baxters had bought the property. It also showed that the rates had been paid meticulously during that period, and the electricity had been connected.

Bridget gave two names on the deed of ownership: Gertrude Richardson and Mavis O'Loughlin, nee Richardson. Their addresses, or at least their last known addresses, had not been updated for twenty years. A search of births and deaths indicated that both were alive, and would be eighty-seven and eighty-five years of age respectively.

Wendy had the addresses, but after so long, they seemed to be a long shot, although both were in London and she could get out to one that day. Glad of the opportunity she informed DCI Cook on the way out. The police constable decided to visit her husband on the way, hopeful that he would be in an agreeable mood, even remember her name. She felt guilt that she was not with him more often, but life has its consequences. Her husband, a loyal local government employee, had not put his affairs in order, and she had to pay for the house and the nursing home. She had to work, and she was glad to. The arthritis that had given her trouble had subsided, although she realised it was only temporary due to the warmer weather.

Bridget, meanwhile, happy to be in the office, continued with the documentation that a murder investigation always entails. As firm a friend as she was with Wendy, as fond of a few too many drinks and idle gossip as they both were, Bridget was an office person, Wendy enjoyed being out in the field.

Bridget set to work with the filing, setting up the databases, collating what they had so far. Even at this early stage, she knew it would be another three to four hours before she could consider going home; not that it concerned her, as she was in her element.

Larry Hill had found himself a desk and was setting it up to suit him. He preferred a desk facing the window. Logging on to the department's intranet was proving difficult, but Bridget had said she would be over in five minutes to sort it out for him.

The team, supplemented by several other officers, were collecting and tagging retrieved goods from the house: precious few as it turned out. Others were preparing a case for the prosecution if a culprit was found and brought to justice. It seemed premature to Isaac Cook, in that so far there was no culprit, but procedures were procedures. Even he, a product of university and police training college, could see that the Metropolitan Police was becoming over-bureaucratised. It had been fine with the former commissioner, Charles Shaw, but he had moved on to the House of Lords.

Richard Goddard was looking for an assistant commissioner's position in a couple of years, and the new head of the London Metropolitan Police did not seem to be overly keen on him. The warm relationship with his predecessor had been good, but the new man did not have the charm or the willingness to respond to Goddard's pandering.

Even Isaac had to reflect on his future. He could see detective superintendent, possibly detective chief superintendent, but commissioner…

He needed a mentor to guide him to the top. He needed Detective Chief Superintendent Goddard, although he needed him to make commissioner first, and that was looking shaky. It was a momentary distraction to reflect on past events. It was the present that was important, and that consisted of a body slowly being unwrapped from its blankets.

Chapter 3

Wendy was clearly the most active as she had a defined task. Isaac, for once at a loose end, decided to visit Gordon Windsor.

Wendy's first address was in Richmond. The address showed it as close to the park. She arrived to find what was, on first impression, an imposing mansion. She entered through the front gate and rang the doorbell. The chimes echoed through the house.

Five minutes later, an old and wizened woman leaning on a stick came to the door. 'What do you want?'

'Constable Wendy Gladstone.'

'Are you after a donation or something?'

Wendy could see that the woman was embittered.

'I need to ask you some questions about a property in Bellevue Street, Holland Park.'

'Sold it.'

'We are aware of that, but there are still some questions we need to ask.'

'Ask then. I don't have all day to stand here talking.'

'Would it be better if I came in?'

'If you must.'

As Wendy moved through the house, the main rooms on either side appeared to be unused. The smell pervading the house was unpleasant – stale urine. Upon reaching the kitchen at the back of the house, she could see why. There were cats everywhere, and they were not fussy where they made their mess. It was clear that no attempt had been made for a very long time to keep the area clean. In the corner of the kitchen was an old camp bed.

'Do you want a cup of tea?'

Wendy could only answer in the affirmative if she wanted the woman to open up, although she couldn't see any clean cups.

The woman reluctantly moved over to the sink and pulled out a cup from the filthy water in the basin. She gave it a quick shake and a wipe with a cloth that a cat had been sitting on. Wendy shuddered at the lack of hygiene, although she knew that a cup of tea invariably loosened most tongues, and she needed this woman to talk.

'What can you tell me about Bellevue Street?'
'Not much.'
'It's part of a police investigation.'
'Nothing to do with me, is it?'
'I don't know. What can you tell me about it?'
'I sold it.'
'You've already said that.'
'What else do you want me to say?'

Wendy could see that the conversation was going nowhere. 'Why did you sell it?' she asked.

'Needed the money.'
'This must be worth more than the house you sold.'
'Can't sell this one.'
'Why's that?'
'You ask too many questions.'
'It's my job.'
'That's maybe, but I don't like people sticking their noses into my business. Every month, the council is around here complaining about the cats. Even gave me a clean-up order.'
'What did you do?'
'Same as I'm about to do with you. I told them to bugger off and leave me alone.'
'I could make it official, take you down the police station.'
'Just you try it.'
'This is going nowhere,' Wendy said.
'Then you'd better leave.'
'Before I go, let me clarify a couple of points.'
'Hurry up, I've got the cats to feed.'
'Your name is Gertrude Richardson?'
'What if it is?'

'Do you have a married name?'

'Never bothered to get married. I shacked up with a few, slept with a few more.'

'You have a sister by the name of Mavis O'Loughlin.'

'I don't have a sister.'

'The records clearly state that you do. She's two years younger than you.'

'If you mean that thieving bitch!'

'That's who I mean.'

'Haven't seen her in forty years, don't want to.'

'Any reason?'

'You're sticking your nose in where it's not wanted again.'

'We know that the two of you had joint ownership of the house in Bellevue Street.'

'Maybe we did. What's that got to do with it?'

'The sale of the house would have required both of you as signatories.'

'Not me. I gave a proxy to my lawyer.'

'Can I have his name?'

'Why?'

'We found a body at the house.'

'What's my lawyer got to do with it?'

'You don't seem very concerned about what I just told you.'

'Should I be? Seen plenty of dead people in my time. One more won't make any difference.'

'The body has been there for up to thirty years.'

'Don't look at me. I haven't set foot in *that* house for over forty years, maybe longer.'

'Any reason?'

'My business. If you're finished sticking your nose in, you'd better leave. The cats are hungry, and I'm tired. Come here talking about dead bodies, upsetting the cats. You're also upsetting me, an old woman of eighty-seven, going on eighty-eight.'

Wendy, sensing that her time had come to a conclusion, rose from the old wooden chair she had been sitting on. 'Just one question before I leave.'

'Yes, what is it?'

'Your sister?'

'Don't have a sister.'

'The one that used to share your surname.'

'I've not seen her since Bellevue Street. Dead as far as I'm concerned.'

'But she signed the sale documents for the house.'

'Somebody did. May have been her, I suppose.'

***

Isaac found Gordon Windsor down at Pathology. The body, now revealed, was clearly male. It was lying flat on a table, or at least in an approximation of flat; years of being bent over had tightened it rigid. The clothing was with Forensics who were conducting fibre analysis, attempting to find any clues that would assist. According to Windsor, a positive ID was proving difficult.

'Too many years wrapped in blankets being shat on by pigeons. Add in the water and the coal dust, and the body and the clothing have almost been mummified. That explains the unusually good condition of the skin.' Isaac, used to dead bodies – not as old as this one, though – could only agree.

'The newspaper? Placed there at the time of death?' Isaac asked.

'It looks to be that way, but why would someone bother to place a newspaper first unless they saw it as a time capsule? Instead of a few artefacts, they thought a dead body was more appropriate. Macabre, if that was the case.'

'The cause of death?'

'We'll need to wait for the autopsy. No visible signs of trauma, although that would be hard to ascertain given the condition of the body.'

'How long before they get back to us?'

'Hard to say,' Gordon Windsor said. 'No point rushing a pathologist. They take their time, afraid to get it wrong in case they have to stand up in court and defend their findings.'

'Give me a call,' Isaac said. He had seen enough, and watching the pathologist slice a body with a scalpel from up near the shoulders down to below the navel was not agreeable, even at the best of times. He had seen a pathology examination during police training; he did not want to see another.

***

Larry Hill, once he had settled in and Bridget had sorted out his IT problems, was anxious to be out on the road. He, like Wendy, did not relish extended periods in the office. He phoned her; she was glad of the call.

'I'm trying to find Mavis O'Loughlin,' she said.

'Address?'

'No one there. Looks unoccupied to me.'

'What's the plan?'

'Ask Bridget, see if she can come up with something.'

'I'll do that,' Larry said.

Bridget spent another twenty minutes before she came up with some additional leads. Larry planned to meet Wendy and to go from there.

Wendy had tried the house in Belgravia with no success. Bridget found another possibility in Primrose Hill, three miles to the north. Wendy agreed to meet Larry at the address.

The location did not look promising on their arrival. It appeared to be empty, although it was a well-maintained freestanding property. To Larry, it looked very expensive. Wendy knocked at the door, Larry walked round to the back. As he approached the back door, it opened abruptly. An elderly woman appeared; she was elegantly dressed. Larry judged her to be in her eighties.

'You can tell that bitch sister of mine that she's getting none of it.'

'Detective Inspector Larry Hill. We are looking for a Mavis O'Loughlin.'

'What's the police got to do with this?'

'We're not from your sister.'

'Why are you here?'

'We need to ask you a few questions about the property you jointly owned in Bellevue Street, Holland Park.'

'She's not getting any more money. I've given her enough already.'

'Your relationship with your sister is not our primary concern. Do you think we could come in?'

'The woman at the front banging on the door?'

'Constable Wendy Gladstone.'

'Very well. I will let her in. You can come in the back door. Remember to wipe your feet.'

Wendy could only reflect on the difference between Gertrude's mansion and Mavis's house. The property was exquisite, with everything in the right place. Wendy, who appreciated a clean house but rarely achieved it, was astonished at the cleanliness.

'Can we confirm your name as Mavis O'Loughlin?' Wendy asked.

'I reverted to my maiden name, Mavis Richardson.'

'Would it be appropriate to ask why?' Larry asked.

'Not really, but I'll tell you anyway.'

'Thank you.'

'I caught the bastard cheating on me. Both of them naked in my bed.'

'What did you do?'

'I kicked them out and then threw his clothes out of the window.'

'How long ago?' Wendy asked.

'Over forty years.'

'Have you seen your husband since then?'

'Not once. Vanished off the face of the earth.'

'Does it concern you?'

'Not really. He always had a roving eye.'

'And the woman?'

'Who do you think it was?' She looked at Wendy.

'Your sister.'

'Who else? Back then she was a terrible tart. She could not find a man for herself, so she took everyone else's.'

'That was a long time ago. Have there been other men in your life since then?' Larry asked.

'Plenty, but I've seen no need for a piece of paper and a name change. A few have moved in here, but none have stayed for long.'

'And now?' Wendy asked.

'I'm eighty-five, what use would a man be to me now?'

'Companionship.' Larry ventured a comment.

'If I were lonely, which I am not, I'd get a dog. Anyway, you did not come here to talk about my love life. What do you want?'

'A body has been discovered at Bellevue Street.'

'Number 54?'

'It was found in a boarded-up fireplace.'

'I've not seen the house for over forty years, ever since that night.'

'Which night?' Wendy asked.

'The night I caught the two of them screwing in my bed.'

'It is a long time to bear a grudge against your sister,' Wendy said.

'I forgave her within a week. It's her who can't forgive.'

'Forgive what?'

'She was in love with him, and he upped and disappeared.'

'Why did he disappear?'

'No money.'

'This house is yours?'

'As well as Bellevue Street and the mansion in Richmond.'

'We were led to believe that the house in Bellevue Street was jointly owned,' Wendy said.

'Legally, not financially.'

'Could you please explain?' Larry asked.

'It's simple. I was careful with my money and my men; she was not. Is this integral to your investigation, the Richardson family history?'

'The body appears to have been placed in the fireplace in early 1987.'

'I moved out in '76.'

'You owned it in 1987.'

'That's true, but it would have been empty.'

'Could you please elaborate on the financial arrangement with your sister?' Larry asked.

'The properties, all of them, were joint ownership. Given to us by our father on his deathbed. Gertrude became involved with a few unsavoury men, who fleeced her while professing love. I bailed her out; the family lawyer kept a record. In the end, she ended up with nothing but a place to live and God knows how many cats.'

'You let her stay there?' Wendy asked.

'That was the last deal. I would provide a roof over Gertrude's head in return for no more demands.'

'And she agreed?'

'She had no alternative. I believe I have given you enough of my time. I've got a social event to attend.'

Wendy and Larry realised there were more questions to ask, but they would have to wait for another time. Besides, their DCI wanted them back at the office.

Chapter 4

Isaac saw the validity of an end of day briefing and an update on activities concluded so far, activities planned for the next day. He knew that once the investigation into the body in the fireplace became more intense, it would become a luxury.

Wendy and Larry were back in the office, as was Bridget, who was enjoying her newly elevated position.

'I'll update on what we know so far,' Isaac said. Larry sat with a coffee in his hand.

'DCI, is it a confirmed murder?' Wendy asked.

'Not yet. We're still waiting for the result of the autopsy.'

'Sir, you've met Gordon Windsor?' Larry asked.

'He was over at Pathology. Forensics is inspecting the clothing.'

'Any identification?' Wendy asked.

'Not yet, and it looks as though the clothing may yield no clues, other than an approximate date when it was purchased.'

'Is 1987 a probable date?'

'It appears to be around that time. Wendy, your update.'

'Bridget found an address for Gertrude Richardson, one of the joint owners of the property before the Baxters bought it.'

'Did they own it in the 80s?' Isaac asked.

'They purchased it in 1972, sold it three months ago,' Bridget said.

'Did they live in it around the time the body was placed in the fireplace?'

'According to Mavis Richardson, she moved out in the 70s,' Wendy said. 'It's best if I conclude my report first.'

'Please do,' Isaac said.

'To reiterate, Bridget found an address for Gertrude Richardson in Richmond. It was a substantial house, mansion even, close to the park. I knocked on the front door. An old woman, later identified as Gertrude Richardson, came to the door. She was in a bad way.'

'What do you mean?'

'She was unwashed, the house showed severe neglect, and it appears that she lives in the kitchen at the back, surrounded by numerous cats that smelt awful.'

'What did she tell you?'

'It's what she didn't say that's important.'

'That's an ambiguous statement. What do you mean?'

'She's an embittered and reclusive woman who does not acknowledge that she has a sister.'

'Senile?'

'I don't think so. More likely a family feud.'

'What else did she say?'

'She stated that she had not been in the house in Bellevue Street for over forty years.'

'Did she give a reason?'

'No, but I believe I know why. Eventually the woman acknowledged, somewhat reluctantly, that she had a sister, but had not seen her for over forty years.'

'Dates coincide with Bellevue Street?' Isaac asked.

'I'll address that in a minute. She explained that she had sold the house in Bellevue Street because she had no money. I asked her why she had not sold the mansion in Richmond as it was more valuable. She said she could not. She was not willing to elaborate. Besides, she cut me short and hustled me out of the door.'

'And the sister?' Isaac asked.

'I'll let DI Hill answer that question.'

'Wendy had drawn a blank on the first address for Mavis O'Loughlin, the sister,' Larry Hill said. 'Bridget found another and I met up with Wendy at the address. A three-storey terrace opposite the park in Primrose Hill.

'Wendy knocked on the door to no avail. I went around the back. A woman opened the back door and started quizzing me, assumed I was from the sister.'

'Why would she do that? You showed her your badge?'

'Eventually, when she calmed down. After that, she let Wendy in at the front, and I entered through the back door.'

'A total opposite to the sister,' Wendy said.

'What do you mean?' Isaac asked.

'Mavis O'Loughlin, who has now reverted to her maiden name, is an elegant woman who keeps her house in pristine condition. Apart from the reason we were there, she was good company.'

'What did she have to say?'

'She has not spoken to her sister since 1976, or thereabouts, and has not seen her husband since then.'

'Related or coincidental?'

'Related. Mavis Richardson came home unexpectedly and found her husband in bed with her sister. She threw both of them out onto the street.'

'And the sisters have not spoken since?' Isaac asked.

'That's unclear. According to Mavis O'Loughlin, her sister had a tendency to become involved with the wrong type of men. Some of them had taken advantage and fleeced her for money. The debts incurred were covered by her sister, who gradually accumulated the properties under her name.'

'She allows her sister to live in squalor, while she lives in luxury?' Bridget asked.

'I don't think we can make that assumption. She forgave her sister for sleeping with her husband a week after the event, or at least, she said she did. Why the squalor, and now the animosity from both women, is unclear,' Wendy said.

'I suggest you find out as soon as possible,' Isaac said. 'Larry, can you assist?'

'No problem. Can you update us when the pathologist's report and forensics come through?'

'Will do,' Isaac said.

***

It was late at night, as Isaac drove home to the flat he shared with Jess, that he received the phone call that was to intensify the focus on the case. 'It's murder,' Gordon Windsor said.

'How?' Isaac asked.

'Signs of trauma, suffocation.'

'Where are you?'

'I've just driven over to the pathologist's. I came as soon as he phoned me up with the news.'

It was unusual for the pathologist to work so late into the night, but this body was important. The media were hovering for information; a thirty-year-old corpse had raised their interest. And now, Sue Baxter had been selling the story to a Sunday newspaper; there, emblazoned on the front page, the photos she had taken. She had dutifully handed over the camera as requested by Larry Hill, kept the memory card for herself. Isaac realised that she could be trouble if she kept talking, and now with a clear murder, the media would be pressing her for more news.

'I'll be there as soon as possible,' Isaac replied to Gordon Windsor. It was already close to ten in the evening, and Jess had made a special attempt to be at home for an intimate meal that night. Isaac phoned her to let her know that he was further delayed; she was not pleased.

Isaac had seen the signs before. How many times had someone moved in, fully understanding the challenges that a senior police officer in Homicide faced? How many times had the woman said that she understood, when clearly she did not? He had hoped that with Jess he could finally settle down. After all, she was the executive producer of a successful and long-running television drama, and as such, used to long hours and broken engagements. Sure, he had been looking forward to the evening with some good food, a few drinks, and an early and romantic night. He had to admit that the romance was withering. And then there was the issue with Linda Harris and the fact that he had slept with her, while he and Jess were only flirtatious. Her name had come up in an argument two nights previously; she was bound to be mentioned again. He had to admit that he loved, had loved Jess before she moved in, and he sensed it was the same with her, but he could see only another three to four weeks before the relationship came to a conclusion. He was sorry, but there was nothing he could do to change the situation.

'It looks like murder to me,' the pathologist, a tall, thin man, said. Isaac judged him to be in his late fifties, maybe early sixties. He had met him before and had found him to be an unusually unsociable man.

'Why do you say that?' Gordon Windsor asked. Both he and Isaac were standing close to the body: internal organs, or at least what remained of them, clearly visible. It was not a sight that Isaac appreciated, and if he was being totally honest, he would have to admit that he could be squeamish, but this was important, and people, senior people, were looking for answers and a resolution to the case.

'Clear sign of trauma around the head, and if I'm not mistaken, evidence of suffocation.'

'Enough to stand up in a court of law?' Isaac asked.

'Not yet. I've just given you my professional opinion.'

'How long before you're sure?'

'Could be weeks. I'll need to get Forensics to run tests.'

'What can they find?'

'Why are you asking me? You are the detective chief inspector. Didn't they teach you anything at the police college?'

Isaac had seen that he was making polite conversation; the pathologist saw it as wasted time. 'Of course, DNA, fingerprints, drugs in the system,' he replied. Isaac realised it was a flippant response, but did not appreciate the pathologist's lecture. *Maybe the friction with Jess is getting to me*, he thought.

'There's trauma around the head, but not the level of bleeding that I would normally expect. Mind you, after so many years, I can't be sure.'

'You are confirming murder?' Isaac needed clarity on that one piece of information.

'Tied up, bag over head, trauma around the cranial regions. It seems conclusive.'

'Any chance of identification?' Isaac asked.

'Not from me. Forensics may have better luck.'

'What can you tell us with some degree of certainty?'

'Male, aged in his late thirties, early forties. Caucasian, height close to six feet. Apart from that, it is hard to tell any more. There is a clear sign of a broken right leg and a dislocated thumb. Apart from that, the body indicates that the man had been in good physical shape.'

'Hair colour, skin colour?' Gordon Windsor asked.

'Dark hair. Skin colour almost certainly white, but that's only because I'm classifying the body as Caucasian.'

'English?' Isaac asked.

'Hard to tell. We live in a multicultural society. Not sure that can be confirmed, although DNA analysis may help.'

'Any indication from his clothing?'

'Bought in England. We found a few labels so it may be possible to localise where it was bought. Some of the clothes looked as though they were made to measure, not out of a high-street store.'

'If it's murder, it hardly seems clever to conceal the body fully clothed,' Gordon Windsor said.

'Or hide it in a fireplace in an empty house,' Isaac said. 'But then, we don't know the state of mind of the person who placed him there, do we?'

'Must have been someone handy with wood to have built the fireplace covering.'

'If you two have finished postulating, I'm off home,' the pathologist said. 'I've spent too many hours here today for you.'

'We're finished,' Isaac replied. 'Many thanks.'

'Don't thank me. Just sign for my expenses when you receive the bill.'

***

Larry Hill and Wendy Gladstone, as agreed with their DCI, visited Gertrude Richardson. It was his first visit, her second. The welcome at the door, the same as before. 'What do you want?' the elderly woman asked.

'We have some more questions,' Wendy replied.

'I told you last time that I sold the place. Why bother me?'

'We've spoken to your sister,' Larry said.

'And who are you? I don't like men coming here.'

'Detective Inspector Larry Hill. I work with Constable Gladstone.'

'That may be, but you're not welcome here, and neither is she.'

'I could make this official,' Wendy said.

'Maybe you could, and then it will be in the newspapers. How you took a prominent member of society, eighty-five and infirm, and carted her off down to the police station.'

'Prominent?' Wendy asked.

'Once I was. Always in the society pages. Even met the King on a couple of occasions.'

'That's a long time ago to be claiming prominence, don't you think?'

'My name still counts for something.'

Both Wendy and Larry were intrigued, although neither said anything, other than to look at each other with a momentary glance and an imperceptible shake of the head.

'Can we come in?' Wendy asked.

'I don't want him near my cats. They don't like men, neither do I.'

'You did once.'

'Long time ago, maybe. Naïve then, not now.'

'Can we use another room?' Wendy asked. The old woman was correct in that they would not be taking her in handcuffs down to the police station, nor would they be forcing her to do or say anything other than voluntarily given.

'If you must. You don't want a cup of tea, do you?'

'I wouldn't mind,' Larry said. Wendy wished he had not answered in the affirmative.

'The room on the left. There are some chairs in there. I'll be back in five minutes.'

Granted entry, Larry and Wendy moved to the room on the left. It was clear that it had not been used for many years. The dust pervaded the air as they disturbed it. Larry found a chair close to the window; Wendy, another near a magnificent open fireplace. The walls were adorned with a selection of oil paintings, some old, some valuable. One of the women portrayed, dressed in the style of the seventeenth century, bore a striking resemblance to the old lady who was now making them a cup of tea. Wendy hoped the hygiene would be a little better this time; realised it probably would not.

Ten minutes later, Gertrude Richardson returned with one cat following. It made straight for Larry and jumped up on his lap. 'I've never seen that before,' the woman said.

'I have a couple of cats at home,' Larry said. 'We're very fond of them, the wife and I.'

'If my cat likes you, then so will I.'

'Do you get many people in here?' Wendy asked. She had made sure to choose what looked to be the cleanest cup.

'There's a woman who comes once a week to check on me and bring my shopping.'

'You don't go?' Larry asked.

'I've not been out of the front gate in five years.'

'That's a long time,' Wendy said.

'There's nothing out there that interests me.'

'Why's that?'

'As long as I've got my cats, then I want nothing else.'

'We met up with your sister,' Larry said.

'I told her.' The old woman looked in Wendy's direction. 'I don't have a sister.'

'The woman with your name,' Wendy reminded her.

'What did she have to say?'

'She told us that you fell out with her over a man.'

'What if I did?'

'It's important.'

'Not to me.'

'Is that right?'

'I suppose it is, but there's more to it than me just screwing him. And besides, she was no better.'

Larry stood up; the cat was using his new suit to sharpen its claws. His cats at home were regularly bathed, this one was not.

'Could you elaborate?' Larry asked.

'None of your business.'

'It is if it is relevant to a murder enquiry.'

'Why should it be?'

'We've yet to identify the body. Any idea who it may be?' Wendy asked.

'I haven't been in that house for a long time. How would I know?'

'We are aware the body was that of a male, aged in his late thirties to early forties, who almost certainly died at the beginning of 1987.'

'No one I know.'

'Last time I was here, you said that you had seen a lot of dead people,' Wendy reminded the old woman, who showed every sign of ejecting them from the mansion very soon.

'I was in London during the war, worked as a nurse.'

'And after the war?' Larry asked.

'We came from a privileged family, employment was for others.'

'What did you do?'

'For a couple of years, voluntary work, but mainly taking our place in society.'

'It doesn't sound much of a life,' Wendy, who had little time for the idle rich, commented.

'Endless parties and fun? It was marvellous.'

Five minutes later, Larry and Wendy found themselves outside the front door of the house. Their eviction had been executed swiftly.

'What do you reckon?' Larry asked.

'None of what she told us is relevant if the body has nothing to do with her or her sister,' Wendy replied.

'There's more she's not telling us.'

'We'll meet DCI Cook and let him know,' Wendy said.

'Until the body is identified, we'll continue probing the background of the two sisters.'

'Agreed. There still remains a strong possibility that the body is somehow tied back to them.'

Chapter 5

'What do we know about this lawyer?' Isaac asked at the late afternoon debriefing back at Challis Street Police Station.

'Only a name,' Wendy said.

'And the name?'

'Montague St John Grenfell.'

'Sounds aristocratic to me,' Isaac said. The key members of the team were assembled: Larry was standing in the corner, his back to the wall, Bridget was holding a large cup of tea and the obligatory chocolate biscuit, Wendy as well. Isaac was sipping on green tea as his weight was starting to cause him some concern.

'We checked him out in *Burke's Peerage*. He is the second son of a lord with no chance of inheriting the title and the stately home unless the incumbent dies soon,' Larry said.

'What do you mean "soon"?' Isaac asked.

'Grenfell is in his late seventies; the elder brother is two years older.'

'Someone needs to go and check him out.'

'You'd be the best person for that, sir,' Wendy said. She remembered how he had charmed Angus MacTavish, the chief government whip, on a previous case. Dealing with the elite of society seemed best suited to Isaac's disarming and pleasant manner. She knew that she was too abrasive, and her speech echoed government schooling at every utterance. Larry, although he spoke more clearly than she did, had a distinctive northern accent.

'I'll deal with Grenfell,' Isaac said. He was glad of the opportunity to get out of the office. As the senior investigating officer, the administrative side of his job was beginning to annoy him. He could see himself asking Bridget to take on a heavier workload and help him out, once she had got her primary responsibilities under control.

'And for us, sir?' Larry Hill asked.

'Keep with the sisters, see what you can find out. Bridget, can you trace this missing husband?'

'Yes, sir.'

'Good. Larry and Wendy can follow up.'

'All this may be circumstantial and irrelevant,' Larry said.

'Moving out of the house in 1986, a body placed there in 1987? It must be tied in to the women,' Isaac said.

'Agreed, sir. That is what Wendy and I thought.'

***

Bridget soon busied herself with finding out what she could about the husband. It was proving to be difficult as there were no recorded marriages in the period before 1986 for Mavis Richardson, which indicated a wedding outside the country.

However, there was a clear record of marriage in 1952 for Gertrude Richardson, which surprised Wendy. Although, Wendy realised, the woman had denied she had a sister, so why would she not deny a marriage, and now there was the question of where her husband was, although records clearly showed that he would be in his nineties now, so possibly deceased. Too many unknowns, too many instances of intrigue and subterfuge, to not believe that somehow, someway, the sisters were not involved directly or indirectly with the body.

Until the body was formally identified, Wendy and the rest of the team realised they were chasing possible red herrings. It was clear that another visit to the old woman in the mansion was required. Wendy did not relish the task.

As there was no phone at the mansion, it was a drive in heavy traffic out to Richmond. The same procedure: ring the doorbell, wait for five minutes, receive verbal abuse about her being an old woman and the cats needed feeding, and then a reluctant entry through to the kitchen.

'I contacted my lawyer about you coming here all the time. He said it was police harassment, and if it continued, then I was to register an official complaint.'

'Miss Richardson, that is your prerogative. I am only doing my job. By the way, how did you contact your lawyer? I wasn't aware you had a phone.'

'I had no intention of giving the number to you.'

'Why?'

'You're knocking on my door every five minutes. I didn't want you ringing as well.'

'There is a record of you being married back in 1952, is that correct?'

'I prefer to forget about it.'

'Why's that?'

'He was a scoundrel.'

'When did you last see him?'

'Thirty to forty years, I suppose.'

'Why did you deny that you had been married, when I asked before?' Wendy could see some softness appear in the old woman.

'It's my business, no one else's.'

'What was he like?' Wendy held a cup of tea that the old woman had given her. It was cleaner than the last time.

'A lovable rogue, charm the birds out of the trees.'

'He charmed you?'

'Yes.'

'And you've not seen him for thirty to forty years?'

'That's correct.'

'Any idea where he is now?'

'He went overseas. Apart from that, I have no idea. He could be dead.'

Although not senile, Gertrude Richardson was, nevertheless, old and frail, and excessive questioning would have achieved little more. Wendy had noticed that the woman's initial disdain at her space being invaded had subdued, and her manner, though still disarmingly blunt, was agreeable.

Realising that no more was to be gained, Wendy bid her farewell, promised to come and see her in a few days. The response was as expected, but it did not have the harsh undertone that had been present on previous visits.

***

Montague St John Grenfell did prove to be aristocratic when Isaac met him in his office. He was, Isaac knew, a man in his late seventies, but surprisingly fit and agile. He was as tall as Isaac, over six feet in height. His handshake was firm and vigorous, his manners impeccable. Isaac was impressed.

'Please take a seat,' the lawyer said. 'I only have Earl Grey. Is that fine by you?'

'Fine,' Isaac replied. As the lawyer prepared the tea, it gave Isaac the opportunity to look around his surroundings. He had to conclude that it was a good office, certainly better than his at Challis Street, but then, his was the office of a policeman, clean and functional, lacking in any charm. Grenfell's office showed the look of age, as though it had been occupied by the one person for many years. Not far from Paddington, the third-floor office was situated on Bayswater Avenue in an office building which Isaac assumed had been built over seventy years earlier. There was no lift which had given him some much-needed exercise. He wondered how Grenfell managed every day, as he noticed that the man limped.

An impressive bookcase stood to one side of the office, overflowing with legal books and assorted memorabilia. Isaac sat on a comfortable chair, Grenfell on a leather chair, a walnut desk separating them. It was clear that the man was busy as legal files littered the desk. Isaac saw no computer which seemed incongruous in the modern age. He wondered how anyone could conduct business without email and access to the internet.

Montague Grenfell returned holding two cups of tea. Isaac noticed the man's hands did not tremble as he carried them. 'You've been looking around my office,' he said.

'It's certainly more impressive than mine,' Isaac replied, aware that he had been seen.

'I've been here for over forty years. More like a home for me than an office.'

'Is it?' Isaac asked.

'Just a figure of speech, but I'd rather be here than at home.'

'May I ask why?'

'Here, I have my books and my studies. At home, there is no one.'

'Your wife?'

'I've been a widower for five years.'

'Sorry about that.'

'No need to be. People get old, people die. None of us is immortal.'

Isaac knew there were questions to be asked, and as congenial as the current setting was, he needed to redirect their conversation. 'Gertrude and Mavis Richardson, what can you tell me about them?'

'I'm not sure there is a lot. Gertrude is semi-reclusive, Mavis is more outgoing.'

'My detective inspector and constable have met them both.'

'Gertrude can be acerbic.'

'Have you known them long?'

'Since my childhood, although they are a few years older than me.'

'Where did you meet them?'

'I'm sure you're aware of my family history.'

'Second son of a lord.'

'*Burke's Peerage* could tell you that. What else?'

'That's as far as we went. So far, we have a body with no identity, and the only people with any link to that period are the two sisters. There's no reason to believe they're involved, but there is a possibility that people close to them could be.'

'My family is extremely wealthy, obscenely so. The wealth resides with my eldest brother, the lord. I'm financially secure due to a bequethment from my father in his will, but compared to my brother, it is a mere pittance.'

'Your meeting with the sisters?' Isaac repeated his earlier question.

'They were regular guests at the family's stately home.'

'Any reason?'

'They are cousins of mine, distant cousins.'

'Are they independently wealthy?'

'They both were, but now Mavis has all the money.'

'That was explained by Mavis. Gertrude denies that she has a sister.'

'Bad blood, goes back a long way.'

'Do you know the reason?' Isaac asked.

'Gertrude made some bad decisions. Mavis, always the smarter, helped her out.'

'We are aware that Gertrude signed over the properties.'

'I ensured it was legal.'

'And that's left Gertrude living in abject misery?' Isaac asked.

'Abject misery in a mansion in Richmond. I do not think so. Regardless of what Gertrude may have said, that is not the truth. There's enough money for her to live well, but she chooses the life.'

'So, why doesn't she accept the money?'

'You'd better ask her. I've offered it to her enough times, so has her sister.'

'According to both women, they have not communicated for a long time.'

'I believe I've said enough on this matter. As you have said, there is no connection between the women and the body at this time.'

'Can I clarify if the women have communicated in recent times?'

'I suggest that you talk to them further.'

Isaac prepared to leave. 'Just one more question, totally unrelated. How do you manage the stairs up to here?'

'With difficulty. It doesn't help only having one leg.'
'I didn't realise.'
'Motorcycle accident in my youth.'

As Isaac exited the building, his phone rang. 'I have some updates from Forensics,' Gordon Windsor said.

'When can we meet to discuss?'

'Your office, sixty minutes.'

***

Isaac hurried back to the office, pushed the car harder than he should have, broke the speed limit a couple of times, but the news from Gordon Windsor sounded important. Upon arrival, he found Windsor comfortably seated with a smug look on his face. Wendy was with him, having just arrived backed from Gertrude Richardson's place in Richmond. Larry was out with the other sister, Mavis.

'What do you have?' Isaac asked.

'Forensics have been able to analyse some of the clothing, even read a tag on a shirt.'

'The significance?' Isaac asked.

'Made to order.'

'Wendy, a job for you.'

'Yes, sir.'

'Anything else?' Isaac asked.

'It appears that the trousers were also made to measure, but so far they've not found a tag. They're conducting an analysis of the fabric, may come up with something.'

'How about the body?' Isaac asked.

'They're still conducting tests, but asphyxiation is looking the stronger of the two means of death, although the trauma to the skull is significant.'

'Regardless of how the man died, we still need a name.'

'I'll get on to it straight away,' Wendy said.

'Any luck with the elder sister?' Isaac asked her.

'Apart from admitting that she had been married, not a lot. She was more agreeable, seemed to appreciate the company this time. The place is a mess, should be condemned.'

'According to her lawyer, there's no reason for her to live like that,' Isaac said.

'Then why does she?'

'Senile?' Gordon Windsor asked.

'Not from what I can see,' Wendy said.

'We need to find out more about her and this mysterious husband,' Isaac said. 'How's Bridget progressing?'

'There are two husbands to find, Gertrude's and Mavis's, although both will be in their nineties now.'

'Possibly dead.'

'It's possible.'

'We need to know what happened to them anyway, but first we need to identify the body. Wendy, you and Larry better make that your priority.'

'As soon as Bridget gives us an address, we'll go and visit the tailor.'

***

'Did you know about your sister's marriage?' Larry asked Mavis Richardson. His entrance into the elegant house, this time through the front door.

'It was a long time ago. Michael Solomon has not been seen for years, same as my husband,' Mavis Richardson replied.

Larry, this time asked to sit in a more comfortable chair than on his previous visit, could only reflect that the woman still had an eye for a man, especially a younger man. The woman was older than his mother, and he was happily married, two young children, another on the way. He knew all about Isaac and his legendary reputation for seducing beautiful women. He felt no need to emulate him and especially not with someone so old, even though still remarkably attractive. Larry assumed her look came courtesy of a healthy bank balance, expensive cosmetics, and a plastic surgeon. All of which may be interesting, but there was a more important issue to consider – the unidentified body.

'Tell me about Gertrude's husband.'

'Attractive, well-spoken, lovable rogue.'

'Did you like him?'

'All the women liked him, that was the problem.'

'What do you mean?'

'He'd screw anything in a skirt.'

'And?' Larry asked, not sure of the response.

'Yes, I'm included.'

'What did your sister say?'

'She never knew. Mind you, she screwed mine, so I suppose it's all fair in love and war.'

Larry, who had been receiving SMS updates from Isaac and Wendy, continued to probe, continued to slowly move away from the woman as she edged along the sofa in his direction. 'My colleague has met your lawyer.'

'A lovely man.'

'Apparently, you have known him since you were children.'

'We're cousins, poor cousins.'

'Poor hardly seems an appropriate word.'

'Compared to his family, we were virtual paupers. Sure, we were not on our uppers, cap in hand, but their wealth was immense. One of the richest families in the country.'

'Your background?'

'Gertrude and I are the only children of Frederick Richardson, a wealthy landowner and property developer in the north of England. My father and Montague's father were half-brothers. One was conceived in the marital bed, the other was not. You must realise which of the two was illegitimate.'

'Then you and your family have no claim to the title and the wealth?'

'My father and Montague's father were brought up as brothers. Their father made no distinction, although the right of succession did. The first claim to the title belonged to the eldest son, assuming he was legitimate.'

'If either you or your sister had a son, then he is in the line of succession?'

'It's a long line, and the legitimate heirs take precedence, and besides, neither of us have had any offspring.'

***

The name on the clothing tag, although faded, had shown up under ultraviolet. Bridget had a printed scan. The name stated *'Clement Jones and Sons. Gentleman Tailors'*. It was not hard to find, located as it was on Savile Row, the address for the discerning and wealthy purchaser of men's clothing in London.

Wendy and Larry left soon after. They showed their IDs on arrival and were quickly moved into a small office at the rear. 'Not good for business, having a couple of police officers out the front asking questions,' the manager said.

'Sorry about that,' Larry said.

'What can I do for you?'

'We need to identify the purchaser of a shirt made in the 1980s. Would that be possible?'

'Difficult, but not impossible.'

As the men spoke, Wendy took the opportunity to look around the office. Everywhere there seemed to be samples of clothing, as well as numerous bookkeeping records. It smelt musty, although not unpleasant, as it was interspersed with the smell of leather and fabric. The manager, a fat, red-faced man, elegantly dressed in a suit with a waistcoat, and sporting a bowtie, seemed ideally suited to such an august establishment. Larry, who had an affinity for dressing well, could only admire what was for sale in the shop at a price he could never afford.

'How much for a suit here?' Larry asked.

'Up to four thousand pounds,' the manager said.

'A lot of money.'

'As you say, a lot of money, but the men who come in here don't look at the price, just the quality.'

'What type of men?' Wendy asked.

'City men, bankers, stockbrokers, the occasional pop star.'
'Any villains?' Larry asked.
'Confidentiality is crucial in our business.'
'Which means?' Wendy asked.
'Everyone who comes in here is treated equally. We don't ask their politics or where the money came from, only their inside leg measurement.'
'You would have records from 1986 or thereabouts?' Larry asked.
'From 1904, if you need. That's how long we've been here.'
'Mid to late eighties is all we need. What do you need from us?'
'A sample of the fabric, a photo of the garment, and a copy of the tag.'
'We can give you a copy of the label now and a picture of the garment. We will need to get a special release of a sample in a day or so.'
'What's so important?' the manager asked.
'We need to identify the owner,' Wendy said.
'Dead?'
'That's correct.'
'Not the body in the fireplace?'
'Confidentiality is crucial in our business, the same as yours,' Larry said.
'Let me have a look at the tag,' the manager said.
Wendy handed over the photocopied image.
'1985 to 1986,' the manager said.
'You can tell that from one glance?'
I remember the tag. We had taken on a new supplier of labels in 1985, but they proved unsatisfactory.'
'Any reason why?' Wendy asked.
'The labels frayed after a year or so, especially if someone had put the garment in a washing machine. We ceased using them in late 1986.'
'And the shirt?' Wendy handed over a photo.
'Long slim cotton with double cuffs, white in colour.'

'Can you give us a name?'

'It was a popular line, maybe sold three to four hundred in that colour. The best I can do is give you a list of all who purchased it. Any idea as to the age of the person?'

'Late thirties, early forties,' Larry said.

'That helps. I should be able to reduce that number to seventy or eighty.'

'When can you give us the list?'

'Ten minutes.'

'That soon?'

'Everything's computerised, and once a customer comes in, we keep him on record. No computers here in the 80s, but we've updated since then.'

'No one after about 1987,' Wendy reminded the manager.

'I figured that. It is still about seventy to eighty. Help yourself to a cup of tea while I sort it out.'

Wendy exited the shop with the list on a USB memory stick. Larry exited with a ready-to-wear shirt, which the manager had let him have for fifty per cent off the list price. Both were pleased with their visit to the shop.

Chapter 6

Forensics were taking a long time, too long for Isaac. He phoned them to see how much longer. They said another week at most. He was a man used to being proactive, and for too long he had been waiting for others to do something, rather than himself. His position within the team at Challis Street meant he had to deal with a lot of administrative tasks. Not that he minded usually, but there was just too much. The new commissioner of the Metropolitan Police had brought in additional procedures, and no excuses would be brokered for failing to comply. The previous incumbent, Charles Shaw, had been a great man, streamlining where possible, and it had helped. Now the paperwork was building up, and he was struggling to stay on top of it. Bridget had been helping as she could, but she was weighed under.

Isaac felt the need to leave the office, and besides, he had female trouble again. Jess, his live-in lover, was causing anguish. They had had another argument the night before, and it seemed inevitable that she was going to move out. It was impacting on his ability in the office, and he knew he would have to confront the issues in a few days. It upset him, as she was a woman any man would be proud to have on their arm.

He thought to visit the Richardson sisters' lawyer again, but it seemed premature, and besides what would he say to him. So far, nothing tied the sisters to the body and their association with the house in Bellevue Street could only be regarded as circumstantial. He could hardly bring the women into the police station based on nothing. He knew that identification of the body was critical, and that lay with Bridget at the present time.

'What do you have, Bridget?' Isaac drew a chair up alongside her. She looked flustered.

'Of the seventy-four on the list, I've eliminated thirty-six.'

'How?'

'They're either Arab or African. Our body is white and Caucasian.'

'That leaves thirty-eight. Can you eliminate more?'

'There'll still be seven or eight left.'

'We can get Larry and Wendy on to searching for them. Any luck with the two women's husbands?'

'Last known addresses. I've passed them on.'

'Is there a name for Gertrude Richardson's husband?'

'Michael Solomon.'

'What do we know about him?' Isaac asked.

'German, of Jewish ancestry.'

'Any ideas where he is now?'

'I gave Wendy the only address I could find, but it's old, and he would be ninety-five. Unlikely that he'll still be alive.'

***

Wendy and Larry decided to visit the last known address of Michael Solomon. The husband of Mavis Richardson, Ger O'Loughlin, was proving elusive. Bridget was struggling to find an address, other than one that was twenty years old, and Google Street View had shown that the building no longer existed.

Michael Solomon had arrived in England in 1945, the only survivor of his family from a concentration camp in Germany. Bridget had managed to find out that he had prospered over the years, and by the time of his marriage to Gertrude, he was successfully running his own jewellery business. The last piece of valid information was when he had sold the business thirty years previously. If that was correct, then the dates did not agree with what Gertrude Richardson had said. Her statement was that she had not seen him for over forty years, but there he was, running a shop not more than three miles from where she currently lived. Wendy saw another visit to the woman.

Wendy and Larry arrived at Solomon's house in Fulham at around four in the afternoon. The house was not as palatial as Gertrude's mansion, not as well maintained as her sister's house.

It looked occupied. Wendy rang the doorbell. A woman in her sixties came to the door. 'What can I do for you?'

'Detective Inspector Larry Hill, Constable Wendy Gladstone,' Larry said as they both showed their ID badges.

'Is this about Daniel?' she asked. Wendy observed that she appeared to be a woman worn down by the stress of life. Her hair was showing grey roots with no attempt to conceal them. She wore a drab dress, unironed and apparently unwashed. She wore no makeup.

'Daniel?' Wendy queried.

'My eldest. A grown man and still he acts like an irresponsible child. Your people were always around here, bringing him home, or taking him down the police station. What's he done this time?'

'We're not here about Daniel.'

'Then what are you here for?'

'We're looking for Michael Solomon. This is his last known address.'

'Maybe it is, but he's not here now.'

'Any idea where?'

'Five-minute walk.'

'Can we have the address?' Larry asked.

'You can, but it won't help you much. He's been dead for eight years.'

'And you are?' Wendy asked.

'Mary Solomon. I was married to him for thirty-five years, until he died and left me with his children.'

'He was older than you when you married?'

'He was twenty-seven years older than me, but he was affluent and a good-looking man. Seemed a good catch at the time.'

'And now?'

'I miss him sometimes, but he was not a good husband.'

'Can we come in?' Wendy asked.

'If you like. Excuse the mess. I'm babysitting Daniel's son, and my daughter has dumped her two on me while she is gallivanting up in the city. No idea what she does up there, although I can imagine. They say "like father, like son", but with Michael, it's both of our children.'

Let into the house, Larry and Wendy found themselves in a small room, neat and tidy, with a television in the corner. Obviously, the one room in the house out of bounds to anyone else. Wendy could only feel sorry for her.

'What do you want to know?' the woman asked.

'What do you know of your husband before you married?' Wendy asked.

'He was married before, if that is what you are intimating?'

'Yes. Do you know any of the history relating to the woman?'

'Only that she was a bitch who kicked him out of the house after he caught her in bed with another man.'

'That we did not know,' Larry said. 'Our information is that he vanished over forty years ago, and went overseas.'

'He may have, but I met him not far from here. Fell for him straight away. Married him within six months, gave birth to Daniel three months later.'

'Tell us about him,' Wendy asked. The woman seemed relieved to have someone to talk to, although the baby crying in the other room was distracting.

'Let it cry. It will stop in a minute. Born with the mother's drug addiction. I've only got warm milk, not what it wants.'

'And your husband allowed your children to grow up like this?'

'Not much he could do, and besides, he was no better.'

'Drugs?'

'With him, it was alcohol and other women, although he always denied it. I could see the smirk on his face, the lipstick on his collar. They may have screwed him, but I was the one who had to clean up after them.'

'The children weren't disciplined?'

'By me, but then he'd come home drunk and forgive them. And then once they reached adolescence, they're out there following in his footsteps.'

'What did he die of?' Larry asked.

'I wake up at six in the morning, and he's lying next to me, dead. Gave me quite a shock. Besides, he was nearly ninety.'

'Are you saying he was still chasing women at that age?'

'He gave up on the women in his seventies.'

'Any violence?'

'Michael? Not at all, although I could have hit him sometimes for his behaviour. As I told you, he was a charmer. I always forgave him.'

It was evident to Wendy and Larry that pursuing Michael Solomon had come to a conclusion. However, they both realised that he could still be the murderer.

***

Bridget, meanwhile, had been ensconced in the office, working through the list of buyers that the manager of the tailor's in Savile Row had supplied. Of the seven that she had focussed on, two were confirmed alive and well. With five left, she started to phone around. She found two more who had answered their phones: one, a successful businessman, the other, a musician. There were three left that she had been unable to confirm; they would need to be handled by Wendy and Larry.

Isaac busied himself in the office, although he wanted to be out on the street. His senior, Detective Chief Superintendent Goddard, was keeping his distance, other than to phone at regular intervals for an update. Apparently, Trevor and Sue Baxter had been complaining about not being able to return to their house, even after the crime scene investigators had concluded their examination. It was still a crime scene, Isaac had tried to explain when they had confronted him at the police station, and as such, the crime scene tape across the front and the uniformed policeman were to stay. He thought they had understood, but there they were on the television complaining and no doubt getting paid, as Sue Baxter continued to come up with little titbits for the media.

Not true, Isaac thought every time she made an unsubstantiated complaint or comment.

Gordon Windsor had phoned to detail the pathologist's final report. It was murder, and a minor blow to the head had occurred before asphyxiation. A second more severe blow had taken place after, although the suffocation had probably killed the man, who would have almost certainly been unconscious. Also, a small tattoo in the shape of a dragon had been found on the right forearm. It appeared to have been skilfully executed.

It was clear that the body needed to be identified. Chasing after missing husbands, delving into the two sisters' relationship was fine, but if they were proven not to be involved, then it was not relevant.

Isaac called the team together for a hastily convened meeting. It was going to be a fateful evening for him, both personally and professionally. He had finally received an ultimatum from Jess O'Neill. She was to make one special effort to put on a romantic meal that night; his non-attendance would signal an end to the relationship. He would have preferred it to have ended on a pleasant note, but he was a senior police officer with a major crime. He could not just leave when it suited him.

***

It was seven in the evening before everyone was assembled back at Challis Street. Isaac had ordered pizzas for everyone. 'We need a name for this body. John Doe is no longer sufficient.'

'We found Gertrude's husband,' Larry said.

'What did you find out?' Isaac asked.

'He's been dead for eight years.'

'We'll discuss this later. For now, we need to identify this body.'

'I've given three names to Larry and Wendy,' Bridget said.

'Fine. When can you start on checking?' Isaac asked.

Wendy knew the answer required, but her husband had taken a turn for the worse. She would need to visit with him first, and then talk to the doctor about additional care, new medicine, and no doubt, an extra cost. She could not see how she could bear the cost without selling the house. 'Tomorrow morning,' she replied. 'Pressing family issue.'

There was no more for her to say, as Isaac was well aware of the situation and sympathised.

'I'll make a couple of phone calls tonight,' Larry said. 'Are we assuming the one we can't find is the body?'

'It's a fair assumption,' Isaac said. He was anxious to leave soon and to see if he could patch it up with Jess before it was too late.

'It's probably best if we call it an early night. There are only three to find, and it would be best to make personal contact rather than over a phone.'

'That sounds fine,' Wendy said. 'I'll attempt to be here early.'

'I'll stay another hour,' Bridget said. 'Tidy up some paperwork.'

'I'll stay with Bridget,' Larry said.

'I'll walk you out,' Isaac said to Wendy. 'I've got some personal business to deal with.'

***

Wendy drove straight to the nursing home. She found her husband sedated and in a confused state.

'It's only getting worse,' the doctor said.

'What can you do?'

'Keep him calm, but he's a big man. We can't have him blundering around.'

'What's your prognosis?'

'There's a heart problem. I give him three, maybe six months.'

'Can he stay here?'

'Under minor sedation, but there is the cost.'

'I'll manage.' She knew that her DCI was attempting to get her made up to sergeant. The extra money would just about cover the additional cost.

Isaac reached home just as Jess was about to give up waiting. He noticed the early signs of packing. 'It's not easy when there is a murder to deal with,' he said.

'I realise that, but sometimes we both have to make an effort. If you want to play the field again, just let me know.'

'I have responsibilities. You knew that before we got together.'

'Even before you slept with Linda Harris.'

Isaac realised the futility of the situation. If he had not slept with the woman, then maybe a longer-term relationship with Jess would have been possible, but it clearly was not. 'It was an error on my part,' he said. 'I can't undo the past, but then I don't think you can forget either.'

'Maybe it's best if we quit while we're ahead,' she said.

'Maybe it is,' he reluctantly agreed.

The meal stayed cold, the bottle of wine unopened. Jess slept on the sofa; Isaac on the bed. He could hear her sobbing, but there was nothing he could say or do. Tomorrow she would be gone. He had hoped it would end better. He was sorry it had not.

Chapter 7

Isaac woke early the next morning after a restless night. Jess had left, a note attesting to the fact on the kitchen table. She clearly stated that she would return during the day and remove her belongings. He sat down for a few minutes, shed a tear in sadness, his momentary remorse disturbed by a phone call.

'We've only got one more person to find,' Wendy said.

'Where are you?'

'In the office. Bridget and DI Hill are here as well.'

'It's only six.'

'We agreed last night to meet at five in the morning.'

'Your husband?'

'Not good.'

'I'm sorry to hear that,' he said.

'And you, sir?'

'The inevitable.'

'I thought it was that, sir. I hope it wasn't too unpleasant.'

'It was.'

'It helps to stay busy, keep the mind occupied.'

'I'll be in the office in twenty minutes.'

'DI Hill and I will be out by then. Bridget will be here.'

'Keep me posted.'

Twenty minutes later, as stated, Isaac arrived in the office. Bridget welcomed him with a cup of freshly-brewed coffee. He could see the motherly touch. Wendy had obviously told her the story.

'Two of the three were easily confirmed on Facebook,' Bridget said. 'DI Hill contacted them. There's only one left, and he seems a distinct possibility.'

'Why do you say that?' Isaac asked.

'He would have been thirty-six in 1987.'

'After 1987?'

'There is no further record of him.'
'Does this person have a name?'
'Solly Michaels. You do understand the significance.'
'Yes, it's clear.'
'Where are DI Hill and Wendy?'
'They've gone to see Gertrude Richardson. Obtain a DNA sample, if she's willing.'
'And if she's not?' Isaac asked.
'Difficult to force a woman in her late eighties, DCI.'
'Almost impossible. We'll deal with it if we come to that hurdle.'

***

Wendy thought it was too early to knock on the door in Richmond. Larry said it was too important to wait any longer. They rang the doorbell three times before the door slowly opened.
'What do you want?'
'There's been a possible development.'
'I'm feeding the cats. Come back later.'
'It would be easier to deal with it now. There are questions to be asked.'
'I sold the house. What more do you want?'
Wendy was concerned that the old woman would not hold up under questioning. She had considered bringing another policewoman skilled in dealing with a medical situation should it occur, but decided against it, as she knew the nature of the woman who confronted them at the door.
'We need to talk to you about your husband.'
'I've not seen him for a long time.'
'We found him,' Wendy said.
'Come in,' the old woman said. 'We can talk in the room we used before.' Wendy could see that the woman was disturbed by the revelation.

The same cat followed them into the room, sat on Larry Hill's lap as before. This time, he did not intend to disturb the conversation by standing up to shake it off.

'Is he dead?' Gertrude Richardson asked.

'I'm sorry, but he died of old age. You must have known.'

Wendy could see that Gertrude was close to tears. She moved over close and put her arm around the woman. Gertrude Richardson nestled her head into Wendy's shoulder, appreciative of her compassion. 'He was a lovely man. I never knew why he left, although he was always playing up.'

'What did you do about it?' Wendy asked.

'Turned a blind eye. It was the way he was, but he always came back to me at night.'

'How many years were you together?'

'Eighteen years, on and off.'

'On and off?' Larry queried.

'Sometimes I'd move out, sometimes he would, but it was a good marriage. Maybe unconventional, but we lived in London during the swinging sixties. A lot of promiscuity then, and we were both guilty. When did he die?'

'Eight years ago, in Fulham.'

'Did he marry again?'

'Yes.'

'We never got divorced.'

'Bigamy?'

'It's a bit late to prosecute him now.'

'Too late,' Wendy said. 'There's another question I must ask. You will not like it.'

'What is it?'

'Did you have a child?'

'Yes,' the woman replied meekly.

'And his name?'

'Garry Solomon.'

'Where is he now?'

'I've not seen him since he turned nineteen. He was wild, always in trouble. Took after his father, I suppose.'

'Did you look for him?'

'For a long time. Even hired a private investigator, but he had disappeared. I received a postcard from India a couple of years later saying that he was fine, but since then, nothing.'

'Did it upset you?'

'For a while, but I was never overly maternal. I was not a good mother, I wanted to party too much, and Michael was not a good example. I thought India was better for him, although I would have liked to have seen him again. I suppose I never will now.'

'I need to take a sample of saliva. Would that be acceptable?'

'What for?'

'We need to collect a sample of your DNA for analysis.'

'Are you saying the body is Garry?'

'We don't know, but we must eliminate all possibilities.'

'I understand.'

After the sample had been taken, Wendy turned to the woman. 'Do you want someone to stay with you?'

'I've got my cats. Besides, I always assumed he would come to an unpleasant end. I never imagined it would be in Bellevue Street.'

'It's not been proven,' Larry said. He had purposely said little during the interview.

'It will be.'

'Why do you say that?'

'A mother knows. I can't explain it.'

***

With a clear reason, Isaac decided to confront Montague Grenfell. As the family lawyer, he should have been more forthcoming about the child of Gertrude Richardson and Michael Solomon. Isaac saw the man as being evasive in hiding information.

'I never spoke of the son because it is part of a confidentiality agreement that I have with the two sisters,'

Grenfell said after Isaac had climbed the stairs to the lawyer's office.

'Why a confidentiality agreement?'

'Do you believe the body to be that of Garry Solomon?'

'It's not proven.'

'But it looks likely?'

'A strong possibility, but why Bellevue Street and why a fireplace? Too many unknowns at the present time.'

'If it is him,' Grenfell said, 'where was he for sixteen, seventeen years?'

'Unknown, although we know he was in India two years after he disappeared.'

'He was trouble.'

'We know, but since he disappeared there has been no record of him, or at least no record of a Garry Solomon. We've not checked for a Solly Michaels, and we've not checked with the fingerprint department.'

Grenfell went to make some tea. He almost spilt it on his return, due to the shaking of his hands. It concerned Isaac as on his previous visit they had been firm.

'Did you know that Michael Solomon was dead?'

'I knew.'

'And you didn't tell his wife?'

'What could I tell her? That he was living not far from her and married to another woman with a couple of children. It would only have caused more trouble.'

'But you're her lawyer?'

'I'm also her cousin and godfather to her son. What kind of bastard would I have been if I had destroyed her belief?'

'What belief is that?'

'That her son is well and happy in India, and her husband is overseas. Better to let sleeping dogs lie. And if I told her that her husband was living in a bigamous relationship, professionally I would have needed to tell the police. I couldn't do that to either Gertrude or Michael Solomon.'

'You knew Michael Solomon?'

'I did.'

'What kind of man was he?'
'He was my friend.'
'Why did he leave Gertrude?'
'That's another story.'
'I could make it official.'
'Confirm the body as Garry Solomon first. Until then it remains a secret.'

***

Larry Hill had been enjoying his time with the team at Challis Street, and he had a great deal of respect for his DCI. He knew some of the truth regarding the death of Sally Jenkins, the murdered woman whose case he had been responsible for. It irked DI Hill that the woman's death had been classified as murder by person or persons unknown. He was aware that his senior knew more, and he had quizzed him on more than one occasion, only to be told that it was classified, and the final report was confidential and came under the Official Secrets Act.

There was not much more that he could do about it, but he saw it as a blot on his career. An unsolved murder invariably reflected on the senior police officer assigned to the case. DCI Cook had told him that it did not, although in this case he even admitted that it irked him as well. Larry Hill saw an inference from Isaac that he knew who the murderer was, but he was not telling either.

Still, Larry Hill had to reflect that working with the team at Challis Street was a lot better than his previous police station. There, it had been office-bound more times than not, dealing with endless paperwork, and the senior man, a detective superintendent, had not been someone he could respect. On the couple of occasions that he had met Detective Chief Superintendent Richard Goddard, he had found him to be a decent man. A little humourless, but he left the team alone as much as possible, and he and Isaac seemed to have a good relationship.

Larry enjoyed being out with Wendy Gladstone, found her to be capable and compassionate, even if she was ageing, and did not move with the agility that he did. He reflected on how well she had handled Gertrude Richardson when she had been told about the death of her husband, and the possible death of her son.

Some secrets were clearly integral to the case. It now appeared that the time spent following up on the two elderly sisters had not been time wasted.

He did not complain about the hours he was working, although his wife, used to him being home at a reasonable time, gave the occasional gripe. He knew that she understood and was always supportive. With the newfound prestige of his position at Challis Street, the possibility of a promotion up to detective chief inspector in a couple of years seemed a distinct possibility.

His time of reflection soon came to a conclusion. 'Are you ready?' Wendy asked.

'Let's go,' he replied. Another visit out to meet the younger sister.

Larry drove. Wendy sat in the passenger's seat, telling him about her husband and his condition. It was not a subject he wanted to hear about, but she seemed to want to talk. He could at least acquiesce and offer comment when required, encouragement when needed.

'They reckon another three to six months,' she said soulfully. He had noticed that she was a cheerful woman until she spoke about her husband. He could only assume they were close.

He understood, as he and his wife were close, although sometimes they argued like cats and dogs. She put it down to her fiery Irish Roman Catholic upbringing; he, to his growing up in a rough area in a rough town in the north of England. Their arguments, he reflected, only lasted a short time, and neither dwelled for weeks on why they had argued in the first place. Money was often the main reason, and a promotion to DCI would help.

'Anyone at home for you?' Larry asked Wendy.

'My last son moved out. All I have there are a television and rising damp.'

'Not ideal.'

'Arthritis,' she said.

'What do you mean?'

'The dampness in the house is playing havoc with my aches and pains. I intend to sell it as soon as possible.'

'And your husband, are you close?'

'We were, but with dementia, it's hard to remember back to that time. Every time I go to visit, I have to take a tablet to calm myself down. Anyway, enough of my complaining. You're a good listener.'

'We're here,' he said.

Exiting the car, they both made their way to the front door of Mavis Richardson's house. The woman opened the door on Wendy's second knock.

'I've had Montague Grenfell on the phone,' Mavis said. She was obviously upset.

'What did he tell you?' Larry asked. Even though the woman was upset, she still managed to ensure they were all seated and had a cup of tea.

'He's had a visit from a Detective Chief Inspector Cook.'

'Our senior,' Wendy said.

'Michael Solomon's dead,' Mavis Richardson said.

'Had you any idea what happened to him after he left your sister?' Larry asked.

'I saw him about ten years ago, purely by chance. I was in the city, and he walked by. We recognised each other instantly.'

'What happened?' Wendy asked.

'We sat down and had a coffee.'

'Anything more?'

'Nothing more. He asked after Gertrude. He seemed to be genuinely concerned. We parted, and I never saw him again.'

'Did you tell your sister?'

'We were not talking, and besides, it would only have brought up unpleasant memories.'

'Secrets best left unspoken?' Wendy asked.

'This is a murder enquiry, you do realise this?' Larry said. He had just poured himself a second cup of tea.

'Garry?' Mavis Richardson asked.

'It's possible.'

'Not proven.'

'We're conducting DNA analysis.'

'You could be forced to give evidence, explain what all the secrets are.'

'Two old women, no more than a few years left for either of us. I don't think the fear of imprisonment would be a catalyst for us to talk. Besides, some secrets must remain hidden, regardless.'

'Are these secrets that important?' Wendy asked. She had helped herself to a small cake.

'Yes.'

Chapter 8

Forensics wasted no time once they had a sample of Gertrude Richardson's DNA. A mitochondrial DNA sequence from the mother and the body matched. Confirmation of the body as Garry Solomon accelerated the investigation. Wendy had the unpleasant task of telling Gertrude. She did not relish it, but she would do it with all haste.

Isaac made an appointment to meet Montague St John Grenfell, the sisters' lawyer. Isaac realised he knew more than he had told them so far; he needed to be pressured. It was now a full-blown murder investigation; the time for evasion belonged in the past.

Wendy, not in the best of spirits, made the trip out to Richmond. Her husband continued to wane, and now she had bad news for Gertrude Richardson, a woman with whom she felt an affinity. Sure, she did not live in a mansion surrounded by cats, but she could empathise with the loneliness of the old woman. Wendy's husband may have been difficult when he had been at home, but he had been there when she arrived. All she had now was a stone-cold house where her voice echoed. Sometimes, she felt like screaming when she got home. Challis Street was not warm and inviting, but at least there were people and noise and activity. The long hours of a murder case suited her fine; telling an old woman that her only child had died thirty years previously did not.

'It's Garry. I'm sorry.'
'I always knew it was.'
'Any more than a mother's instinct?' Wendy asked.
'Too much dirty laundry, too much history,' the woman said. Wendy could see the sadness etched on her face, regardless of the brave manner in which she laboured around the kitchen, stroking one cat and then another. She offered Wendy a cup of

tea; Wendy accepted, even offered to make it for her. Gertrude Richardson declined.

'I'd like to see him.'

'It's thirty years.'

'I've seen dead bodies before, and he's still my son.'

'You said that before. What did you mean?'

'I can't talk about that now. I just want to see my son.'

'I'll arrange it for you. Do you want me to stay here with you?'

'There's a room upstairs. I would appreciate the company.'

Wendy had prepared for such an eventuality; she had brought a change of clothes and a washbag just in case. Isaac told her to stay, do what was necessary, and to keep asking questions, no matter how gentle, how innocuous.

***

Isaac realised that Montague Grenfell, even though he was in his seventies, was mentally and physically stronger. He had scheduled the appointment for two o'clock in the afternoon at the lawyer's office. As he walked briskly up the three floors to the office, he realised that an early morning jog before coming to work was doing him good.

It had been a couple of weeks since Jess had moved out, and in that time there had been no one else in his flat. He had to admit he missed her, and the only time she had contacted him was to let him know that she had paid the electricity, as they had agreed when she had moved in. An independent woman, she had intended to contribute to the upkeep of their shared accommodation.

She also let him know that she still loved him, and if…

Isaac felt sadness talking to her, but realised that the if… was not going to happen. And besides, he felt better, if sadder, being a free man. He wanted to settle down, realised he probably never would. He was not sure how it would impact on his career with the Metropolitan Police, but realised it probably would not. After all, he, the son of Jamaican immigrants, had made detective chief inspector in record time, in a society that stated equality for all, but rarely was equal. He was still after the top job at the Met, and if he was single and black and the son of immigrants, so be it. And besides, he would achieve it in record time.

'How's Gertrude?' Grenfell asked.

'You've not spoken to her?'

'I phoned. She said she was all right.'

'But you're not sure?'

'Not totally, but she was always harder to read than her sister. Mavis is an open book, what you see is what you get. With Gertrude, you could never be sure what she was thinking.'

'Constable Gladstone said she took the news as well as could be expected.'

'Ambiguous statement, don't you think?'

'My constable thought the woman looked sad. That's why she offered to stay the night with her.'

'In that awful house?'

'There's a room upstairs that's in reasonable condition.'

'Your constable can keep asking questions.'

'Her reason to stay is compassionate, no more.'

'True, true,' Grenfell said.

'Coming back to the reality,' Isaac said, 'what don't I know that I should?'

'I'm not sure where to start.'

'Let's start with the women's childhood.'

'I'll make some tea first,' the lawyer said. Five minutes later he returned. Isaac noticed that his hands were not trembling.

'They came up to our home, you would call it a stately home, every summer for two weeks. I am ten years younger than Mavis, twelve years younger than Gertrude. They treated me well, made sure I was fed and bathed as a baby. They were like sisters to me, and we were all fond of each other.'

'Gertrude and Mavis, good friends?'

'They were inseparable until their late teens.'

'What happened?'

'The inevitable. Gertrude was the more promiscuous of the two, although Mavis was far from perfect.'

'Were there many opportunities in those days for promiscuity?'

'Amongst the aristocratic and the idle rich? A different set of values for the upper classes to the proletariat. I was as much a part of it as anyone back then. I was ignored by them after they reached the age of seventeen. My chance to play up came later.'

'Did you see them much after they reached adolescence?'

'Just family occasions: weddings, deaths, the occasional baptism.'

'And then what?'

'I never saw them for many years, heard about them in the gossip columns. Both of them were regarded as beauties, and they were always popping up at Ascot for the races or at some club or another. Invariably squired by the son of a lord or a duke, sometimes in the company of a minor royal.'

'So why did Gertrude marry Michael Solomon?'

'Beauty fades, and a royal wants a virgin, and the son of a lord wants someone reasonably chaste. Gertrude did not qualify on either count. Rumours of an abortion at one stage, but I don't know if that is true or not, never asked either.'

'Was Michael Solomon wealthy?'

'Successful in trade. I suppose he was. Remember, their father was still alive then, so they only had an allowance. From what I know, Gertrude fell heavily in love with Michael, and they married within a couple of months. Her father disapproved until he met him, and then he was quickly charmed. Finally gave them his blessing and a house in Twickenham.'

'Mavis?'

'She travelled in Europe for a few years after the war.'

'And her husband?'

'I never liked him.'

'Any reason?'

'Irish.'

'Is that sufficient?'

'She met him in Italy. He wooed her, bedded her, and eventually married her once he realised that her father was on his deathbed, and she was about to get a half-share in a substantial fortune.'

'Did she?'

'It was substantial. I handled the legal paperwork, assigned each sister their proportion.'

'And the husband?'

'He lasted for a few years, until he realised that Mavis was no fool, and that his good life came with limitations, but no claim to the fortune.'

'Back then, the husband would be entitled, wouldn't he?'

'Not according to their father's last will and testament. He knew that Gertrude was susceptible to unscrupulous men, and that Mavis had made an unfortunate choice in a husband. As I said, I dealt with the legal aspect to protect the women.'

'But it didn't protect Gertrude?'

'Legally and financially, it did, but there were other problems.'

'Michael Solomon?'

'Not at all. He had his problems, but he always came back to Gertrude. He would never have taken advantage of her.'

'Was there someone else?'

'Some years later there was an issue.'

'What kind of issue? Why did Solomon leave and take up with another woman in Fulham?'

'It's best if you talk to Gertrude on this one. Otherwise, I'll need her permission to tell you.'

'I could make it official.'

'It doesn't need that. Give me a day or so to clear the way. In the meantime, look after Gertrude. She has had a rough time over the years.'

***

Garry Solomon's body was still with the forensic pathologist. Apart from a desiccated shell, some hair and the tattoo, there were no other identifying marks. Isaac checked to ensure that the body would be available, to ensure there was some clothing, and that an attempt would be made to make the corpse's face acceptable to view. They stated that it would be impossible, and the best they could do would be to ensure a darkened room, and a veil covering the face. He ran it past Wendy, who spoke to the mother.

Two days after the mother's request, both Wendy and Gertrude Richardson found themselves outside the address where the body was stored. It was the first time outside the mansion in Richmond for five years for the old woman.

'Are you sure?' Wendy asked.

'I'm sure.'

They entered the building, met a well-mannered laboratory assistant who escorted them to the viewing area. The corpse rested in a coffin which the laboratory had secured for the viewing; the lid was open. The mother approached the casket timidly and looked in. She slowly pulled the veil from the face to look at her son. It was not a pleasant sight. Wendy approached and looked in as well; it upset her greatly. She saw what looked to be an Egyptian mummy. Gertrude Richardson could only see a son; her mind drifted back to him as a child, then a boy, then an adult of nineteen, which was the last time she had seen him alive. He had died at the age of thirty-six. If he had lived, he would have been in his late sixties, drawing his pension, presenting her with grandchildren. She was very sad, although she did not show it.

'Thank you,' she said to Wendy. 'I always wanted to see him again, if only for a minute. I am exhausted. Would you please take me home.'

Wendy drove her home, put her in a bed upstairs, promising to feed the cats. She then went downstairs to make the old woman a cup of tea, and prepare some food for her. When Wendy returned twenty minutes later, the old lady was lying on her back, her eyes wide open, her mouth slightly ajar. She was dead.

***

'You did well, Wendy,' Isaac said on her return to the office several hours later. As sad as it was, Gertrude Richardson had died of natural causes. There would be an autopsy, as she was an integral person in a murder investigation, but Wendy saw it as a formality. The woman, old and frail, had held on to see her son. She had died soon after as a result. Wendy had stayed at the mansion until the body had been removed. She then phoned the Battersea Dogs and Cats Home to come and take care of the cats. She counted twenty-three. Larry said he would take the one that kept sitting on his lap. Wendy decided on two that would provide company for her when she got home at night. The rest she surmised would be adopted out, more likely euthanised.

'It doesn't feel that way at the moment, sir,' she said.

'It will in time. Are you free to talk about the case?'

'It will help to take my mind off what happened. No wonder she died after what she saw in that casket.'

'You said she was used to dead bodies.'

'She never explained why. It was her son she was looking at, but she stood there showing no emotion.'

'Her lawyer said she concealed her feelings well, never knew what she was thinking. Mavis, he said, was the opposite.'

'Where's DI Hill?'

'He went out to inform Mavis Richardson. Apparently, the woman became quite emotional. Larry's still there.'

'Maybe I should go there as well, sir.'

'Not necessary. Larry took her to a formal identification of her sister. He will be here within the next hour.'

Bridget, sensing that Wendy was grieving, took her under her wing. She settled her down on a comfortable chair and gave her a strong brew of tea and a couple of chocolate biscuits, as well as some cake she had brought from home. Ten minutes later, Wendy was much better.

'She identified the body,' DI Hill said on his return to the station.

'Where is she now?'

'Back at her house. Her lawyer is with her.'

'We should go out there,' Isaac said to Larry.

'Yes, sir.'

'I'll go as well,' Wendy said.

'Go home and take it easy for the rest of the day,' Isaac said.

'She's coming home with me,' Bridget said. 'I don't think she wants to be on her own tonight.' Wendy thanked her.

It took forty-five minutes to make the trip out to Mavis Richardson's house. Larry reflected that it would only have taken twelve on the train. Isaac could only agree.

They saw Montague Grenfell's car in the driveway of the house on their arrival, a late model Mercedes. They knocked at the door.

'Come in,' Montague Grenfell said. 'Miss Richardson is composing herself. She will be down in a minute.' Isaac reflected that the man seemed at home in the house.

The woman joined them soon after. She was relaxed and agreeable, although there were signs of crying around her eyes.

'I'm sorry about your loss,' Isaac said.

'Thank you, DCI Cook. We didn't always see eye to eye, but she was still my sister.'

'There are questions to be asked, answers to be given. Is this an appropriate time?'

'There will never be an appropriate time.'

'Are you able to elaborate?' Isaac asked.

'Another time would be better,' Grenfell said.

'The truth will come out sometime. It is best to clear the air now,' Mavis Richardson said.

She went to make tea for everyone. Isaac accompanied her to assist. She appeared to appreciate the gesture.

Upon their return, Isaac placed the tray in the middle of the coffee table. Everyone helped themselves to the tea and the small cakes. 'Baked them myself,' she said.

'They're delicious,' Larry and Isaac said in unison. Everyone knew that it was small talk, the sparring before the main event. There was a secret, possibly secrets that were crucial to solving the murder of Garry Solomon aka Solly Michaels. The person most likely to know had died. Isaac was hopeful that those remaining knew as much.

'Miss Richardson, were you aware that Garry Solomon was in London during the 1980s, and possibly the years preceding?'

'I never saw him again, but he knew that he would not be welcome.'

'Did your sister know of your ambivalence?'

'Yes.'

'Can you elaborate?'

'Must I?'

'Yes. This is a murder enquiry.'

'Very well.' She sat down, perched herself on the edge of a chair. She looked unsure of herself. 'Garry had always been a disruptive child, even when he was very young. A cruel streak as well. Gertrude always made excuses; Michael always forgave. We were sharing the mansion in Richmond. It was the sixties, the swinging sixties, free love.'

'You were part of that scene?' Isaac asked.

'We were still young enough to enjoy it. We were promiscuous, always screwing around when we were in our teens, and it had carried on as we got older. It was what the elite used to get up to, although most everyone will deny it. We used to have some wild parties. Mainly alcohol, but some drugs, and often people would pair off, car keys in a bowl, that sort of thing.'

'Gertrude was married,' Isaac said.

'So was I, but it didn't seem to matter. I would pair off with her husband or someone else. She would do the same. No one appeared to be affected by it, apart from Garry. It was our mistake really, too interested in our pleasures at the expense of a minor, although he was in his early teens by then. We always ensured he was at boarding school during the week when we had the parties. Whenever he came home, it was just one happy family: picnics on the lawn, games around an open fire. Even then, he would quickly lose his temper if the game did not go his way.'

'Why your ambivalence towards him?'

'He came home early while we were having one of our parties. Supposedly, he had picked up an infection in the school swimming pool. Usually, someone would have gone and picked him up, but for some reason it had not happened this time. It was a long time ago, and I forget the details. He comes into the house; those who are not upstairs paired off are out for the count on alcohol and drugs. Not finding anyone that he knows, he climbs the stairs and enters the first room he finds.'

'What did he find?' Larry asked.

'Two naked bodies entwined.'

'Who were they?'

'His father and me, who else?'

'And then?'

'He goes crazy, starts hitting me with an iron poker used to stoke the fire. I was on top. Eventually, my husband comes in and restrains him, and I'm taken off to the hospital.'

'Serious injuries?'

'Bruising, black and blue for some weeks, but I recovered.'

'And your husband? What did he say finding you with Michael Solomon?'

'Nothing. He was off with someone else. Gertrude was with Montague.'

'So why the ambivalence? It seems he had every right to be upset.'

'Of course, but then he gets back to his school, and tells all his friends who tell their parents. It is just bad breeding. The upper classes keep their dirty laundry to themselves, but then Garry never understood that. Just common, I suppose.'

Isaac saw clearly that Mavis Richardson was a snob who saw breeding and class as paramount. He decided that he did not like her, regardless of how polite and friendly she had been towards him.

Chapter 9

Mavis Richardson's husband continued to be an enigma. The name of O'Loughlin did not automatically conjure up thoughts of aristocracy and breeding. Isaac realised that he needed to be found. He was the one person missing out of the key group.

There was also the question of what happened to Garry Solomon, or Solly Michaels as he seemed to have been known. He had come from a privileged background, but police records showed behaviour not akin to influence and importance. There were police reports available, indicating that a Solly Michaels had been picked up for drug trafficking, occasional violence, and receiving stolen goods.

Isaac felt it was necessary to find out more about him. And then the question remained, why a fireplace in a house belonging to the Richardson sisters? It was evident that the body would be found at some stage and an identification secured. Too many variables, too many unanswered questions. He needed Larry and Wendy out and about, aiming to reduce the unknowns. Wendy seemed best placed to find the missing husband, Larry better placed to find out if anyone knew the story of Garry Solomon. From all indications that would require him entering the underbelly of society, going into places where a woman might not be welcome.

'Surely Garry Solomon is more important,' Larry Hill said at the evening meeting.

'Outline your thought process,' Isaac said.

'He disappears for all those years, and then he ends up in the fireplace of the house in Bellevue Street.'

Bridget wanted to say something. Isaac waved his hand at her, a gesture to keep quiet for the moment. Wendy had questions to ask, but she knew Isaac's style. He was a team player who did not steal someone's thunder when they were on a roll.

Larry continued after taking a quick sip of his coffee. 'Garry Solomon is here in London, a petty villain. There's a fortune to be had, yet he decides not to come forward to claim any of it.'

'What about the antagonism from Mavis Richardson?' Wendy asked.

'What about it?' Larry replied. 'Garry Solomon was a villain, and by all accounts a nasty piece of work. Do you think he would care who he upset?'

'Probably not, and then there is his mother. Why didn't he contact her at least a few times over the years?'

'Maybe he did, but we'll never know now as both mother and son are dead,' Isaac said.

'I've obtained his full criminal record. It may help to fill in some of the blanks,' Bridget said.

'Great,' Larry said. 'Let me finish first.'

'It looks as if we're in for a long night. Do I need to phone for some food?' Isaac asked.

Bridget and Wendy were quick to raise their hands. Isaac knew his keep fit regime was to suffer. Jess had left a message, wanting to meet up. He quickly sent her a message stating that he was busy until ten that night. Her reply was curt.

Larry took the floor again. He stood up and leant against the wall. 'We know he's a villain, but why does he end up dead in a fireplace? The address would indicate that his murder was committed by someone he knew, someone who had access to the house.'

'But why?' Isaac asked. 'Hiding a body in a fireplace, hoping it would not be disturbed, makes no sense.'

'It must have been temporary, and for some reason the person never returned.'

'It still makes no sense,' Wendy said. 'If you intend to hide a body for a short period, there must be better places than the house.'

'Do we know where he was murdered?' Bridget asked.

'Good question,' Isaac said. 'The assumption is that it was in the house, but that's not been confirmed. After thirty years, it may be difficult to ascertain.'

'The crime scene examiner, what did he say?' Wendy asked.

'Not his call. He checked the body, and then handed it over to his crime scene investigators.'

'There are still another few variables,' Larry said. 'If Garry Solomon did not contact his mother, what about his father?'

'Another dead witness,' Isaac said.

'But his wife, or should I say his bigamous wife, is still alive,' Wendy said. 'I'll go out there tomorrow.'

'If somehow Garry Solomon had managed to avoid any contact with his parents, then why does he appear all of a sudden, only to be murdered?' Larry asked.

'Larry's right,' Isaac said. 'All those years, and not once has he contacted his parents. It seems unlikely that he had not seen his father. They both moved in the same area of London.'

'Their lawyer appears suspect,' Larry said.

'That's my thought,' Isaac replied. 'He said that there was a secret, and if the body tied in with the sisters, he would reveal it to me.'

'Now's the time, sir,' Wendy said.

The pizzas had arrived, and everyone was eating. Isaac had promised himself to keep it down to two slices, although he snuck in a third.

'Garry Solomon is murdered for a reason. Asking for money hardly seems sufficient,' Larry said.

'Montague Grenfell is the key to this,' Isaac said.

'I'll go out and see the grieving sister tomorrow,' Larry said. 'She must know something.'

'I'll meet Michael Solomon's widow.' Wendy reiterated her earlier statement.

'Bridget, can you check out Garry Solomon's movements over the missing years? See if there is anything of interest,' Isaac said.

'And you, sir?' Wendy asked.

'Montague St John Grenfell is going to give me some answers tomorrow, Earl Grey tea or no Earl Grey tea. I remain convinced that he knows something. The dead man had found out something which was dynamite. It was what got him killed. Grenfell must know something, although we must not discount Mavis Richardson.'

At eleven in the evening, the meeting concluded. Isaac sent an SMS to Jess. She sent one back to tell him it was too late, and she would talk to him another time.

Isaac went home to a cold bed and a hot drink, which was not how he liked his day to conclude.

At nine o'clock the next morning, Isaac made the climb up to Montague Grenfell's office. He had managed to have an early morning jog, and this time he ran up the stairs.

Grenfell had not been expecting a visit from the DCI. He did not seem pleased to see him.

'Sad business about Gertrude,' Grenfell said.

'Why was her son murdered?' Isaac asked. He was not in the mood for procrastination. It was clear that the shock of Gertrude Richardson seeing her son no more than a mummified shell, manifestly unrecognisable except to a mother, had been the reason for her death.

'I don't know.' Montague Grenfell, as usual, prepared tea. Isaac was aware that the man was hiding a secret. A secret that had remained hidden, unspoken, for many years. With Garry Solomon's identity confirmed and his murder proved, the secret needed to be revealed.

'We can do this down at Challis Street Police Station if that would help you to give me a straight answer.' Grenfell was perturbed by the change in the policeman's manner.

Grenfell had relaxed back in his chair, looking up into the air, resisting the need to make eye contact with Isaac. 'Neither of the two women had any other children,' he said.

'Is that a fact?' Isaac asked. 'You failed to tell me about Gertrude's son before. You could be omitting some information now.'

'I failed to mention her son before because it was not relevant.'

'You suspected it may be him in the fireplace. Am I correct in that assumption?'

'From the information you had given me about the body, it seemed likely but highly improbable.'

'Why do you say that?'

'He disappeared when he was in his teens. No one had heard from him since, except for a postcard to Gertrude to say he was in India.'

'Is it confirmed that he was in India?' Isaac asked.

'I remember seeing it. There was an Indian stamp on it. Gertrude was delighted when she received it.'

'And you felt that your suspicions about the body did not warrant informing the police?'

'There were no suspicions. He had disappeared many years before the body was placed in the fireplace. The fact that the age appeared to be about the same as Garry seemed circumstantial. I know that he was in Australia for a short period.'

'How do you know this?'

'I am the family lawyer. It's my business to know.'

'But how? And more importantly, why?'

'If both of the sisters die, then Garry Solomon would have inherited their money and assets.'

'What about their husbands?'

'Mavis was smart enough to make sure that wouldn't happen. She married for love, but she was still a realist. She knew the family wealth would make them an attractive target for smooth-talking Romeos.'

'But Gertrude lost all her money to this type of man?' Isaac said.

'She lost plenty, but not all.'

'You'd better explain that statement.'

Montague Grenfell went to make another cup of tea.

The lawyer returned and sat upright on his chair. 'I suppose I should confess something here,' he said.

'If you're about to confess to the murder, then I should caution you.'

'Nothing like that,' Grenfell replied.

'When Gertrude was in her twenties, she fell madly in love with an Italian she had met on holiday in Italy. Both Mavis and I were aware of Gertrude and her momentary fantasies, falling for the wrong kind of man only to realise very quickly that it was more lust than love. Gertrude at that time had access to half of the Richardson family fortune. In the moment of greatest love, the man could ask for anything and she would agree. This Italian gave her a story about his ailing mother back home. Gertrude, an easy target then, not the embittered woman that she became, fell for the story. He had letters and photos, even arranged for her to phone his mother. The outcome of this was that Gertrude arranged a transfer of twenty thousand pounds to his account. Remember, this is the 1950s, so in today's money that would be over two hundred thousand pounds.'

'A lot of money,' Isaac said.

'As you say, a lot of money.'

'And the Italian?'

'After it had been made clear that no more would be forthcoming, he soon disappeared.'

'And what of Gertrude?'

'Broken-hearted for a few weeks. Some years later, she found someone else.'

'Another scoundrel?'

'Not this time, but he had issues.'

'What sort of problems?'

'He couldn't keep it in his pants.'

'Unfaithful?'

'Eventually bigamy.'

'Michael Solomon?' Isaac asked.

'Yes.'

'You mentioned a confession.'

'It was clear that Gertrude, given the opportunity, would have given all of her money to one man or another.'

'You said that Michael Solomon was a friend of yours,' Isaac reminded Grenfell.

'He was, but I did not want to see Gertrude lose all her money to him.'

'But he was a good businessman?'

'Eventually, but he would take some risks, go into substantial debt. Gertrude had to be protected.'

'What did you do?'

'Mavis knew the details, and we hatched a plan. The best protection for her sister was to ensure that she had no noticeable wealth. Then any smooth-tongued man that came hunting for a wealthy woman would not find it with Gertrude.'

'I was under the assumption that she had lost all her money, and that Mavis had covered the debts.'

'Not all of it. Gertrude still had sufficient, although she was never interested in asking or checking. To her, money was there for spending. I doubt if she looked at a bank account once in her life.'

'Mavis?' Isaac asked.

'Total opposite. Mavis could tell you her bank balance down to the last pound.'

'But the hatred between the sisters?'

'There was no hatred from Mavis. She loved her sister. The problem was with Gertrude. She blamed Mavis for her life, her parlous state, even the health of her cats, the condition of the mansion. And especially for her son leaving.'

'Are you saying that her hatred was invalid?'

'If Garry had not seen his father with Mavis on the bed, then maybe he would not have disappeared, but that's past history. As I said, Michael Solomon was a friend, even if he could waste money, Gertrude's money, at times. Garry, for whatever reason, was not as the father. Mavis always saw him as common, but it was not that.'

'What was it?' Isaac asked.

'Being shuffled off to a boarding school at an early age may have been part of the problem. The belief that he was unloved, especially by his mother. But mainly because he was not a good person. His character, even from an early age, was disruptive, argumentative, and by the time he was nineteen, he was already getting into trouble with the police. He had been to three boarding schools, all very expensive and exclusive, and he had been expelled from the first two for stealing from the other boys. He was destined to turn out bad, and his father knew that.'

'His mother?'

'She made excuses, but she was not a good mother. Always interested in the pursuit of her own pleasures, and she was promiscuous, even more so than Mavis.'

'The parties at the mansion?'

'Harmless fun for those who partook.'

'You included?'

'Why not? I was young, and there were always plenty of women.'

'You stated before that you ensured that Gertrude had no visible wealth.' Isaac returned to Grenfell's earlier statement.

'It was clear that Gertrude would give her half of the fortune away eventually. Each time that she came to her sister for money, we would take some more and put it into a trust account.'

'And this money?'

'It's all there. The records are meticulous. Gertrude and eventually Garry were still wealthy.'

'If Garry had lived, he would have inherited money?'

'Yes.'

'Enough money to kill for?'

'I suppose so. The money was not the issue then as Gertrude still had plenty.'

'If Gertrude had so much money, then why did she live so poorly? Why did her sister allow it?'

'But she didn't. That was Gertrude's choice. She was always eccentric. The crazy old woman with the cats suited her. I had offered to fix up the mansion for her, even take the cats to the vet for check-ups, but she wouldn't have any of it.'

'Who owns the mansion?'

'Gertrude and Mavis own it jointly.'

'But Mavis said she did, and Gertrude believed it did not belong to her,' Isaac said.

'That may be, but there was an incident some years ago when Gertrude wanted her half-share to help out Michael Solomon.'

'And you didn't give him the money?'

'There was already money in the trust fund. We used that and kept the mansion. Believe me, there was never any attempt to cheat Gertrude. It was all done out of love to protect her.'

Isaac realised that Montague Grenfell had explained the situation satisfactorily. It all sounded plausible to him, but it would need to be checked out.

'Due to the seriousness of the matter, would you be willing to allow the trust fund records to be examined?' Isaac asked.

'Yes.'

Isaac intended to pass them over initially to Bridget. His instinct told him that Grenfell had acted honourably. He was still not sure about Mavis Richardson.

Chapter 10

Wendy met Mary Solomon at a restaurant close to where the woman lived.

'My daughter is looking after her children,' the woman said. Wendy noticed that she looked a lot better away from the oppressive house in Fulham.

'Mrs Solomon, I have a few questions,' Wendy said.

'Call me Mary. Besides, I am not sure if I am legally Mrs Solomon.' Wendy chose not to comment.

'Are you aware of a child from his previous marriage?' Wendy asked.

'He mentioned that there was a son.'

'Did you have any suspicions that your husband may not have been divorced?'

'None. It was never mentioned when we applied for a marriage licence. I always assumed it was legitimate.'

'And the previous wife, what did you know about her?'

'He never spoke about her. I don't even know her name.'

'She died last week,' Wendy said.

'I'm sorry to hear that.'

'Does the name Solly Michaels mean anything to you?'

The reaction on Mary Solomon's face indicated that it did.

'I met a person by that name, a long time ago. He was friendly with my husband.'

'Do you remember the year?'

'Not really. He would have been about my age.'

'What age would you have been?'

'In my early thirties.'

'Did you meet him many times?' Wendy asked.

'Only a couple of times. I assumed it was to do with my husband's business. Why did you ask about Solly Michaels?' Mary Solomon asked.

'Subject to confirmation, it was his son.'

Mary Solomon sat back on the chair, visibly shrunken. 'What else did my husband not tell me?' she asked.

'Unfortunately, we need to find out,' Wendy said.

'My eldest son is always in trouble with the police. Was Michael's first son?'

'It appears so.'

'It must be genetic. Michael's first son, and our son and daughter.'

'Your daughter?'

'A bad drug habit. She tells me she's working up in the city, but I know the truth.'

Wendy could see that the woman had been dealt a bad hand, and that life had not treated her well.

'Tell me more about your daughter,' Wendy said.

'I followed her once. She's working in a club up there, selling herself to feed her habit.'

'Does she know that you know?'

'I confronted her. She told me to mind my own business. Then she lands her mongrel spawn on me to babysit. They are only children, but I can see it already. Michael's genes have infected another generation. They'll grow up same as the mother and the grandfather.'

'What about the father of the children?' Wendy asked.

'Some mongrel or mongrels she sold herself to, no doubt. One of the children looks half-Chinese.'

'Your son's child?'

'The mother walked out on Daniel after he had hit her once too often. I am the child's mother now, although he looks fine. Maybe with this one it will be my genes and its mother.'

'Good woman, was she?'

'Lovely, but Daniel doesn't know how to treat women. His father did.'

'Solly Michaels, is there any more you can tell me about him?' Wendy asked.

So far, they had not ordered any food. Wendy rectified the situation and ordered for them both. The woman sitting opposite appeared glad to be taking a break from the drudgery of her domestic situation. Wendy was thankful that her children were fine and adult and not causing trouble. Even her husband had treated her well until his dementia kicked in.

'Michael's son by this other woman, what happened to him?' Mary Solomon asked.

'He's dead.'

'I'm sorry to hear that. He was a nice-looking man. Now I think about it, he did bear a resemblance to Michael. I must have been stupid not to notice, although he always called my husband by his first name.'

'He died in 1987.'

'How sad. Do you think Michael knew?'

'We don't know.'

'I'll let you know if I remember any more, but it could not have been Michael, not his own son.'

'I only hope you are right.'

After finishing their meal, Wendy walked with Mary Solomon to her house. The woman gave Wendy a hug as they parted. Wendy realised that Michael Solomon knew more than he had ever told Mary. She hoped he was not involved in Garry's death as Mary Solomon had enough to deal with. She had learnt that her husband had been a bigamist, her marriage certificate was probably not valid, and then she had two children and their offspring, and none of them looked fine. To find out that her husband was a murderer as well, a murderer of his own son, Wendy thought, would be more than Mary Solomon could be expected to bear.

***

Mavis Richardson was extremely cordial when Larry Hill knocked on her door. He had some trepidation about visiting her on his own, but everyone was busy, and besides he did not need a nursemaid to look after him.

'On your own?' she asked. Larry noticed a nice spread of food laid out on the coffee table. He had questions to ask, not the time to partake of a feast, and besides, he needed to keep his distance from the woman.

Larry seated himself in a chair close to the fireplace. Mavis Richardson sat close by in another chair. 'There are some questions,' he said.

'A lot of questions, I suppose.'

'According to Montague Grenfell, Gertrude's money was intact.'

'A lot of it was wasted, but we saved her from herself.'

'We?'

'Montague and I.'

'There was animosity between you and your sister, though.'

'Only from her side. As I told you before, I forgave her.'

'Was she aware that financially she was secure?'

'No.'

'Any reason?'

'If she had known, she would have taken action to secure her share. She was an easy touch for a charming man.'

'Michael Solomon?'

'He was exceedingly charming.'

'And he took her money?'

'He did, but he was still a good man. I'm sure he loved Gertrude, as much as she loved him.'

'Then why did he leave?'

'He loved too many women. Eventually Gertrude tired of his dalliances. And there was a scene. After that, he left.'

'They never divorced, yet he marries again?'

'What's the problem with that?' Mavis asked.

'It's illegal for one thing.'

'And the other?'

'It just seems unusual. He could have divorced Gertrude officially, and then he could have married the other woman.'

'Divorce would not have been an option for Gertrude.'

'Did he ask her?'

'Montague alluded to that fact. I never asked for the details. I had problems of my own.'

'Your husband?'

'Ger O'Loughlin.'

'And where is he now?'

'Not here.'

'Have you seen or heard from him since?' Larry asked.

'Infrequently.'

'We have no record of children. Is that correct?'

'I never had children. Never wanted them anyway. My social life was more important. A child would only have hampered my lifestyle.'

'And your husband?'

'He wanted children. My reluctance doomed the marriage.'

'And where is he now?'

'Ireland, surrounded by his brood.'

'How do you know this?'

'He occasionally contacts me. I've not seen him though.'

Larry realised that his questioning was not progressing. Ger O'Loughlin did not seem relevant, and Bridget had found proof that he and Mavis Richardson were legally divorced. The death of Garry Solomon aka Solly Michael was the only issue. Mavis Richardson's husband was not relevant unless he could be tied in with Gertrude's family.

'Did your husband know Garry Solomon?'

'Yes. I told you that he pulled him off me.'

'We know that Garry Solomon disappeared when he was nineteen, but what about Michael Solomon?'

'He stayed around for another six months, but by then the parties at the mansion were starting to wither. Everyone was tired of the same people to swap car keys with. At first it had been fun, a titillation, but eventually it became routine.'

'Is that when you fell out with Gertrude?'

'Around that time.'

'Why?'

'She wanted money for Michael, a lot of money.'

'And you wouldn't give it to her?'

'I knew what he was up to. It wasn't financially sound, so Montague falsified the accounts to show that she didn't have that much money.'

'You effectively broke up her marriage,' Larry said.

'I couldn't let her bankrupt herself. Believe me, it was in her own best interest.'

'Did she eventually find out?'

'No.'

Larry took advantage of the spread placed in front of him, and he was only eating because he was hungry.

'A glass of wine, beer?' she asked.

'On duty. Can I come back to Garry Solomon?'

'If you must.'

'Did you ever hear from him again?'

'No, although Michael did.'

'Why do you say that?'

'Remember, I told you that I ran into him once in the street.'

'Did he mention his son?'

'He asked after Gertrude, I asked after their son.'

'His reply?'

'He said he had seen him on a couple of occasions. I asked him if the son had contacted his mother.'

'What did he say?'

'Garry could never forgive her.'

'Forgive her for what?'

'No idea. Maybe the lack of love he received from her, maybe the fact that his mother slept with other men, perhaps he was just angry, but I was the one screwing his father. He was not aware that Gertrude was off screwing someone else, although he was a smart lad. He probably assumed she was.'

'Tell me about that night,' Larry asked.

'It's old history. I am with his father, Gertrude is with Montague. Is this important?'

'I want to ascertain what happened after Garry put you in the hospital.'

'He ran out of the house. Five hours later, in the early morning, he returns.'

'And then what?'

'Nothing.'

'What did his father say to him?'

'Nothing. Garry's reaction was understandable. Michael and Gertrude took him to the Caribbean for a couple of weeks, acted the loving parents for once.'

'Did you see him again?'

'Never. Whenever he was there, I made sure to be somewhere else. That night was the last time that I saw him.'

'You never forgave him for what he did to you?'

'I've explained this before. It was his returning to school, and bragging to his friends about what he did to me that I could never forgive. As far as he was concerned, his father was welcome to screw whoever he wanted.'

'And his mother?'

'Typical male chauvinist attitude. Very prevalent in the sixties. It's alright for the man to screw around, but not the woman.'

'What did he say at school?'

'He told everyone, even the sons of friends of ours, that I was a slut. I could never forgive him for that. A sign of bad blood, Michael's blood. That's what happens when you breed outside of your class.'

'When did he finally leave home?'

'He was nineteen, hormones raging. He comes home with a female in tow and says he is off to India. He makes sure to score some money out of his parents and a bank transfer from Montague.'

'Your money?'

'Both Gertrude's and mine, although she did not know that it was.'

'Why did you agree?'

'He was still Gertrude's son.'
'And the female?'
'Supposedly he married her in India.'
'Where is she now?'
'I've no idea. Montague may know.'

Mavis Richardson excused herself and left the room for a couple of minutes. Larry took the opportunity to update Isaac regarding Garry Solomon's wife. If anyone knew what had happened in India and on their return, it would be her.

Isaac could see that information was still being withheld. It was almost as if the Richardson family and Montague Grenfell were intentionally obstructing them.

Larry continued at Mavis Richardson's house on instructions from Isaac. 'Keep probing,' Isaac said. 'What else are they withholding?'

Mavis Richardson returned with a fresh pot of tea. 'Who were you talking to?' she asked.

'My boss, DCI Cook.'
'What did he have to say?'
'He was curious as to what else we don't know.'
'I've told you everything that I know.'
'That may be, but until we started probing, we did not know that your sister had been married, or that her son had returned to England.'

'We are a private family. We don't air our dirty linen in public.'

'But this is a murder investigation into the death of your nephew.'

'That may be. My family, as with Montague's, goes back hundreds of years. There are a lot of secrets during that time, secrets best kept hidden.'

Chapter 11

'Bridget, what's your situation?' Isaac asked at the regular end of day meeting.

'Apart from collating all sundry information, I've had a cursory look at the documents the Richardson sisters' lawyer supplied,' Bridget said.

'What do you reckon?'

'I'm not an expert, but they appear to be in order.'

'Any transfer of money to Garry Solomon during the period mentioned by Mavis Richardson?'

'There were some transfers to him.'

'Can you check for a marriage certificate for Garry Solomon?' Larry asked.

'In India?' Bridget queried.

'I suppose so.'

'Almost impossible to find unless they legalised it in England. In India, it could have just been a Buddhist ceremony on a mountain top. It would not stand up in an English court of law.'

'Look anyway,' Larry said.

'What are your thoughts?' Isaac asked.

'If Garry Solomon had a child, legitimate or otherwise, then that child is due to inherit a substantial amount of money.'

'It is substantial if the records are correct,' Bridget said.

'How substantial?' Isaac asked.

'Gertrude Richardson may have regarded herself as a pauper, supported by a sister she abhorred.'

'She didn't even acknowledge that she had a sister,' Wendy said.

'According to the records, she still had a half-share in the mansion and five million pounds,' Bridget said.

'Substantial, as you say,' Isaac said.

'And it belongs to the widow is no longer alive. We need the will of Gertrude Richardson,' Larry said.

'Bridget, another job for you,' Isaac said. 'Check with the National Will Register. Otherwise, Montague Grenfell will have a copy.'

'Do you trust him, sir?' Wendy asked.

'Not particularly, that's why I'd prefer Bridget to see if she can find the will without letting him know.'

'I could do with some help. I am not an accountant. It needs a skilled person to check the documentation from Grenfell,' Bridget said.

'Wendy, your update,' Isaac said, momentarily ignoring Bridget's comment.

'Mary Solomon, the second wife of Michael Solomon, remembers meeting a Solly Michaels. She was not aware of his significance.'

'How old would he have been?' Larry asked.

'The woman can be a little vague. She has led a tough life, but from memory, she remembers him as being about the same age as she was. She thought he was in his early thirties.'

'A few years before he was murdered,' Isaac said.

'I will spend more time with her. Maybe she will be able to pinpoint the date more accurately.'

'You suspect his father?' Bridget asked.

'We're not forming an opinion on flimsy assumptions, not just yet,' Isaac said. 'We have proven that Garry Solomon was in London and that he had been in contact with his father, but not his mother.'

'She acted as though she had not seen him since he left when he was nineteen,' Wendy said.

'You were there when she formally identified the body?' Larry asked.

'She was convinced it was him, but visual identification was not possible. The body was far too decayed. It was purely DNA and dental records that proved who it was. The shock of seeing him killed her.'

'But you took her.'

'It was her son. She had a right to see him.'

'No issue from me,' Isaac said. 'What's important now is to find out more about Garry Solomon. Larry, can you focus on his criminal record, known haunts, known villains that he may have been in contact with. Wendy, it may be best if you work with Bridget and see if you can find Garry Solomon's widow.'

'And you, sir?' Wendy asked.

'Three flights of stairs and Montague Grenfell again. He knows a lot more than he's telling us.'

'Don't tell him we're looking for Gertrude Richardson's will,' Bridget reminded Isaac.

'Not at all, and find someone from Fraud to help you with the trust agreements and bank statements.'

***

Isaac saw clearly that Montague Grenfell was still withholding information. The murdered man and the lawyer shared a common ancestor with the father of one, the grandfather of the other. Montague Grenfell came from the legitimate line. Garry Richardson, however, came from the other side of the bed, in that his grandfather had not been legitimate. But as Grenfell had freely admitted, his father and the Richardson sisters' father had been brought up as brothers.

Isaac understood Grenfell's reticence, but this was a murder investigation. The time for propriety had passed, and a full and frank admission of all the skeletons in the cupboard was needed.

'I've been totally open with you, DCI Cook,' Montague Grenfell said when Isaac reminded him of the facts, and that withholding information, especially in a murder enquiry, was a criminal offence.

'You failed to mention that you had sent money to Michael Solomon and Gertrude Richardson's son, and you did not reveal that he had probably married in India. Do you deny that fact?'

'Michael told me, although I had no contact with him.'

'Garry Richardson's wife?'

'Michael assumed it was someone he had met at school, although he never met her.'

'Were there any children?'

'I have no idea.'

'Unfortunately, you have not revealed other information which we have subsequently unearthed. Is there any more that you are not telling us?'

'I have been open with you. I gave you full access to all legal and financial documents relating to Gertrude.'

'That is true. They appear to be in order.'

'You will find no errors there.'

'From what we can ascertain, Gertrude Richardson was a very wealthy woman, and subsequently her son would be. Yet you withheld that information from her.'

'As I said before, my intentions and those of her sister were totally honourable. I have no reason to reproach myself.'

'The woman lived in squalor.'

'Detective Chief Inspector, we've been over this before. Where she lived would have been restored to a liveable standard if she had wanted. I offered enough times.'

'And why did she refuse?'

'She was an old woman set in her ways. She liked the squalor and the cats defecating in the house. There was no way I, or her sister, could force her to change her ways, nor would we.'

'And what about the son? Was he entitled to any money?'

'If he had asked.'

'He didn't?'

'Never. Supposedly, he had returned from India with this woman, now his wife as a result of a wedding in a commune or on a hill top. No idea if it's legal, but it is probably not relevant under English law.'

'Children?' Isaac asked.

'I have already told you that I don't know. It is possible. If Garry was anything like his father, then she may have had a child. We looked after Gertrude even if she did not want our help. The son was young enough to look out for himself. Where he went, I never asked or cared.'

'Did Gertrude realise that her sister wanted to help her?'

'Impossible to say. Mavis, as you know, is concerned with appearances and breeding. Gertrude was not bothered by any of it. As long as she had her cats and some food, then she wanted no more. It was not Mavis and me who were the issue. It was the old woman.'

'And her money?'

'It is in trust until probate is resolved.'

***

There seemed to be two major issues confronting the investigation. Isaac summed them up at the evening's meeting. So far, they had managed to hold it every night during the investigation, even managed to take one Sunday off. Not that is helped with Jess O'Neill as she was gone and no longer answering his phone calls. He put it down to the fact that she was busy. Isaac, never a fan of television, had watched the programme she produced a couple of times in the last week, and it was clear that its standards had been maintained, although he regarded his opinion as subjective.

'We need to find out about Garry Solomon's wife,' Isaac said. Wendy, as usual, was nominated for the task.

'But why would someone murder him?' Larry asked.

'Unknown,' Isaac answered. 'How do we find out why? According to the family lawyer, there was no issue with money if he had come forward and asked.'

'Then his death is illogical,' Larry replied.

'Any ideas?' Bridget asked.

'I'm not sure about their lawyer is being totally honest,' Isaac said. It was dark outside and getting late, but he was in no hurry to get home. Larry was, as his wife was complaining about the hours he was working. Wendy's problems were more severe as her husband's hospital bills were way above her salary. She had secured an additional loan against her house, but she knew that it would not be long before she had to sell it.

Bridget revelled in the office environment with its endless challenges, and as long as Wendy was in the office, she was happy to stay. The two women's night out, invariably an excuse for too much gossip and too many drinks, had been postponed due to Wendy's visits to her husband. They were scheduling again for the weekend, but the pressure of work was now starting to eat into their socialising. Not that either woman complained too much as they both enjoyed the camaraderie of the department and the challenge of the job, even if at times it could have its sad moments.

Wendy had been with Gertrude Richardson when she had looked at the mummified, skeletal remains of her son. She had also been in her mansion preparing some food when the old woman had died, and now she had two of the woman's cats in her home, and they were still not domesticated enough to exit the house to conduct a call of nature. Bridget had her own problems at home; her layabout live-in lover, a council worker, was becoming lazier and more slovenly. She always prided herself on a tidy mind, a tidy house, and now he wasn't even washing the dishes after inviting his equally slovenly friends over. She could see that she was about to show him the door. The two women had discussed moving in together once Wendy's husband had passed away.

Larry, a happily married man, did not envy his DCI the lifestyle that he lived, although he knew of his reputation for beautiful women; who did not in the police station in Challis Street.

It was nine in the evening before the meeting concluded. Wendy had to leave to visit her husband, say goodnight to him, not sure if he would recognise her or not. Such a vibrant, active man in his younger days, then senility, then bitterness, and now a shell of a man 'waiting for the final call from his maker' as Bridget would say; not that Wendy was religious, but Bridget was. Wendy did not need the religious overtones, but it was good to have a friend who cared.

Larry took the opportunity to go home as well, promising to be in the office very early in the morning and to follow up on Garry Solomon.

Bridget, in no great hurry to go home, had another cup of coffee in her hand. 'I'll stay a couple of hours, do some preparation work for tomorrow,' she said.

'I'll keep you company,' Isaac said. He had no wish to hurry home. The only things that welcomed him there were a hot chocolate and a cold bed. *Not the ideal arrangement*, he thought.

He remembered Linda Harris's comment, the last time they had spoken, a brief phone call when she had denied responsibility for the murder of Jess O'Neill's boss: 'We could have been something more.'

Isaac wondered if that could have been possible. He had been attracted to her, even slept with her that one time, but she was MI5, a minor cog in the organisation according to her.

On reflection, he realised that she would have been an ideal woman for him, but she came with too many secrets. He thought to ask his boss if he could find out what had become of her. Richard Goddard would know who to ask, but it was just idle speculation on his part. Isaac knew there would be other women, but it was now a drought after plenty. There had been Sophie White, and then Jess O'Neill, and now, nobody.

Chapter 12

With the office empty apart from Bridget, Isaac returned to his office. He picked up the necessary paperwork, put it down again. It was not that he had an issue with it, although there was too much. It was because they had a murder and no motive.

Garry Solomon, a criminal when he had no reason to be one, had died thirty years previously and had been stuffed behind a wooden structure crudely built around the fireplace.

But why? Isaac asked himself. The body would be found one day, although thirty years seemed a long time. If it had been placed there temporarily, then why attempt to conceal it, and why had the body not been found before now. Could the house have been unoccupied, unvisited in all those years? It seemed illogical. Bridget had evidence showing that the utility bills and rates had been paid during that time.

The newspaper placed under the body at the time of incarceration had been clear enough, and the date of vacating the house and the murder were within months of each other. The house was empty when the Baxters had moved in, but what was the condition when they had first seen it? Was it full of cobwebs, creaking doors, rats?

Isaac regretted not having his previous DI, Farhan Ahmed, with him. Then it would have been the two of them late at night, putting forward the imponderables, throwing up ideas, some valid, some crazy, but somehow it worked.

Larry Hill, Farhan's replacement, was an excellent detective inspector, but he was a family man and intended to stay that way.

Farhan had been too, but his staying late in the office had cost him his marriage, an occupational hazard all too common in the police force. Even the break up of the relationship with Jess,

Isaac reflected, had to a large part come about due to his job taking precedence over his emotional responsibilities.

Bridget interrupted Isaac's train of thought. 'I've found an address for Garry Solomon's wife,' she said.

'Current?'

'Twenty years old, I'm afraid.'

'At least it will give something for Wendy to work on. Do you have a name?'

'Emily Solomon.'

'Any children?'

'None that I can find.'

'The last known address of Emily Solomon is after the death of her husband, Garry?'

'By a few years,' Bridget said.

'How do you know that it is the same woman?'

'She claimed unemployment benefits. There are documents on record showing that she was the legal wife of Garry Solomon, even a marriage certificate.'

'Married in England?'

'Registry Office, but it's legitimate. There are even copies of their birth certificates.'

'In that case any children, even Emily Solomon herself, would be legally entitled as beneficiaries of Gertrude Richardson's estate.'

'That would be correct,' Bridget said.

'Did you find a copy of Gertrude Richardson's will?'

'Not yet. Her family lawyer will have a copy.'

'I would prefer to obtain a copy from an independent source,' Isaac replied.

'First thing in the morning. Is that okay?' Bridget asked. Isaac looked up at the clock. It was midnight.

'Fine,' he replied. 'Larry needs to follow up on Garry Solomon. Any luck with his criminal record?'

'Larry already has a copy,' Bridget replied. Isaac realised what a great asset she had become to the department, always one step ahead.

***

Isaac was in the office early the next day, as was the team. Wendy was first out of the door, following up on an address for Garry Solomon's widow. She took the opportunity to smoke a cigarette, once she was free of the office.

Larry was not long after, and he was heading to Garry Solomon's last known criminal haunt, although after thirty years it seemed unlikely he would find too many people who remembered him.

Isaac, at a loose end, decided that Montague Grenfell was worth another visit.

Wendy's address for Emily Solomon was close to the centre of London in an upmarket area of Mayfair, which seemed incongruous as the woman had been claiming unemployment at one stage, and Garry Solomon had never risen above being a petty criminal and small-time hooligan.

Regardless, Wendy knocked at the door of the house. It was a very elegant townhouse, even better than Mavis Richardson's.

'Emily Solomon?' Wendy asked.

'Who's asking?' The accent was working class, not upper-class Mayfair.

'Constable Wendy Gladstone, Challis Street Police Station.'

'Long way from there, aren't you?'

'That may be, but I still need to contact Emily Solomon.'

'Why?'

'Once you confirm that you are Emily Solomon, I will tell you.'

'Long time since I've heard that name mentioned,' the woman said. Wendy could see that she was an attractive woman, who prided herself on her appearance but had not dealt with her speech.

'Are you admitting that you are Emily Solomon?'

'You'd better come in.'

Wendy entered, noted the grand hallway, the staircase at the rear. She was ushered into a side room and given a chair. It was not so much a request, more of a command.

'Nice place,' Wendy said.

'It's all mine.'

'You said it was a long time since you had heard the name Emily Solomon.'

'Twenty years at least.'

'Why?'

'I'm not pleased with you being here. Nothing personal, but the past is the past.'

'Any man here?'

'What do you mean? Husband, lover, an idle screw?'

'Yes.'

'There's the occasional man when I feel the need. Other than that, I'm here on my own.'

'Where did the money come from?'

'What business is that of yours?'

Wendy noted no attempt to offer a cup of tea. It was clear that the woman had money, or at least someone did, but the room was cold and unwelcoming. None of the ornaments indicative of a family were on show: no family photos, nothing to suggest any emotional involvement of the woman with another.

'When did you last see your husband?'

'Which one?'

'Garry Solomon.'

'Sometime in the eighties, I suppose.'

'I need you to be more specific.'

'Why? It is not a period in my life that I wish to remember.'

'Let's get the date correct first and then you can tell me why. Any chance of a cup of tea?'

With the woman in the kitchen, Wendy took the opportunity to look around the room. She rustled through some photos albums but was soon interrupted. She thought she had seen a photo of a man and a woman in Indian clothes, but could not be sure. If it were important, she would claim the album as vital evidence at a later date.

'1979.'

'Are you certain?'

'The bastard left me high and dry, not a penny to my name.'

'Garry Solomon?'

'Who else?' Emily Solomon replied.

'Did you divorce him?'

'Why? We weren't married, not in this country.'

'There's a marriage certificate.'

'His idea, not mine.'

'So you were married?'

'I only went through with it because he threatened me.'

'Did he do that often?'

'Often enough, almost strangled me once.'

'But why?'

'Caught me with another man.'

'Why marry you then?'

'He said it was important for the children.'

'You have children?'

'One son, but he's just the same as his father. I haven't seen him for a few years, don't want to.'

'And your name now?'

'Emma Hampshire.'

'Married?'

'I took his name and his money.'

'This house?' Wendy asked.

'I ensured that when he died it was mine.'

'Tell me about your husband.'

'Garry? We met when we were young. We travelled over to India, sat on a mountain top, the usual hippy stuff.'

'Smoked some weed?'

'Part of the spiritual experience. All Garry could see from it was the chance to screw some of the other women. Free love, they called it.'

'And you?'

'I was guilty as well.'

'And when you returned to London?'

'Garry set himself up in business and life was good. Then our son comes along, a beautiful bouncing boy.'

'What happened?'

'Garry fell in with a bad crowd: drinking, gambling, screwing the local tarts.'

'What do you know about his family?'

'I met his father once.'

'And his mother?'

'He said she was crazy. Why are you asking these questions?'

'Mrs Solomon, I am afraid that your husband is dead.'

'As far as I'm concerned, he has been dead for over thirty years.'

'You're not upset?' Wendy asked.

'After his treatment of me? What do you think?'

'Mrs Solomon, I believe we need to discuss this. Another cup of tea?'

'Call me Emma.'

Wendy's initial impression of the woman, something of a painted tart, had dissipated. Emma Hampshire appeared to be a woman whom life had initially treated badly, but it was now treating her well.

'What can you tell me about Garry Solomon? Let's start with his family background.'

'His father I met just the once. I could see where Garry had got his manner from.'

'A charmer?'

'Father and son alike.'

'And the mother?'

'No idea about her, other than she supposedly had money. Not that I saw any of it.'

'Life was tough?' Wendy asked.

'Not really. We were happy on our return from India, and Garry soon charmed himself into a good job before he set up his own business. I found out later the first job came about after he had screwed the female owner.'

'Like the father,' Wendy commented.

'Precisely.'

'Anyway, apart from his inability to keep it in his trousers, Garry was a good provider and a good father.'

'What happened?'

'Started running with the wrong crowd. He liked to socialise, and with a few too many drinks his behaviour would become erratic. Even hit me on a couple of occasions.'

'His mother died.'

'Sorry to hear that.' Emma Hampshire appeared to be genuine in her comment. 'It can be hard to have a child and never see them.'

'Is that the same with you?' Wendy asked.

'With Garry, it was alcohol; with Kevin, it's drugs.'

'You never see him?'

'Not for a couple of years.'

'Upsets you?'

'Of course, but what can I do? It's worse when I see what he has become. He had his father's charm, and then he gets himself addicted. I caught him shooting up in here once, threw him out on the street.'

'Can we come back to Garry? He changed his name to Solly Michaels. Was there any reason?'

'With me, he was Garry. With his criminal friends, he was Solly. No idea why.'

'Tell me about the criminal activities.'

'Not a lot to tell. He was running a motor repair business, good quality cars. Business was good, and apart from the drinking and the womanising, everything was fine.'

'You accepted the womanising?'

'It used to upset me, but as I said, he was a good father and a good provider.'

'Not such a good husband.'

'Not at all. He was a good husband at first. It was later that he changed.'

'Tell me about it.'

'All of a sudden, he's flush with a lot of cash, enough to pay off our house. I asked him about it. He told me just to be thankful and not ask questions.'

'What did you think?'

'What anyone would think.'

'Drugs.'

'He said it was gambling.'

'What was your reaction?'

'I told him that dealing with drugs was unacceptable and that it was either me and his son or the money.'

'His reaction?'

'He said okay for the first couple of times, but then there's a fancy car outside, and a tart sitting in the passenger's seat. I threw a scene, and he threw me out.'

'Literally?'

'He put us into a two-bedroom flat, ensured all the bills were paid, and that I had money to spend.'

'And then?'

'He was caught, spent two years in jail, and the money dried up. I'm out on the street with nowhere to go.'

'After that?'

'I was desperate for money. I had a baby in one arm and nowhere to live.'

'Your parents?'

'I was no longer in communication with them after I took off to India with Garry. They were very religious and could never accept free love, living on a commune, and meditating on a mountain top. They had told me before I left not to come back. Both dead now, car accident some years back. They had cut me out of their will, so I never bothered to visit their grave.'

'You're out on the street, so what did you do?'

'I found a women's refuge, worked two jobs a day, slowly recovered my life, and then I met Bob.'

'Bob Hampshire? How long were you with him?'

'Twenty-five years until he died of a heart attack.'

'Tell me about him?'

'He was older than me by a few years, but we were a great couple, and he ensured that Kevin went to the best schools. Even offered to marry me, but there was still the marriage with Garry, and besides, the church's blessing meant nothing to me. And when Bob died, he left money to his previous wife and their children, this house and enough money to me.'

Chapter 13

Larry's day had been spent finding out what he could about Garry Solomon. His criminal record indicated periods of incarceration starting with a two-year stretch in 1978. The date aligned with the information that Solomon's widow had stated.

It was clear that he was then using the name of Solly Michaels, initially reported at his arrest, although shown as Garry Solomon at his court case. From there on, there had been two periods of incarceration interspersed with periods of freedom. The records indicated several addresses over the years, each one progressively less salubrious than the other. Why he had not contacted Grenfell, the family lawyer, and his ex-wife, at least, from about 1981 was still unanswered. The litany of crimes, some minor, some major, indicated an unsavoury character with few moral restraints.

The last known address, 62 Bakewell Street, Greenwich, close to the Royal Observatory and the site of the Greenwich meridian line, was not what Larry had expected. It had been thirty years since Garry Solomon's death, but the almost derelict building could not have looked much better then. It was clearly uninhabited and had been that way for some years. Larry phoned Bridget for her to do some checks.

The information that Bridget had managed to put together had shown addresses firstly in Paddington then slowly moving eastwards and downwards in quality and suburb. Judging by the condition of the house in Greenwich, this had been his last address. There seemed little possibility of finding anyone who remembered him from that time. Without much more to be achieved he visited the local pub. The Green Elephant had seen better days, but it was run down enough to offer the possibility that someone may have known the hapless Garry Solomon.

'A pint of your best,' Larry said to the man behind the bar. The man reflected the condition of the pub; he was as run down as it was.

'Comin' up,' the singularly unfriendly reply.

'One for yourself,' Larry said.

'Don't mind if I do.'

There were a few others in the pub, some slowly getting drunk, some surfing the internet on their phones, but generally it was quiet. Larry wondered how it managed to stay financially viable.

'Did you ever know a Solly Michaels?' Larry asked. He realised it was a long shot, but it had been a fruitless trip out to Greenwich, and then he had a tiresome trip back to Challis Street afterwards.

'It doesn't ring a bell.' The publican had moved closer, taken a seat on his side of the bar.

'How about Garry Solomon?'

'Are you the police?'

'Detective Inspector Hill.'

'Any problems concerning me?'

'Not at all. Bakewell Street is the last known abode of Garry Solomon, also known as Solly Michaels.'

'How long ago?'

'Thirty years.'

'I've been here for forty. If he was a drinker, then he would have been in here.'

'Why's that?' Larry ordered another two pints: one for him, the other for the publican.

'Thirty years ago, we were the busiest pub in the area. Nowadays, as you can see...'

'What changed?'

'The boutique pubs. This pub no longer suited the up and coming trendies.'

'Bitter about it?' Larry asked.

'Not really. I own the lease and the building, and as long as enough people come through the door to pay the bills, then I'm fine.'

'Garry Solomon would have probably been down on his luck, although he would have dressed well.' Larry knew that the body in the fireplace was expensively dressed, which did not tie in with the house and the area Garry Solomon had been living in.

'There was a Solly that used to come in here, but that would have been back in 1984.'

Larry checked his records. In December 1983, Garry Solomon had been released from prison after serving twelve months, with time off for good behaviour. The charge, possession of a prohibited drug.

'Looks to be the same person,' Larry said. He noticed that the advice came at the cost of two more pints of beer.

'There's not a lot to tell you. He came in here every night for a couple of months, drank his fair share of alcohol, and then he disappeared.'

'What date would that have been?'

'February 1984, give or take a few weeks.'

It would take another two pints before Larry concluded with the publican. It was clear that the time difference between Greenwich and Garry Solomon's death was relevant. The period prior to Greenwich, while it may have some bearing on his demise, did not seem as important.

Larry phoned Isaac, explained the situation, and the reason why he was not in a condition to drive back to the office.

It had happened a few times to Isaac as well, and he fully understood. He told Larry to take an early night, and he would see him in the morning. At least Larry's wife would see him at a sociable hour, but not in the best condition.

***

The following day, Larry had to find out where Garry Solomon had gone after leaving Greenwich and before his untimely death. There was a period of three years and a change in fortune to be accounted for. In Greenwich, he had been destitute, an ex-prisoner. At the time of his death, he had been affluent; at least, that was the assumption judging by the clothes that he had been wearing at the time of his death.

Bridget was checking out the ownership of the house in Greenwich, and Isaac had another planned meeting with Montague Grenfell. Isaac's suspicions, as always, came back to the family lawyer. Wendy had found Garry Solomon's wife, now she had to find his son.

Neither were regarded as primary suspects in his death, as the construction of the fireplace surround at the house in Bellevue Street had required someone of strength, and Wendy could not envisage Emma Hampshire as being capable, and the son would have only been thirteen at the time.

As Bridget was still checking on the information Larry wanted, he decided to contact some of Garry Solomon's earlier contacts. His criminal career had not been particularly long, lasting from his first prison sentence in 1977 through to his death in 1987. There had been two terms in prison, the first lasting twenty-four months, the second, twelve months. Seven years of freedom out of ten, which to Larry seemed to be statistically correct for the average villain.

If he had become involved in drug trafficking, it could only indicate one thing, that he was short of money. But then, there was Montague Grenfell stating that money was available for the asking, but Garry Solomon had never asked, which seemed illogical.

From what the team had managed to source, neither the father nor the son was short of charm or the willingness to stick their hand out for assistance. According to Gertrude Richardson, she had not seen Michael Solomon since he left in the seventies and her son since 1970.

'There's a secret,' Isaac said to Larry on his arrival in the office.

Bridget was checking the title deeds for the house in Greenwich, and yet again it was all leading back to Montague Grenfell. The ownership was not clear, but the attempts at obscuring it were. It was obvious that it would have required a smart legal mind to put it all in place. And why was the house derelict, when it was worth a lot of money? Anyone smart enough to obscure the ownership would have been smart enough to appreciate its value.

'Are we ruling out Garry Solomon's widow?' Isaac asked.

'He treated her badly at one stage,' Larry said.

'I'm trying to find the son,' Wendy said.

'Is he important?' Isaac asked.

'Not for the murder, but he may know something.'

'But he was only thirteen when Garry Solomon died.'

'That may be, but so far we have a body, apparently affluent, but no motive, and why hide it in a fireplace?' Wendy said.

It was a question that had concerned Isaac since the case began. Why not in the basement under the floor, and then covered with concrete, or a grave in the backyard. It was almost as if the discovery was to be expected.

'Let us look at who could have placed the body in the fireplace,' Isaac said to the team.

'The body would have required one person, but sealing the fireplace? That would have probably required two people,' Larry said. He had propped the back of his chair up against the wall, the two front legs not touching the floor.

'Are we assuming one person?' Bridget asked.

'So far, we've being looking for a motive, not how many people could have been involved,' Isaac replied.

'Could be one or two,' Larry said.

'But why the fireplace?' Wendy asked.

'It seems illogical unless they intended to come back and seal the fireplace with bricks.'

'Whoever placed the wooden structure around the fireplace must have been physically strong, so that discounts any of the women that we know of. The only people capable would have been Michael Solomon and Mavis Richardson's missing husband, Ger O'Loughlin,' Isaac added.

'And Montague Grenfell,' Larry said.

'Of course, there's always the family lawyer. It always comes back to him.'

'Ger O'Loughlin is not missing,' Wendy said.

'Can he be contacted?' Isaac asked.

'Mavis Richardson will know how to contact him.'

With no more to be discussed, the team went back to their work. Wendy had spoken to Emma Hampshire, told her that it was important to contact her son. She had been reluctant to comply, but had given Wendy the address.

***

Kevin Solomon, a man of forty-three, was not difficult to find. The address, a two-bedroom flat in Hampstead, was in remarkably good condition for a man who had a history of drug abuse. Bridget had checked out his criminal record, found a history of drug possession, a few arrests for being drunk and disorderly, but no prison sentences, and no major crimes.

'The flat, is it yours?' Wendy asked. She had been invited in after showing her badge.

'Out of my price bracket,' Kevin Solomon replied. Wendy had to admit he was a good-looking man, not what she had expected.

'What is your price bracket?'

'Cheap, exceptionally cheap.'

'No money?'

'If I have some, I spend it.'

'A remarkably frank admission,' Wendy said.

'Honesty, it's part of my rehabilitation.'

'What do you mean?'

'I'm a drug addict, heroin mainly. For years, I was crazy for it. I would do anything for the next hit.'

'Crime?'

'Petty sometimes, or else I would hire out as a male escort.'

'Pay well?'

'Well enough for the next injection.'

'That doesn't explain the accommodation.'
'It's owned by the family.'
'Which family?'
'My grandmother's.'
'We were not aware that you had any contact with them.'
'My father didn't, although I knew from my mother about the family lawyer.'
'Montague Grenfell?'
'Yes, him.'
'Have you met him?'
'Once, when he came here and gave me the key to the flat.'
'Did your father have any contact with his mother or Grenfell?'
'He hated them. I doubt if he made contact.'
'And you?'
'Whatever the issue was between my father and his mother, I never knew.'
'Did you meet her?'
'I knocked on her door once. I was drugged out, attempted to explain who I was. She slammed the door in my face.'
'Why would she do that?'
'Living in a mansion fit for condemning. She must have assumed that I wanted to steal her money.'
'Did you?'
'Not really. I am not an ambitious man, lazy would be a more apt description. I knew I was in trouble with my addiction, and I was looking for somebody, anybody, to help.'
'There was your mother.'
'She wasn't much help.'
'I met her,' Wendy said. He had made them both a cup of coffee. Whereas he had given up drugs, he had not given up cigarettes. Both were sitting in the main room of the flat smoking, a luxury both obviously enjoyed.
'What did you think?' Kevin Solomon asked.

'I liked her. She seemed genuinely concerned about you.'

'Maybe she is, but I don't see her often.'

'Any reason?'

'She was quick enough to ship me off to boarding school.'

'She said your father walked out on you two.'

'After he had caught her screwing another man. Did she tell you that?'

'Tell me about your father.'

'He disappeared when I was three or four. I don't remember him.'

'You never saw him again?'

'Once, when I was about ten or eleven, but never again.'

'Did Bob Hampshire treat you well?'

'He was a good man, more like a father than my father.'

'Why the bitterness towards your mother?'

'She shipped me off to boarding school.'

'Only that?'

'It's enough.'

'I'm afraid that your father is dead.'

'I'm not surprised.'

'Why do you say that?'

'I knew about the drug trafficking and the prison sentences. From what my mother told me, he ran with the wrong crowd. He was always bound to get his wings clipped at some time.'

'Your father died in 1987 when you would have been thirteen.'

'Unpleasant death?'

'Murdered, unfortunately.'

'His death means nothing to me. I was upset when Bob Hampshire died, but my father's death leaves me cold. Does that sound callous?'

'Not at all,' Wendy replied.

With no more to be gained, Wendy left. Again, the hand of Montague Grenfell had interceded. She phoned Isaac to update him, as well as to inform Bridget. If the flat currently occupied by Kevin Solomon belonged to Gertrude Richardson, then what else belonged to her.

There was the property in Greenwich, and there was every reason to believe it belonged to Gertrude Richardson or her sister, or both. And was Gertrude as eccentric as everyone said? And what of the money and all the properties in Mavis Richardson's name? What did Grenfell know?

It was clear that Montague Grenfell needed to be brought into Challis Street Police Station, cautioned, and given a chance to explain the truth in detail.

Chapter 14

Larry followed up on Garry Solomon's earlier life. The evidence unfolding indicated that before 1976 he had been an honest man, but somehow he had become involved in selling drugs.

Larry visited Garry Solomon's business before he had turned to crime. It was located down a side street in Hammersmith. The company was still involved in servicing luxury motors, attested by the Mercedes and BMWs lined up on the forecourt.

'Garry Solomon, remember him well,' the owner, Graham Nicholson, said. A distinguished-looking man, he spoke with the accent of the well-educated.

'What can you tell me about him?' Larry asked.

'I bought this place from him back in 1976. Paid plenty for it.'

'Good buy?'

'It's kept me solvent.'

'Why did he sell it to you?'

'No idea. He said he wanted to move on, bigger fish in the sea.'

'What did you believe?'

'I wasn't concerned as to what he said, only if the business was viable. Everyone distorts the truth when they're selling or buying.'

'Can you speculate as to what was the truth?'

'He was a young man. Obviously smart and a competent businessman, but he seemed to be in a hurry to set the world on fire. He was probably a little immature to be running a business such as this.'

'Did he keep in contact?'

'Not really. He honoured the agreement we had made: introduced me to his suppliers, his customers, and then left. I never saw him again.'

'Did you ever wonder what had happened to him?'

'Why? Should I have?'

'I'm just curious. We're tracing his whereabouts from 1976 through to 1987, that's all.'

'Why 1987?'

'He died in 1987.'

'Suspicious?' Graham Nicholson asked.

'He was murdered.'

'Not a good way to end your days.'

'Apart from that, do you have any idea where he went to?'

'You're pushing the memory here. It's been many years. I vaguely remember hearing that he had fallen on hard times, but apart from that, there's not much I can tell you.'

Larry returned to Challis Street Police Station. Montague Grenfell was due within the next hour, and Isaac wanted him to be present in the interview room with him.

***

Montague Grenfell arrived at Challis Street at 3 p.m. He was not in a good mood and felt the need to verbally abuse Isaac.

In his usual manner, Isaac shrugged off the lawyer's rhetoric. As the senior policeman involved in the murder of Garry Solomon, he had a job to do, and whether Montague Grenfell was pleasant or abusive made little difference.

Isaac opened the interview with Grenfell, following all the procedures. Isaac sat on the right-hand side of the table, with Larry on his left. Grenfell sat on the other side, facing Isaac. He had not brought additional legal representation.

Detective Chief Superintendent Goddard watched from outside. He had made a special trip to come and see Isaac. The case of the body in the fireplace was not occupying the media, except on an infrequent basis. The fickle public had been diverted by world events, terrorist activity in the north of England, and the inclement and unseasonal weather in the country.

'Mr Grenfell, there are anomalies in statements that you have made to me,' Isaac said.

'I have always been truthful when asked.' Isaac realised it was Grenfell's predictable reply. A man who, by his own admission, looked out for the Richardson family's interests, even if that meant obscuring the truth from the police during a murder investigation.

'According to Gertrude Richardson's grandson, you supplied him with a flat in Hampstead.'

'That is correct.'

'When I asked you on a previous occasion, you denied any knowledge of Garry Solomon's family.'

'That is correct.'

'Why did you not tell me?'

'Firstly, you had asked me in my office, not in an interview room, duly cautioned.'

'And secondly?'

'The son has no recollection of his father, other than a fleeting childhood meeting when he was ten or eleven. He did not seem relevant to Garry's murder.'

'That is for the police to decide, not you,' Isaac said.

'I disagree. The son would have been thirteen or fourteen when his father was murdered. He cannot be implicated in the man's death,' Grenfell said. Isaac noticed that the man had tensed, almost verging on anger.

'That may be, but it is clear that you are withholding information.'

'If you ask formally, then I will answer. Apart from that, the Richardson family's personal business, and by default mine, remains sacrosanct.'

'Even when a murder has been committed?'

'Even then.'

'I don't understand.'

'My family has a history stretching back for hundreds of years. English aristocracy keep their dirty linen to themselves. It is not there to be bandied across the internet and in the media.'

'The house in Greenwich?' Larry asked.

'Bakewell Street?' Grenfell sat up at the mention of Greenwich. 'How did you find it?'

'Last known address of Garry Solomon,' Larry said.

'Who owned it, owns it?' Isaac asked.

'Gertrude.'

'And if she's dead?'

'It's a matter for probate.'

'In your legal opinion?' Isaac asked.

'I cannot answer that question.'

'Why not?'

'I represent the Richardson family. It is a matter for them.'

'You mean Mavis?'

'Yes, Mavis Richardson.'

It was evident to Isaac that Montague Grenfell would remain a hostile witness, only willing to give the truth when asked directly.

'Would Garry Solomon's widow be eligible to inherit Gertrude Richardson's assets?' Isaac asked.

'And her debts.'

'You are aware that his wife uses the name of Emma Hampshire?'

'Yes.'

'Which means that you are aware of the movements of Garry Solomon, the two prison terms, the convictions for drug trafficking.'

'Yes.'

'Then why are we spending the time to find out when you could have supplied us with that information?'

'If you ask, I will answer. Otherwise, what I know remains secret.'

'I don't understand,' Isaac said.

'No offence, but you are not of aristocratic birth.'

117

Regardless of Grenfell's statement, Isaac saw it as a slur on his good character and that of his parents.

'Let us come back to Garry Solomon.'

'What do you want to know?'

'You are aware that he and Emily Solomon were married legally in England?'

'Yes.'

'You denied any knowledge of it on a previous occasion.'

'Yes.'

'Are you aware that you may well have committed a criminal offence by your persistent lies?'

'I am well aware of the law.'

'Was Garry Solomon murdered because of something he knew?'

'Why ask me? I am the family lawyer, not his murderer.'

'Could they be one and the same?' Isaac knew he was baiting the man, attempting to get more from him than a curt reply.

'Repeat that in public and I will sue you for slander.'

'Judging by the way in which the body was concealed, there are only three people capable of committing the murder, or at least hiding the body in the fireplace: you, Michael Solomon, and Ger O'Loughlin.'

'From what I've been told, the construction around the fireplace was substantial,' Grenfell said.

'It would have required someone with the skill to build and the strength to put it in place,' Isaac said.

'That rules me out. I've only got the one leg, and as for handyman skills, I can barely change a light bulb.'

'What about Michael Solomon?'

'It's possible. He was certainly strong enough, although I never saw him do anything practical around the house.'

'Ger O'Loughlin?'

'He could have done it, but why? He had nothing to gain by Garry's death, and besides, he's long gone.'

'And you know where he is?'

'Mavis does.'

'And you?'
'Yes.'
'We need the address.'
'I'll send it to you.'

Isaac concluded the interview, knowing full well that yet again Montague Grenfell had not been forthcoming with the truth.

***

'I need you to visit Ger O'Loughlin,' Isaac said.

Normally, Wendy would have been delighted with a trip out of London, but her husband was worrying her greatly. The doctor was giving him just four to five weeks, and now she was off to Ireland. Still, she couldn't refuse as it was her job, and her promotion to sergeant was soon to be confirmed. For once, the expense account and the ability to use it did not excite her, but, as always, she would do her duty.

A flight was booked with British Airways at eight the next morning. Wendy's eldest son offered to come over to the house to feed the two cats, and to visit his father every day.

Arriving in Dublin, she picked up a hire car at the airport. The address for O'Loughlin was recent, and she had no difficulty finding him. She had even phoned in advance, and informed the Irish police, the Garda, that she was coming. It was a formality, and as no arrests were to be made, she was free to question O'Loughlin on her own.

Any extraditions and they would be involved, but that looked unlikely, as when she had phoned the previous day, the phone had been answered by a softly-spoken woman with a distinctive Irish accent. 'My father is dying,' she had said.

Ger O'Loughlin, as explained by his youngest daughter on Wendy's arrival, was suffering from lung cancer after a lifetime of chain smoking.

Wendy found the man sitting up in bed, a ventilator forcing air into his destroyed lungs.

119

'How is Mavis?' Ger O'Loughlin asked, his voice rasping but weak.

'She's fine,' Wendy said.

'Still attractive?'

'Still.'

'She was a looker, couldn't keep my hands off her when I was younger.'

'She still acts younger than her age. Are you aware of her sister's death?'

'Grenfell phoned.'

'Do you hear from him often?'

'Rarely.'

'When did you last see Mavis?'

'It must be twenty-five years at least. We have spoken a few times, but both our lives have moved on. We're long-distance friends, nothing more.'

'Did he tell you about Garry Solomon?'

'Yes, and he told me that Michael Solomon had died, but I knew that already.'

'How?'

'I kept in contact with him. We used to meet from time to time over the years. When he died, his second wife phoned.'

'Did you know he was not divorced from Gertrude when he married the second wife?'

'I never asked if he had married again. I assumed they were living together and she had taken his surname.'

'Don't you go tiring my dad. He needs to rest,' O'Loughlin's daughter said after poking her head around the door.

'I won't,' Wendy said.

'Always fussing, that one,' O'Loughlin said after the young woman had retreated.

'How many children do you have?'

'Four, and a good wife as well. She'll be back in later today.'

'According to Mavis, she did not want children.'

'That's why we broke up. It was important to me, not to her.'

All Wendy could see was a tired old man close to death, but she had not travelled to talk about life now, but life back when he was younger, when he was married to Mavis Richardson.

'Sorry, but I need to ask about Garry Solomon.'

'The last time I saw him would have been around 1963, the night he walked in at the party.'

'When Michael Solomon was in bed with Mavis?'

'Wild days.' Ger O'Loughlin managed a thin smile.

'And you didn't object?'

'We were young. It was the age of free love and permissiveness. Mind you, Garry went crazy with hitting Mavis. It took all my strength to pull him off.'

'Were you a strong man?'

'I used to work out at the gym.'

'What can you tell me about the structure around the fireplace in Bellevue Street?' Wendy asked.

'Nothing. I never went around to the house after that day.'

'When she caught you in bed with Gertrude?'

'You've done your homework. Who told you?'

'Mavis. So why was she upset if you had both been indulging in wife swapping?'

'As she saw it, a wife-swapping party was by mutual consent of all parties, whereas my sleeping with her sister was a private agreement.'

'How did you see it?' Wendy asked.

'An afternoon screw, nothing more. It was not the first time that I had slept with her.'

'Mavis kicks the two of you out, subsequently forgives the sister, but not you.'

'She forgave me, but the trust that Mavis had for me was broken. We both moved on.'

At that point, the young daughter came in and asked Wendy to leave as her father needed to rest. There seemed no reason for her to stay longer in Ireland. There was a late-night flight; she intended to catch it.

Chapter 15

Larry decided to focus on Garry Solomon. His whereabouts between 1984 and 1987 were still vague, apart from the times he visited the clothing shop to buy some hand-made shirts and trousers. Solomon's last visit had been in 1986, approximately one year before his murder.

There were no criminal activities registered against either of the two names he had been using, which meant he was either honestly employed or out of the country. Or, possibly, he had managed to evade the long arm of the law. Larry saw that option as remote, as Garry Solomon had shown himself to be a small-time criminal of limited abilities. The man had received a good education, was apparently articulate and intelligent, yet he remained a petty criminal. It all seemed incongruous to Larry, who was a strong believer that a person should make the best of what was given at birth and in their life, and should always strive for more.

It was a philosophy that drove him on in his career within the London Metropolitan Police. He was aiming to make detective chief inspector within a year, superintendent in three, and chief superintendent in five. He knew that he needed one or two university degrees to achieve his final goal, but working with Homicide was demanding and he knew he was not keeping up with his studies.

The only way to achieve the degrees was to take six months off work and to study to exhaustion, sleep and study again. However, he had a family and another child on the way. It would be another five years before he could see any financial relief.

Montague Grenfell, when questioned, had offered no information as to where Solomon had gone, but Larry and Isaac had regarded that as further obstructive behaviour.

Bridget had managed to find records of a driving licence issued to Garry Solomon, the address in Knightsbridge. It seemed an upmarket location after Greenwich.

Larry saw it as a long shot, but there were no other leads. He made his way out to the property in Montpelier Square. The house was as opulent as the house in Greenwich had been rundown. He knocked on the door. A woman in her sixties answered.

'Detective Inspector Larry Hill, Challis Street Police Station.'

'What can I do for you?'

'I need to ask you some questions.' Larry showed his ID badge. The door opened fully to let him in. He observed that the house was beautifully decorated, and the woman was very attractive.

'Your name?' Larry asked once he was seated in the main room of the house.

'Barbara Ecclestone.'

'Have you lived here long?'

'It was my parents' house. I grew up here.'

'I'm looking for a Garry Solomon, or as he was also known, Solly Michaels.'

'So was I, for a long time.'

'You knew him?'

'We lived together.'

'What can you tell me about him?'

'Is he dead?'

'I'm sorry.'

The woman, obviously distraught, sat down to compose herself.

'I'm not surprised,' she said.

'Are you alright?' Larry asked.

'He walked out on me a long time in the past. I was upset back then. Now, it's just the shock of facing reality.'

'Did you look for him?'

'Everywhere I could think of.'

'Did he have many friends?'

'Not in the two years that he was here with me. We spent most of the time here, occasionally walking up to Harrods to buy the groceries.'

'What do you know about his past life?'

'He became involved with a criminal element, started trafficking drugs. He did time for that on a couple of occasions.'

'Were you involved with him then?'

'On and off. I went through a wild period, but, as with Garry, I settled down. Got older, I suppose.'

'What do you know about his family life?'

'He mentioned his father once or twice, although I never met him. Any mention of his mother and he would get upset. No idea why. My mother was a bitch, but I still miss her. Are they still alive?'

'The father died some years ago; the mother, recently.'

'Did she know that her son had died?'

'She did. She died soon after.'

'How sad.'

'Do you know the date when he disappeared?'

'January 21st, 1987.'

'Good memory.'

'It was my birthday. I had made a special meal, bought some champagne, but he goes out for a couple of hours and never comes back. In the end, I threw the meal in the bin and drank the champagne. Is the date significant?'

'It was the day he died.'

'And there I was getting angry, yet it was not his fault. How did he die? Car accident?'

'Unfortunately, he came to a tragic end. He was murdered.'

The woman sat down and put her face in her hands, overcome with emotion. Larry found a bottle of whisky and gave her some. Five minutes later, she revived.

'I'm sorry,' she said.

'It's an understandable reaction.'

'It's been thirty years. I've moved on since then, got married, had a couple of kids.'

'And the children?'

'They have both left home. One's married, the other one is overseas.'

'Either of them belong to Garry Solomon?'

'No.'

'Tell me about the day he disappeared,' Larry said.

'Do you want a cup of tea?'

'Yes, please.'

Five minutes later, with the tea poured, Barbara Ecclestone spoke about her time with Garry Solomon.

'I first met Garry in 1979. He was just out of prison, and I was a social worker. I was there to help him readjust to society and to ensure he went straight.'

'Did he?'

'My first ex-prisoner, my first failure.'

'What happened?'

'He called himself Solly Michaels. Soon after his release, he was back with his criminal mates. If you had met him, you would have wondered why.'

'Why?'

'A charming man, articulate, generous, great company.'

'Did you become involved then?'

'You mean lovers?'

'Yes.'

'Not at all. I was very prim and proper, still am.'

'And then what?'

'Three years later and he's back in prison. We had kept in contact over the years, and occasionally we would meet up. I think he enjoyed my attempts at reforming him.

'I started to visit him in prison, and we spoke about our lives. He was from an affluent background, shipped off to a boarding school, as was I. We were both bitter about the neglect, although, with me, it didn't affect me as badly as it did Garry.'

'Greenwich,' Larry said.

'You've been there?'

'And the local pub.'

'It was awful out there.'

'Still is.'

'Why didn't he come here instead of Greenwich?'

'My mother was still alive. And besides, Garry still had some unresolved issues to deal with.'

'Such as?'

'He was a ladies' man.'

'He was playing the field?'

'I'm sure he was. As long as I didn't know, I was fine. I loved him, foolish as it was, and I was willing to wait.'

'While he was here with you?'

'We were together virtually twenty-four hours a day.'

'Did he work during his time here?'

'He seemed to have some money coming in. I quizzed him once. He said it was from his family.'

'Did you work during that time?'

'No. We were just very happy, planning our future together.'

'Did you know about his past personal relationships?'

'His wife and son? Yes, I did. Apparently, she had upset him once, but he had forgiven her. He said that she had moved in with a good man and that his son was fine. Apart from that, he did not speak about his past.'

'Did he see them?'

'I don't think so. For some reason, past memories were always difficult for him. He dealt with the present and the future.'

'Is there any more?' Larry asked. 'The day he disappeared, what happened?'

'He went out, never returned. I've no idea where he went or who he met.'

'Thanks. I may come back to you if there is any other information that I require.'

'My husband is due back in fifteen minutes. Please stay till then. I don't want to be on my own at the present time.'

Fifteen minutes later, the husband returned. Barbara told him why a police inspector was in the house. Larry left soon after and headed back to Challis Street.

***

Detective Chief Superintendent Goddard was in Isaac's office on Larry's return to Challis Street. From Larry's side of the glass partition, it appeared to be an animated conversation.

'Isaac, how much longer is this going to take? We've other murders requiring your team's attention, and this thirty-year-old corpse is still garnering more attention than it should.'

'We're still collating the facts,' Isaac's reply.

'What have you got?'

'We now know where Garry Solomon was before his murder. His murderer is still uncertain, and why a fireplace remains a mystery.'

'Surely you must have a motive.'

'No motive is apparent.'

It was clear from DCS Goddard's visit that he was under pressure to provide a result. Isaac had ceased to relish his superior's visits. Questions as to when the case was going to be wrapped up always grated. The team were working hard, attempting to resolve it, but everyone was jaundiced by now. Their previous cases had been long and gruelling, and before Garry Solomon's body had been discovered, they had been hoping for a break from the routine. It sometimes seemed to DCI Isaac Cook that they were in a growth industry.

Wendy's promotion, due to Isaac's efforts and her good work, had come about. She was now Sergeant Wendy Gladstone, and to Isaac, a title well earned. Not that it helped with her husband who continued to wither. Under normal circumstances, she would have been entitled to compassionate leave, or at least to forbearance from the London Metropolitan Police as she juggled the emotional and financial needs of her husband and the professional needs of a policewoman involved in a murder investigation that defied logic.

Regardless, Wendy had been insistent that being at home or at the nursing home were non-constructive, and that an idle mind did no good. On several occasions, Bridget had gone home with Wendy to keep her company.

Garry Solomon's body in a house owned by his family indicated that a relative or relatives were involved, but which? Isaac had ruled out the two Richardson sisters as primary suspects: one was his mother, the other would not have had the physical strength to secure his resting place in the old house.

Ger O'Loughlin seemed a likely culprit, but why? The man had been close to death when Wendy had met him; although by his own admission he had been a strong man in his earlier years, his motive seemed weak. There appeared to be no financial gain to him. He had married Mavis Richardson, divorced her, or she had divorced him. She was a wealthy woman, but he had gained no benefit.

Isaac pondered who could have killed the man. At the time of his death, Garry Solomon was no longer involved with his criminal friends, and he was living with Barbara Ecclestone. He had money in his pocket, and besides, if he had been killed by persons other than his immediate family, they would have taken him out into the countryside, weighed him down with concrete and thrown him in the river.

Isaac realised that the motive was the key element. So far, that remained a mystery, although why Garry Solomon had remained detached from his mother was a concern. It had been his father that he had seen in bed with his aunt, yet for some reason he had maintained infrequent contact with the father, but not the mother.

It was clear that the mother, Gertrude Richardson, had been eccentric, even in her younger years. It hardly seemed a reason to maintain a hatred towards her; there had to be something more.

At the evening meeting in the office, he raised his concerns. 'I've had our boss over here grilling me,' he said.

'Not happy?' Larry asked.

'What do you think?' Wendy said. Her mood fluctuated with her husband's condition. Today she was not in a cheerful frame of mind.

'Detective Chief Superintendent Goddard is concerned that we are going nowhere with this case.'

'He's right,' Larry said.

'What do we do?' Isaac was not a man who sat in isolation issuing commands and demanding answers. He knew that a team discussion was often the best way to come up with a resolution.

'Find the motive,' Larry's reply.

'Easier said than done,' Isaac said.

'Are we certain that it's a family member?' Wendy asked.

'Who else knew about Bellevue Street, and why has the body been undisturbed for so many years?' Isaac replied.

'Records indicate occupancy of the house since 1987 when the body was incarcerated in the fireplace,' Bridget said.

'Detailed records?' Isaac asked.

'Not totally. The house had been divided up for most of the time as low-cost accommodation, each bedroom equipped with a fold-down bed and a basic kitchen.'

'What about the room where the body was found?'

'No information on that.'

'Who would know?' Isaac asked.

'The family lawyer,' Larry said.

'I don't think he will be too pleased to see me after the last time we met.'

'It doesn't concern you, does it, sir?' Wendy asked.

'Not at all. Tomorrow morning, I will go out there with Larry.'

Again, the answers gravitate towards Montague Grenfell, Isaac thought.

'Wendy, Bridget, focus on Montague Grenfell: family history, background, personal relationships, financial information. Whatever you can find.'

Both of the women nodded their affirmation.

Chapter 16

The next day at nine in the morning, Larry and Isaac drove out to Montague Grenfell's office. Isaac prepared to march briskly up the stairs to his office. He managed the first two flights before stopping abruptly. There, at the base of the third flight of stairs, a man's crumpled body, the head at an awkward angle. Larry quickly dialled 999 for an ambulance, although he could see it was a formality.

'Another body for you,' Isaac said on the phone to Gordon Windsor.

'Identity?'

'Montague Grenfell.'

'I'll be there within fifteen minutes,' Windsor said.

'This changes everything,' Larry said after Isaac had ended his phone call. Larry called the local police station. They were sending around a uniformed police officer to be stationed outside, and a local detective to secure the scene.

'It depends on if it was murder or not,' Isaac said.

'Any doubt on your part?'

'The man had one leg. It's possible he slipped.'

'Or was pushed.'

'Let's wait for Gordon Windsor. He'll be able to tell us.'

'We need to meet Bridget and Wendy to discuss this,' Larry said.

'Agreed, but first we need to meet Mavis Richardson. She needs to be told, once Gordon Windsor has brought us up to speed.'

Isaac phoned his boss. 'It's just become a lot more complicated. Garry Solomon was an old murder; this one is recent, and they are both related.'

His boss's reaction: 'Wrap this up soon. Grenfell was well connected. There are bound to be more questions, and the media will be sticking their collective noses in again.'

Fifteen minutes later, Gordon Windsor arrived. He donned his overalls, gloves, and mask before approaching the body.

'Broken neck,' he said, even before kneeling down to examine the body.

'Are you sure?' Isaac asked.

'Judging by the angle of the neck, I would say that I am correct.'

'Is it the cause of death?'

'Probably, but I will need to conduct my examination, and then the autopsy will confirm if it was or not. Whatever the cause, he died here.'

'Was he pushed?' Larry asked.

'Give my team sixty minutes, and it should become clearer.'

Isaac and Larry, realising that there was no more to be gained from their presence, left the scene.

Grenfell's family needed to be informed. Bridget would be able to supply the contact details. It was known that Montague Grenfell had no children and his wife was dead.

Mavis Richardson was excited when she first met Isaac, although deflated when told the reason for his visit.

'Were you close?' Isaac asked.

'I trusted him implicitly,' she replied. She had sat down in a corner chair, showing every year of her advanced age. It was the first time that Larry had seen her like this. He went to pour her a brandy, leaving Isaac alone with the old woman.

'I'm told that you had known him since you were children.'

'He was like a brother to me.'

'And he handled all your financial matters?'

'Totally. He had a proxy to act on my behalf.'

'Did he have many friends?'

'None that I know of. He was very close to his wife, but she has been dead for a few years.'

'Family?'

'Two brothers.'

'Do you have their contact details?'

'The elder brother, the lord, but he's senile.'

'And the younger brother?'

'I don't know where he is. I liked the elder brother, but not the younger.'

'Any reason why?'

'He was the black sheep of the family: always gambling, whoring, that sort of thing.'

'Do you have anyone you can call to come over and be with you?'

'I have plenty of friends. At my age, you get used to people dying. Is it murder?' Mavis asked.

'It is too early to speculate,' Isaac replied. 'Any reason to believe that it might be?'

'Not really, but Garry had been murdered. I wondered if it was related.'

'We have not made a connection between the two deaths yet.'

'But you will.'

'Why do you say that?' Larry asked.

'Montague knew everything. If you wanted to keep our family secrets, then all you had to do was rid yourself of Montague.'

'Secrets worth killing for?' Isaac asked.

'None that I know of.'

Isaac wondered if the woman knew something that she was not telling him, but realised she probably did not. She was a old woman, feeling every one of her eighty-five years, and just talking.

'Did Garry know any secrets?' Isaac asked.

'He may have found out something, but I don't know.'

'Are you hiding some information from us?'

'No.'

'Then why talk about secrets?'

'Garry died, Gertrude died, and now Montague.'

'Are you assuming they are related?'

'Not really. I'm only sorry that I never saw Gertrude before she died.'

'You cared about her?'

'Of course I did.'

'And Garry?'

'He was her son. Personally, I did not care for him, but I always made sure that he came to no harm, and that he had money and a place to live when he needed it.'

'You knew about his marriage and child?'

'Montague kept a look out for him, hired a private investigator sometimes.'

'And the rest of Garry's history?'

'The prison terms, the house in Greenwich, and Barbara Ecclestone. Yes, I knew.'

'And Kevin Solomon?'

'He's always had someone watching out for him, although he never knew it. Who do you think paid for his drug rehabilitation?'

'Very generous of you.'

'Not generous. That's what families do for each other; at least, my family.'

'What about Garry's wife?' Isaac asked.

'She's fine.'

'Any contact with her?'

'None, but she lived with Bob Hampshire for many years. He treated her well.'

'You knew him?'

'I met him once or twice, nothing more. I even met Emily, or Emma as she calls herself now. There's nothing to make of it. We moved in the same social circles, that's all.'

'Did Emma Hampshire know who you were?'

'No. I was known as Mavis O'Loughlin.'

'Constable Gladstone went to Ireland.'

'She met Ger?'

'Yes.'

'He's dying,' Mavis said.

'You know?' Isaac asked.

'His daughter phoned, asked if I wanted to visit him.'

'And what did you say?'

'I declined.'

'But you wanted to?'

'Yes, but he has his family with him. I spoke to him on the phone for five minutes. That's another one who's dying.'

Mavis Richardson then made a phone call. Five minutes later, another old woman arrived. 'Sheila will stay with me. Would you please leave.'

Larry and Isaac could see that there was another person who was going to die soon. The recent events had sapped the life out of the woman. Larry felt sad as he left the house.

***

Wendy and Bridget were in the office when Isaac and Larry arrived. Wendy was looking more cheerful, a clear indication that her husband had been more cheerful than on her previous visit to see him.

'What can you tell us, Bridget?' Isaac asked.

'Montague Grenfell was the second son of Lord Penrith. The other sons are Albert, the eldest and the current lord, and Malcolm, the younger. According to reports, the current Lord Penrith is close to death. Malcolm is the result of a second marriage of the previous lord to a younger woman.'

'The younger son's mother?'

'She's dead.'

'Someone needs to tell the Grenfell family about Montague,' Isaac said.

'A job for you, sir,' Wendy said.

'What else, Bridget?'

'All three men are childless. The title will expire on the death of Malcolm. On the passing of the eldest son, the title would have passed to Montague Grenfell. The records indicate that Lord Penrith has no money, other than a stately home and the money to maintain it. Montague Grenfell was only affluent due to his own abilities.'

'Where can we find Lord Penrith?' Isaac asked.

'Leicestershire,' Bridget answered.

'Wendy, are you up to meeting aristocracy?' Isaac asked.

'I'll need to practise my curtseying,' Wendy replied.

'Larry, can you follow up with Gordon Windsor and check out the crime scene at Bellevue Street again? See if you can figure out how a body lies undisturbed for thirty years.'

***

Sue Baxter was not pleased to see DI Larry Hill. 'I thought we were free of you,' she said.

'It is still a crime scene,' Larry said.

'One room is.'

'As you say, one room.'

Larry noted that renovations were proceeding. A body in the fireplace had given the place some notoriety and the house had been renamed 'The Mummy's Recline', a somewhat macabre reference to the body's condition and its position.

The room where the body had been discovered had been sealed off with metal bars, and police signs to the effect that it was a crime scene. Otherwise, the house had a sense of normality, a television on in another room, a dog barking, and the sound of children. He was not sure that he would want to live in a house where there had been a violent murder, but the Baxters appeared to have no issues.

'Can you tell me about the first time you wanted to enter the room?' Larry asked. He had moved with Sue Baxter to the modern kitchen at the rear of the house.

'It was sealed with a metal grille. It took us some time to get it off.'

'Was there any explanation given why?'

'None.'

'Did it concern you?'

'We thought it strange, but the house was in our price range, and the location was excellent.'

'When you first entered the room, any sense of foreboding?'

'None at all. We just thought it was a lovely room.'

'No smell?'

'It was musty. We opened the windows, and it soon freshened up. I dusted the room; ran a wet mop over the floorboards.'

'No suspicion as to why the fireplace was covered?'

'Why?'

'It seems unusual.'

'All the bedrooms had covered fireplaces. It had been sublet for years.'

'We're at a loss as to why someone would have expected the fireplace to have remained untouched for thirty years,' Larry admitted. 'It seems crucial to know. To us, it seems illogical.'

'We wondered as well,' Sue Baxter said.

'Any thoughts?'

'You're the police officer, what do you think?'

'Did you keep the grille?'

'It's down in the basement.'

'I'll get someone over to look at it. Make sure it remains untouched,' Larry said.

Chapter 17

Lord Penrith, as Wendy and Isaac found out on their arrival at his home, a decaying remnant of Georgian architecture, was beyond caring about his younger brother or anyone else.

'His mind has gone,' Katrina Smith, the pretty young nurse who had shown them into his lordship's bedroom, said. The man was propped up in bed, a television in the corner showing a melodrama.

'Anyone else in the house?' Isaac asked.

'There's a cook and a handyman. Apart from that, no one.'

'Who employed you?'

'Montague Grenfell. I met him in London, but apart from that he has not been near. I have a bank account to draw from as needed. Each month, I send him an itemised list of my costs, and he ensures to put my salary into my account. To be honest, it's a cushy number, although it will not last for much longer.'

'Why do you say that?' Wendy asked.

'His lordship is dying. He could go anytime.'

'And when he does, what do you do?'

'I'm to phone the local police and the local undertaker. After that, I am to phone the family doctor and Montague Grenfell, the new Lord Penrith.'

'Except that he won't be,' Isaac said.

'Why's that?' Katrina Smith asked.

'Unfortunately, Montague Grenfell has died.'

'He seemed a nice man.'

'What will you do now?' Wendy asked.

'Hopefully, someone will pay the bills, but anyway, I'll stay for now. I've grown fond of Lord Penrith, even if he doesn't remember me one day to the next.'

'There's another brother,' Isaac said.

'Malcolm.'

'Have you seen him?'

'The proverbial black sheep of the family. Every aristocratic family has one of them, as well as a ghost or two in the stately home,' Katrina Smith said. Isaac had to admit he liked her humour, even under trying circumstances.

'Have you seen any?' Wendy asked.

'Late at night when the wind blows it can be eerie, but no.'

'You don't believe in the possibility?'

'A healthy sceptic. If there are any here, I've not seen them.'

'What about Malcolm? Any ideas as to where he may be?'

'Montague Grenfell would have known, but I've no idea.'

'You said he was the black sheep of the family?' Wendy asked.

'Montague Grenfell mentioned him when we met in London. He asked me to phone him if Malcolm turned up. Apart from that, he told me nothing.'

It was ten in the evening when Isaac and Wendy left Lord Penrith's residence. There seemed little reason to spend the night in Leicestershire. They arrived back in London just after midnight.

Wendy had noticed Katrina Smith handling Isaac's business card, and saying she would give him a call the next time she was in London. She saw Isaac smile in return. Wendy knew Isaac would not be on his own for much longer.

***

Gordon Windsor was on the phone early the next morning. 'The door frame to Grenfell's office has scuff marks from his clothing, indicative of his being manhandled through it. And then, there are marks where he had attempted to force his shoe hard against the wall at the top of the stairs. We also found two sets of shoeprints that show a conflict situation.'

'The evidence is convincing enough to hold up in a court of law?' Isaac asked.

'The final report will state that he had been forced to the top of the stairs, and almost certainly pushed down them.'

'The broken neck killed him?'

'Yes. There was a clear break above the fifth cervical vertebra. If he had not died instantly, he would have died soon after from asphyxiation.'

Isaac phoned DCS Goddard. He was over within minutes.

'What are you going to do about this?' Goddard asked. 'The Penriths are an important family in this country. History goes back for centuries. There's bound to be media scrutiny.'

'Lord Penrith is close to death, and now his brother has been murdered' Isaac said.

'What has the media been told?'

'We have made no official statement.'

'Who could have killed Grenfell?'

'We don't know.'

'Well, you'd better find out soon.'

Goddard left soon after. The two men were firm friends, but sometimes Isaac's senior could rile him. As Isaac saw it, he had a competent team, everyone was giving one hundred per cent, but until there was a breakthrough, they were going nowhere. They knew the identity of the body, although why he died remained a mystery. Montague Grenfell had been integral to providing the reason, but now he was dead, and according to Gordon Windsor and his team, he had been pushed down the stairs outside his office.

Isaac knew full well that falling down a flight of stairs was not an automatic neck break, and there remained a possibility that his death was unintentional. However, the reason why he was at the bottom of the stairs was important, as was the identity of the person who had scuffled with him.

The main suspects were all ageing, and it was hard to believe they would have had the strength. Even with his false leg, Montague Grenfell was a fit man. He was ten years younger than

Mavis Richardson, only seventy-five, and as fit as a man of sixty-five.

There was still one key person unaccounted for: Malcolm Grenfell, the soon to be Lord Penrith.

According to Katrina Smith, the bed-ridden incumbent lord was a decent man, even if he could be snobbish and she had grown fond of the man. Regardless, the next weekend she was taking time off to come and see her mother in London and to meet up with Isaac. Isaac realised that the mother might not receive many hours of her time. He smiled at the thought, which caused Bridget to look his way.

'Good thoughts?' she said.

'I suppose so.' Isaac did not intend to elaborate. 'We need to find Montague Grenfell's younger brother,' he said.

'Yes, sir.'

'Any ideas?'

'What did you find out in Leicestershire?' Bridget asked.

'Not a lot. Only that he had not been there for some time. His current whereabouts are unclear.'

'I have conducted some checks already.'

'What did you find?'

'Malcolm Grenfell is twelve years younger that Montague. That would give his age as sixty-three.'

'Anything else?'

'There appears to be no record of work, although there is a Mercedes registered in his name and a driving licence.'

'A man of independent means, is that it?' Isaac said.

'More likely a scrounging parasite, sir.'

'You may be right. Regardless, we need to find him. How is Wendy's situation?'

'Still with her husband.'

'A job for Larry.'

'He'll be in soon,' Bridget said.

***

'I was going to Bellevue Street this morning,' Larry said on his arrival at the office.

'The grille in the basement?' Isaac replied.

'Yes, sir.'

'What is its condition?'

'It's been damaged, but our people should be able to work with it.'

'What's your feeling?'

Both men were sitting in Isaac's office. The relationship between the two men continued to warm.

'Obviously, it was put there to deter people from entering the room.'

'The whole scenario is illogical. How does anyone expect to keep a body hidden indefinitely in a fireplace?'

'Maybe it was only meant to be there temporarily,' Larry said.

'And then it became impossible to remove, so someone puts up the grille in an attempt to conceal what was inside the room.'

'It makes some sense, but it's still bizarre. And then there is the wooden structure around the fireplace.'

'Focus on the grille for now. The reasons will become clear later.'

'Okay. I'll see you later,' Larry said. He put his empty cup on the sink in the kitchen area in the main office and left.

Isaac walked over to Bridget's desk. 'Let me have Malcolm Grenfell's address,' he said. He was glad of the opportunity to get out of the office.

***

Larry Hill arrived at the house in Bellevue Street at nine thirty in the morning. Gordon Windsor's people were already there, as was Sue Baxter, camera in hand. The woman was becoming a nuisance, and neither Larry nor Isaac had forgiven her for sounding off to the local newspaper about matters which would have been best kept confidential.

Larry reminded her again that it was a murder investigation, and what she saw and heard was not to be repeated outside the confines of the house. As usual, she said that she fully understood, and it was only for a record of the renovations on the house.

Larry had to admit that the Baxters had done a good job, and apart from a few rooms, the murder room included, the house was looking good. Larry realised that it was as well that his wife was not present, as she had been niggling him for the last few months to spend more time at home and to commit to painting the inside, at least.

He could not see the problem as their house was warm and pleasant, and the last thing he wanted at the weekend was to take hold of a paintbrush. Still, he realised on seeing what the Baxters had achieved that maybe his wife was right.

What was the more pressing problem, though? The current murder investigation was taking all his time, and the most he wanted at home was a good sleep. And judging by the way the deaths kept occurring, and the long hours that Isaac committed everyone in the department to, the time for home renovations was not possible.

His wife had made it clear that if he did not have the time, then she would get in a handyman to do it. Larry had said fine until he realised how much that would cost.

'Where's the grille?' Grant Meston asked. He was a good-looking man with flaming red hair and a ruddy complexion. Gordon Windsor had recommended him as the best crime scene investigator in his department.

'Down in the basement. They put it down there, part of Trevor Baxter's wine cellar eventually.'

The two men walked down the stairs off the hallway, followed by a camera, followed by Sue Baxter. The area downstairs was small and lit by a single light bulb hanging from the ceiling.

'We need extra lights down here,' Meston said. 'I've some out in the car. I'll go and fetch them.'

'Why don't you take it upstairs?' Sue Baxter asked.

'Not if we want to avoid more damage.' Grant Meston was already annoyed by the camera and the woman. Larry had forewarned him to keep his detailed findings to himself until they were clear of the house.

The crime scene investigator climbed the stairs and went to fetch the lights. Larry, eyes adjusting to the dim light, looked around the area. It was clear that Trevor Baxter's aspirations to a wine cellar were in the early realisation stage. Baxter had cleared a small corner, a mop and bucket testament to the fact. On the floor, some wine shelves, the sort they sell in the shops, were already holding several bottles of wine.

'My husband's hobby,' Sue Baxter said.

'The looking at them or the drinking?' Larry asked.

'Both.'

'Any good wines here?'

'Better than the average. Leave them for a few years, and they will be great.'

Grant Meston returned. He had run an electric cord down from a socket in the hall. Soon, two powerful fluorescent lights lit the area. No longer needing to focus to see the detail in the basement, Larry could see the grille. It had been pushed up against the far wall. Judging by the marks on the faded paintwork, it had suffered some damage when it had been removed.

'What can you find out from that?' Sue Baxter asked.

'There may be some stamps on the metalwork that will give us a year,' Meston replied, cognisant of Larry Hill's warning about Sue Baxter.

'Any chance of a cup of tea?' Larry asked.

'Sure.' Sue Baxter left for upstairs.

'Would it be easier to take it down to your office?' Larry asked.

'Normally, I would agree, but the grille's been in place for thirty years. Any fingerprints, DNA, will have long been destroyed.'

'Your initial observations?'

'Late 80s, I would say. Give me ten minutes while I check it out. Distract Mrs Baxter if you can.'

Larry left and went upstairs. He found Sue Baxter in the kitchen. 'Grant's fine. He doesn't want tea.'

'Coffee?'

'No, he's okay. He just wants to be left alone to conduct his investigation. He will be up here later.'

'My husband wanted to use the grille for his wine cellar.'

'It is part of a police investigation now, as is the basement. At least, it is for the time being.'

'When can we have the front room back?'

'It doesn't upset you as to what was found in there?' Larry asked.

'The first day it did.'

'And now?'

'Not anymore. It's as if the house had a character, almost like a haunted house.'

'It's not haunted, is it?'

'No. Not at all. 'Have you found the murderer?'

'Not yet.'

Larry sipped his tea. The woman continued to probe.

'We found some old photos,' she said.

'Of the house?'

'They were hidden at the back of an old wardrobe. Slipped down the back, I suppose.'

'Why didn't you reveal this to the police?' Larry asked, aware yet again that the woman would have sold them to the newspapers if she could.

'I never thought any more about them.'

Larry decided to ignore her blatant lie. Sue Baxter was as sharp as a tack, he knew that, and she never forgot. Regardless, he needed the photos.

'Can I see them, please?'

Sue Baxter opened a drawer in the table where she was sitting and handed them to Larry. There were four photos in total, all of them heavily marked from years of neglect.

It was clear that one showed the garden at the rear, another a picture of a child on a bicycle, and the other two a gathering of a group of adults. The adults appeared to be sitting on a sofa.

'We think that is the room where the body was found,' Sue Baxter said.

'What makes you think that?' Larry asked.

'The window at the rear. The curtain material seems to be the same as we found in there the day we opened the room.'

'And the people?'

'No idea.'

'You realise that these photos may become a crucial piece of evidence, yet you decided to keep them from the police.'

'I forgot, honestly.' Sue Baxter went on the defensive, regretting that she had told DI Hill about the photos.

'I need to take them for evidence.'

'Will I get them back at some stage?'

'In time.'

Grant Meston had come into the kitchen before Larry had a chance to remind Sue Baxter that withholding evidence was a criminal offence, as was talking to the media without receiving clearance. It was a moot point as her offences could not be proven to be intentional.

'Cup of tea?' Sue Baxter asked.

'Yes, please,' Meston replied.

'What did you find?' Larry asked, mindful that he had asked Grant Meston not to reveal too much in front of Sue Baxter.

'The age matches. I have taken some numbers off the hinges. It should be possible to match them to a date.'

'Anything else?'

'Nothing more. I have put crime scene tape across the grille, and across the door leading down to the basement. Mrs Baxter, please do not go down there.'

'My husband's wine?'

'He will have to leave it alone for the time being.'

Larry had to admit that although Sue Baxter could stick her nose in where it was not wanted, she was an excellent hostess. The two men stayed for another cup of tea and some sandwiches. Twenty-five minutes later, they stood outside the front gate of the house.

'What's the true story?' Larry asked.

'I found a piece of paper under one corner of the grille. It had been painted over initially, but with time, the paint has lifted.'

'Did you take a photo?'

'I sent one to your email.'

'What does it show?'

'It's a receipt for the grille, or at least, that's what I assume it is.'

'Date?'

'As best as I can tell, February 1987.'

'One month after the murder,' Larry realised. 'Could one person have installed it?'

'With some difficulty. The person would need to know how to use a drill with a masonry bit for the Ramset bolts.'

'A woman?'

'Unlikely, unless they were very practical.'

Chapter 18

By the time, Larry arrived back in the office, Wendy was there. He could see that she had been crying. Bridget was consoling her. 'It was for the best,' she was saying.

'I know, but he was a good man.'

Larry, realising what had happened, came over and put his arm on Wendy's shoulder. 'I'm sorry.'

'Thank you,' she replied meekly.

'You'd better go home,' Larry said.

'DCI Cook's already said that,' Bridget said.

'I prefer to be here. Too many memories there,' Wendy said. 'Tell me about the case.'

Larry had experienced the same feelings when his mother had died five years previously. Sitting around remembering helped little. It was best to keep the mind busy and elsewhere.

'Do you need any help with the arrangements?' Larry asked.

'Thanks for offering, but my sons will deal with it.'

'If you want to work?'

'I do. Please update me.'

'Sue Baxter, the lady of the house in Bellevue Street, has found some photos.'

'Are they relevant?' Wendy asked.

'They are old and grainy, but I think they are.'

'When did she find them?'

'Long enough ago to have informed us before.'

'Have you seen them? What do you reckon?'

'There is one with a child on a bicycle. It may be Garry Solomon. Another two photos show a gathering of adults. We need to identify them.'

'Leave it with me.'

'You will look after Wendy?' Larry said to Bridget.

'Don't worry. She'll be all right with me.'

Isaac arrived back in the office soon after, his search for Malcolm Grenfell curtailed due to the death of Wendy's husband.

'I'm so sorry, Wendy,' he said.

'Thank you, DCI. He was old and barely recognised me, but we had been together for a long time. To me, he was still the strapping young man that I met when I was nineteen. I was a bit wild then, but he soon settled me down.'

'We're here for you. Whatever you want, just let us know.' Isaac put his arms around Wendy and gave her a hug.

DCS Goddard arrived soon after to offer his condolences.

Wendy, not wishing to feel sorry for herself, an understandable reaction under the circumstances, obtained the photos from Larry. She passed them over to Bridget, who had soon found a programme on her computer to enhance them, and to remove some of the marks. Within twenty minutes, the photos were immeasurably improved.

Wendy could see the resemblance of the young boy on the bicycle to the more recent photo of Garry Solomon at nineteen. Under normal circumstances, the mother would have been the ideal person for a positive identification, but Gertrude Richardson was dead. Failing that, there would have been Montague Grenfell, but he was dead as well. Mavis Richardson would have been the next logical choice, but the team had decided that the knowledge of the photos should, at least for the time being, remain concealed from the Richardsons and the Grenfells.

The team had agreed that two of the adults were Gertrude and Mavis Richardson, and Michael Solomon and Ger O'Loughlin were probably two of the men, but there were three others in the photos. Isaac thought that one bore similarities to Montague Grenfell, but he was not sure. As to the other man and woman, no one had any ideas.

Isaac, after he had updated his senior, resumed his search for Malcolm Grenfell.

Wendy thought Garry Solomon's widow, Emma Hampshire, would be a good person to talk to about the boy on the bicycle. Larry said he would go with her.

Wendy acted as though she was fine, but everyone in the office could see through the veneer. Her sons had phoned, asked how she was. The eldest had spoken to Bridget, who put Isaac on the phone.

Isaac told them not to worry as they would look after their mother and bring her home at night.

***

Emma Hampshire was preparing to go out when Wendy and Larry knocked on her door.

'Can we take a few minutes of your time?' Wendy asked. 'This is Detective Inspector Hill.' Larry briefly flashed his ID badge.

'I was just going to the gym,' Emma Hampshire said. 'Personal trainer, so he charges me if I am there or not.'

'Sorry about that,' Larry said.

'What can I do for you?'

'I want to show you a photo,' Wendy said. Larry had to admit that she was holding up well, better than he had when his mother had died.

'Fine.'

'It's old, and the condition is not great, but do you recognise the boy on the bicycle?'

Emma Hampshire studied the photo for a couple of minutes. 'It's Garry.'

'Are you certain?' Wendy asked.

'He looks just the same as Kevin at that age.'

'You took a while to answer,' Larry said.

'It just made me sad that Kevin is not here.'

'He is fine,' Wendy said.

'You've seen him?'

'Last week.'

'Drugs?'

'He was clean and living in Hampstead.'

'Can I have his address?' Emma Hampshire asked.

'He seems to blame you for boarding school, and breaking up the marriage with his father.'

'That's unfair, but he doesn't know the full story. The boarding school was strong on discipline, and Kevin needed it. He was difficult, the same as his father. It was for his own protection, not because I wanted to spend more time with Bob.'

'And the other issue?' Wendy asked.

'Garry poisoned his mind with a story about my screwing another man in his bed. I was not the guilty party, but a young child is susceptible to manipulation. Kevin believes his father's version, not mine. Besides, I would like to see my son.'

'I will talk to him and see if he agrees.'

'You couldn't just give me the phone number?'

'I'm afraid it's privileged information.'

'I understand. Please let him know that I care.'

'I will.'

Sitting outside in Larry's car, he asked Wendy what she had thought of Emma Hampshire's reply relating to the marriage break up.

'Who knows the truth. It's what the son thinks that's important, and she seems genuine in her affection towards her son.'

'Is that why you slipped her the phone number?'

'Yes.'

'What about the people in the other photos?' Larry asked.

'Mavis Richardson is the only one who would know.'

'Why?'

'If it was one of their wife-swapping parties, the other people may want to maintain their confidentiality. Mavis Richardson may not answer, or possibly give us false information.'

'We only know of two who are still alive, Mavis Richardson and Ger O'Loughlin,' Larry said.

'I'm not up to a trip to Ireland,' Wendy said.

'That's understood. We'd better go and see Mavis Richardson. If she lies or is elusive, then I will need to go to Ireland.' The idea of a trip appealed to Larry.

'You'd better make it soon.'

Mavis Richardson, as always, was accommodating and sociable. Even though their visit was arranged with at short notice, she still prepared some food and tea. Wendy nibbled at a biscuit, her eyes welling up with tears. Mavis Richardson asked if she was alright.

Wendy wiped her eyes with a handkerchief and thanked her for her concern.

'We have two photos. We would appreciate it if you will look at them carefully and tell us who you recognise,' Larry said. Wendy sat quietly, stoically putting on a brave face, not certain if she was able to talk without showing emotion.

Mavis Richardson took the photos and placed them on the table. She went to a cupboard in the corner of the room and returned with a magnifying glass. She looked at them for a few minutes.

'The woman in the floral dress is Gertrude. The other woman in the pale blue dress, that's me, although a lot younger.'

'The other woman?' Larry asked.

'The photos must be fifty years old. I can't remember.'

'1962 or 1963?'

'That sounds about right.'

'What about the men?'

'Michael Solomon and my husband, Ger, but you must have recognised them.'

'We needed you to confirm,' Wendy said. She had managed to compose herself.

'There are two other men and a woman,' Larry said.

'It's over fifty years. My memory is not as good as it used to be,' the old woman said. Larry realised that it was the first time that she had alluded to her advanced years, a clear indication that she knew exactly who the other people in the photos were.

Further encouragement from Wendy to Mavis Richardson to think hard came to no avail.

'Was it one of those parties?' Wendy asked indelicately.
'Keys in a hat?' Mavis Richardson replied.
'Yes.'
'Probably, but formal introductions were not always necessary. The people who came changed from time to time.'

Larry and Wendy stayed for another twenty minutes, but realising that the woman was not going to identify the other people, they left.

'She is probably on the phone now,' Larry said once they were clear of the house.

'And those others will be covering their tracks.'

'What about Ger O'Loughlin?'

'You'd better take a flight today,' Wendy said. 'I've got to deal with some issues.'

Larry took her home. He phoned Isaac on the way to update on Mavis Richardson and to get his approval for a flight that day. Bridget, in Isaac's office when Larry called, spoke briefly to Wendy.

'Are you sure you're okay?' Larry asked as he dropped Wendy at her front door.

'The funeral director is here. My sons are here as well. I will be okay, and besides, Bridget is coming over later. Have a safe flight.'

Larry drove to his house, picked up some clothes and an overnight bag, and made his way out to the airport. He rang the O'Loughlins' phone number. The voice on the other end, of a softly-spoken Irish woman, told him to hurry, as her father would only last a few more days.

***

Larry arrived at the O'Loughlins' house at eight in the evening. He had checked into a hotel near to the airport on his arrival. His plan was to show the photos to O'Loughlin, spend the night in Ireland, maybe have a drink or two, and then catch an early morning flight back.

'He can't talk to you tonight,' a pleasant middle-aged woman said as he entered the house.

'Tomorrow?'

'Let's see how he is. He has had a relapse. He is on some medication, but tomorrow morning around nine should be fine.'

Larry phoned Isaac to tell him about the delay. Isaac, as usual, was still in the office. Bridget had left to be with Wendy.

'We need to know the names,' Isaac said.

'Malcolm Grenfell?' Larry asked. 'Any luck finding him?'

'The first address did not check out. Bridget is trying to find somewhere else, but she's distracted with Wendy.'

'You can't blame her, sir.'

'I realise that.'

Larry took the opportunity for a few drinks that night and a good meal. The next day, he arrived back at O'Loughlin's house at 9 a.m. as agreed.

'He's better, but you can only have five minutes.'

'Thanks,' Larry said.

He was shown into Ger O'Loughlin's room. Wendy had said that the man, although incapacitated and connected to a ventilator, was coherent. The man that Larry saw seemed incapable of speech, barely raising his head to acknowledge him.

'Detective Inspector Larry Hill. I'm a colleague of Constable Wendy Gladstone.'

'Please sit down,' the man said in a whisper.

'I have two photos. We need to identify the people in the photos.'

'Show me.'

Larry gave the man's daughter the first of the photos. She placed a pair of glasses on her father and held the photo in front of him.

'Mavis, Gertrude,' the old man said.

'The other woman?'

'Albert Grenfell's wife, Elizabeth.'

'The men?'

'Michael, myself.'

'The other two men?'

'Albert Grenfell and a friend of his. I don't recall his name.'

'My father needs to rest.'

'I need to know who the other man is.'

'I don't know,' the man said feebly. Larry could see that he was fading fast. He now had two more names: names that would cause the investigation to look in new directions.

By 3 p.m. Larry was back in the office in Challis Street.

Isaac was back as well, after looking for the mysterious younger brother of Montague Grenfell.

'We need someone to question Lord Penrith,' Isaac said.

'You've met him,' Larry said. 'It has to be you.'

'What do we hope to gain from this?' Isaac posed a rhetorical question.

'We know he was an attendee at Bellevue Street, as was his wife.'

'What about her?' Bridget asked.

'She has been dead for ten years.'

'It is the unknown man that we need to identify. Do you think his lordship knows?' Larry asked.

'It's a reasonable assumption.'

'But he is suffering from dementia.'

'With dementia, people tend to remember events and people from years before. It's possible he may remember.'

'Is he communicative?'

Isaac made a phone call. Bridget smiled quietly to herself.

'According to his nurse, he comes and goes. A visit there is always uncertain, but regardless, I will go up in the morning,' Isaac said. 'Larry, can you look for Malcolm Grenfell?'

'Wendy will be back in the morning,' Bridget said.

'All three of you focus on this man.'

Chapter 19

Isaac phoned Katrina Smith to tell him of her plans.

'Come up tonight. There are plenty of rooms in the house.'

Isaac left the office early, ostensibly to take advantage of a few more hours of possible coherence from the lord.

He arrived at eleven in the evening. Katrina made him a light supper and showed him to his room. It was ageing, as was the rest of the house, but it had a four-poster bed and a view overlooking a lake at the rear. Katrina never made it back to her room that night.

Refreshed and feeling a lot better the next morning thanks to the nurse, Isaac made his way downstairs to the kitchen. Katrina was already there with an English breakfast for him: eggs, bacon and two sausages. A pot of coffee was brewing on the Aga cooker.

'You'll need to keep your strength up,' she said.

Isaac had to admit that he liked her.

'His lordship is not too well,' Katrina said.

'Later?' Isaac asked.

'Maybe after I have had a chance to get some food into him.'

Isaac ate his breakfast as they talked. Normally, he would have an orange juice, sometimes a bowl of cereal, but today he was going to be well-fed. After he had finished with the main course, there were two slices of toast and home-made jam.

Katrina left and went to look after her patient. Isaac sat down with his laptop and connected to the internet using his phone.

Wendy was soon on the phone.

'How are you?' he asked.

'Better for being in the office. Bridget and Larry are making a fuss of me.'

'Good. You know what is required?'

'Malcolm Grenfell.'

'Judging by the condition of the current lord, he is about to inherit Penrith House and a title. No idea if there's any money involved.'

'Old money,' Wendy said. 'They don't like to flash it around, but there will be plenty of cash somewhere.'

'Which reminds me,' Isaac said. 'Montague Grenfell's legal and financial records.'

'Bridget has someone on them. Do you want to speak to her?'

'Put her on the phone.'

'Bridget, you've been working on Grenfell's papers. Anything interesting.'

'Keith Dawson is here. He's over from Fraud.'

'Yes, I realise.'

'He's not here at the present moment, but I can give you an update.'

'Please do.'

'Grenfell's papers are meticulous. Not only does he look after the Richardsons' legal and financial matters, but he also looks after the Grenfells. All that he told us regarding Gertrude's and Mavis's relationship and financial status appears to be correct. Gertrude was wealthy, although did not know or chose to ignore it.

'Garry Solomon kept in contact with Montague Grenfell on an infrequent basis, and when requested, Grenfell would send him money. However, it was infrequent, and there is no reason to believe that they actually met. Kevin Solomon, the son of Garry Solomon, has been looked after as well. The drug rehabilitation, the flat in Hampstead, all paid for by Gertrude Richardson.'

'Did she know?' Isaac asked.

'Impossible to say. Grenfell had full authority in relation to Mavis's and Gertrude's legal and financial affairs. There is no indication that he abused that privilege. Also, the Grenfells are extremely wealthy, even if, as you say, the house where you currently are does not indicate that.'

'Is there any more?'

'Keith Dawson will update you with more detail as you require.'

'Thanks. Put Wendy on the phone again.'

'I'm here, sir,' Wendy said.

'Malcolm Grenfell, find him today. It's important.'

'How is Katrina Smith?' Wendy asked.

'Take that smile off your face, or your promotion next week to sergeant will be delayed.'

'Yes, sir.' It was the first time that anyone had seen Wendy smile in the office since her husband had passed away.

'Your husband?'

'The funeral is next week.'

'I would like to attend.'

'I would appreciate that, sir.'

Isaac put down the phone, smiled at Wendy's cheeky comment.

***

'You can try now,' Katrina said as she walked back into the kitchen at Penrith House.

Isaac could see the resemblance to the man in the photo, although the man in the bed was old and decrepit and drooling, whereas the man in the picture had been young and vibrant with a full head of jet-black hair.

'How can I help you?' the man asked, lying almost horizontal on his back in the bed. His head was propped up by two large pillows.

'I've explained to Lord Penrith as to why you are here,' Katrina said.

'We need to identify a man in an old photo,' Isaac said.

Katrina took the photo and held it in front of the old man.

'Michael Solomon.'

'We have identified Michael Solomon, Ger O'Loughlin and yourself. There is another man there.'

'George Sullivan.'

'Do you know where we can find him?'

'Haven't seen him in years.'

'Where was the last time?'

'He has a house in Berkshire.'

'Does he have a title?'

'George, no way. Good man, good in business, but no title.'

'That's all you are going to get,' Katrina said.

Lord Penrith closed his eyes and fell asleep.

'I doubt if he will last more than a few days. I'm not sure if I can make this weekend.'

'It was a good job I came up today. I'd better get back to London.'

'Do you fancy lunch before you leave?'

'What's for dessert?' Isaac asked.

'What do you want?' Isaac smiled at Katrina's suggestive response. At two in the afternoon, he left for the drive back to Challis Street. He would be in the office before 5 p.m. He needed Malcolm Grenfell, as well as George Sullivan, assuming he was still alive.

The key players were dying at an increasingly frequent rate, and the one reality of the case was that the murderer, if not dead, may soon be as a result of the ageing process.

Whatever way Isaac looked at it, he realised there was hardly likely to be a conviction, only a conclusion to the case.

Isaac walked into the office just before the end of day meeting started. Bridget was there, fussing over him as he entered. As soon as he had sat down at his desk, there was a cup of coffee in front of him.

'Grenfell's financial and legal dealings? Anything new?'

'No more than what I told you before. It appears that for the last fifteen years, his only clients have been the Grenfells and the Richardsons. What he had told you before he died seems to be correct.'

'The only problem,' Isaac said, 'is that he only gave truthful answers to questions asked. If I didn't ask, he never answered, and now he is dead.'

'There is only one anomaly,' Bridget said.

'Yes. What's that?'

'Malcolm Grenfell.'

'What about him?'

'The records show that Malcolm Grenfell was receiving a substantial payment each month for basically doing nothing.'

'How was it recorded?'

'Purely listed as expenses.'

'I don't see anything unusual,' Isaac said. 'From what we know of the Grenfells and the Richardsons, they look after their own, black sheep or no black sheep. Even Michael Solomon when he left Gertrude remained friendly with Montague Grenfell, and Garry Solomon, whether he was in trouble with the law or not, always had the possibility of help from his mother, Gertrude.'

'Even if she didn't know?' Bridget said.

'The truth as to whether she did or did not has gone to the grave with Gertrude and the family lawyer.'

'Wendy and Larry have been looking for the younger son.'

'Were you able to help them?'

'I believe they have found him, sir.'

'Good. We need to meet him soon.'

'Is he a suspect, sir?'

'Everyone is a suspect, whether they are alive or not.'

***

'Malcolm Grenfell?'

'Yes. Who are you?'

'Detective Inspector Larry Hill, Constable Wendy Gladstone,' Larry said.

'What do you want?'

'You're a hard man to find,' Wendy said.

'I value my privacy.'

To Larry and Wendy, it hardly seemed their idea of privacy. The man lived well. An attractive house in Henley to the west of London, its back garden running down to the River Thames. In the driveway, there was a Mercedes, the same registration that Bridget had found against the man's name.

'You've changed your address,' Larry said.

'I've lived here for five years.'

Wendy felt that she did not like the man, but then she had little time for the class structure that pervaded the country. If she had admitted to it, she would have stated that she was a socialist.

It was clear that there was a woman in the house, her shrill voice shouting for Grenfell to come back.

'I have a visitor. This is not a convenient time. Come back later.'

'Are you used to the police knocking on your door?' Wendy asked.

'Too often for me.'

'Why?'

'The neighbours don't agree with the parties I have here.'

'Loud, are they?' Larry asked.

'They are welcome to come, but they are all frustrated, members of the local golf club, regular churchgoers.'

'And you are not?'

'Hell, no. You only get one shot at life. I intend to enjoy myself.'

'And if that includes women and drinking and making a noise?' Wendy asked.

'Not so much for the drink, but the women, yes.'

'We are from Homicide,' Wendy said.

'Wait a minute. I'll tell her to make herself presentable before you come in.'

Two minutes later, Malcolm Grenfell returned. 'Come in.'

The woman sat on a chair in the kitchen. She was wearing an evening dress, even though it was early in the day. In her hand was a glass of champagne.

'Hi, I'm Lucy,' she said. 'Is Malcolm in trouble again?'

Wendy thought she was in her early twenties. Larry could not but look at her more than he should. Both of them would have agreed that she was vivacious, although only Larry would have appreciated the visible bare breast.

'Go upstairs,' Grenfell said. 'I'll be there shortly.'

'You'd better be hard when you get there,' Lucy said.

Wendy realised that the woman had said it to tease Larry.

'She's had a few too many drinks,' Grenfell said.

'A friend of yours?' Wendy asked.

'One of many. I make no pretence as to what I am.'

'And what is that?'

'A lecherous old man who should know better.'

The three sat down at a dining table.

'Tell me why you are here?'

'Are you aware of certain events pertaining to your family?'

'Albert is dying, and Montague will inherit the title.'

'Anything else?'

'I have no contact with Albert, and very little with Montague.'

'Why is that?' Larry asked.

'They disapprove of me.'

'Because of your lifestyle?'

'They belong to the past. They see that a title and position requires a person to devote himself to a life of sobriety and service to the community. I don't.'

'They still pay you to live the life they despise?' Larry said.

'No option. They could not have a family member of theirs demeaning himself with taking a menial job, even living with the proletariat.'

'I am sorry to tell you that Montague has died,' Wendy said.

'No, that cannot be. I spoke to him the week before last.'

'What did you talk about?'
'Albert.'
'Why?'
'Albert was the one who insisted on maintaining my lifestyle.'
'And Montague would have stopped your allowance?'
'Probably not, but I wanted to check.'
'Are you sad that Albert is dying?'
'Why? Should I be? Look at the life he led – boring and pointless. Married to the same old shrew for years.'
'She's dead.'
'A long time. The best thing she did for Albert.'

The frivolous rent-a-lay poked her head around the corner of the door. 'I need you,' she said to Grenfell.

He told her to watch the television or to have another glass of champagne. She left and went back upstairs, complaining as she went. Wendy was certain that she was snorting cocaine.

'Mind you, I did like Montague, even if he was stuffy.'
'What do you mean?' Wendy asked.
'He always had his head in a book, or was fussing over money.'
'Highly regarded by your family and the Richardsons.'
'The Richardsons,' Grenfell sighed.
'What is it about the Richardsons that causes you to sigh?' Larry asked.
'I never understood the relationship.'
'They are cousins.'
'I realise that, but we have other cousins. I never saw any of them receive the same benevolence.'
'Did you know them?'
'Twenty to twenty-five years since I've seen the two sisters.'
'The eldest one is dead.'
'Gertrude?'
'Yes.'
'I'm not surprised.'

'Why?' Wendy asked.

'Highly promiscuous.'

'She was eighty-seven when she died.'

'At least she knew how to enjoy life.'

'Not for the last few years. She had become reclusive.'

'Unhinged after her son disappeared.'

'What do you know about the son?'

'We were about the same age, shipped off to the same boarding school. He was a decent person, although he had some of Gertrude's madness.'

'What do you mean?'

'He had a wild streak. Always getting into trouble.'

'What sort of trouble?'

'At school: graffiti when he could get hold of some paint, smuggling whisky into the dormitory, even managed to seduce the headmaster's daughter. The old man caught him in bed with her, expelled him immediately. Made himself a legend amongst the pupils that day.'

'Do you know why he hated his mother?'

'Hate? He didn't hate her, quite the opposite.'

'What do you mean?'

'He loved her, but never wanted to see her.'

'Do you know why?'

'No.'

'On the death of your brother, you will become Lord Penrith,' Wendy said.

'I suppose so.'

'What are your thoughts?'

'No need to worry about the neighbours up there.'

'You would move in to the family home?'

'It will need fixing up first, but yes. Why not?'

'You intend to enjoy yourself?' Wendy asked.

'For as long as I can.'

'Garry Solomon. What do you know about him?'

'No idea what happened to him.'

'It's been on the news.'

'Too busy to watch the news.'

'Garry Solomon is dead.'
'How?'
'He was murdered.'
'Somebody's wife or daughter, I suppose.'
'We don't know why.'
'When?'
'1987.'
'That's a long time. How did Montague die?'
'He was pushed down some stairs.'
'Murdered?'
'Murdered. Or an unfortunate consequence of a fight.'
'Fight? Montague? He was a pacifist.'
'His death clears your way to the title,' Larry said.
'The title means little to me.'

The two police officers left soon after. The young woman was becoming restless again, and Malcolm Grenfell looked more in need of her services than talking to them.

Chapter 20

'George Sullivan,' Isaac said in the office on Wendy and Larry's return. 'He is the other man in the photo.'

'And you want us to find him, sir?' Larry asked.

Wendy, once back in the office, had moved over to near Bridget. Isaac could see that Wendy was in need of her friend's ministrations. For the moment, it was only Isaac and Larry.

'Any ideas about him, DCI?'

'Nothing to go on. His lordship gave the name just before he fell asleep.'

'How much longer before he dies?'

'According to Katrina?'

'Katrina?' Larry asked, knowing full well who Isaac was referring to. The office always liked a little bit of gossip, even if it was discreet.

'Katrina Smith, his private nurse.'

'How long?'

'One week, give or take a few days.'

'And then Malcolm Grenfell is the new Lord Penrith.'

'Is he excited?'

'Not sure.'

'What do you mean?'

'He professes not to care, but he's a member of the idle rich. With Albert and Montague dead, he gets the title, the stately home, and the money.'

'A good enough motive to murder Montague Grenfell.'

'As you say.'

Wendy, feeling slightly better, came over and joined the conversation. 'I didn't like him, sir,' she said.

'Malcolm Grenfell?'

'A man his age messing around with a girl in her twenties.'

'He likes young women?'

'He's a total waster, sir.'

'But is he a murderer?'

'If it affected his lifestyle, he might feel inclined.'

'Could he have killed Montague?'

'To ensure the title?' Larry asked.

'Why not?' Isaac answered.

'Montague Grenfell had control of the money, the titles to all of the properties. Did he set up a proxy in case he was indisposed?'

'It's a question that needs answering. We should ask Bridget to check.'

Wendy leant over to the door entrance and shouted for Bridget to come over.

Bridget brought a sheet of paper with her.

'Bridget, who will take control of Montague's legal and financial responsibilities?'

'I have a copy of his will, sir.'

Isaac scanned the document. 'Albert, the first executor, then Mavis Richardson. The wealth stays within the Grenfell family, so Malcolm's claim on the money and the house is secure. There is also a generous amount of money to be taken from his estate and given to Mavis Richardson.'

'What does it mean?' Larry asked.

'He trusts Mavis, but not Malcolm,' Bridget said.

'That is fine, but everyone in this will, except for Malcolm Grenfell, is over eighty years of age. Any one of them could die at any time.'

'In that case, full control would probably go to Malcolm.'

'The man has a strong motive, at least for the murder of his brother.'

'Is Mavis Richardson at risk?' Larry asked.

'DCI, you mentioned George Sullivan,' Wendy said.

'Lord Penrith identified him as the unknown man in the photos.'

'Who is he?'

'That's up to you and Larry.'

'Are we saying that Albert Grenfell and his wife attended the wife-swapping parties?'

'The photos may be unrelated. George Sullivan may know.'

'Where do we look, sir?'

'According to the elder Grenfell, he had a house in Berkshire. Not much to go on, but that is all there is. Maybe check Montague's records.'

***

Albert Grenfell died two days after Isaac had spoken to him. Wendy and Larry informed Malcolm Grenfell by phone. They could hear the sound of people and music in the background. The new Lord Penrith did not turn the music down.

The new lord was delighted and intended to enjoy his good fortune with more drink and more food. The frivolous twenty-something that Larry and Wendy met had been replaced by another.

Mavis Richardson took the news badly when Wendy told her. 'He was a good man. Old fashioned, but genuine. Who's left now?' Mavis said. Wendy thought she looked a lot older than when she had previously seen her.

'Did he attend any of your parties?'

'Yes. On a couple of occasions.'

'And his wife?'

'Once.'

'What can you tell me about George Sullivan?'

'He was a friend of Albert's.'

'He was at one of your parties?'

'We never invited him again.'

'Why?'

'He was a coarse man.'

'Would you care to elaborate?'

'We only agreed that he could come if he brought a woman with him.'

'And he did?'

'No. He came on his own.'

'But he stayed?'

'He was an attractive man. Gertrude wanted him immediately, but I could see he was trouble.'

'How?'

'He started putting his hands on me.'

'Was that a problem?'

'In front of everyone?'

'Are you saying that behind closed doors it was okay, but not in front of the guests?'

'It's basic good manners, and he had very few of them.'

'Did you sleep with him?'

'Gertrude did.'

'Why didn't you?'

'He wanted to, and if he had been more of a gentleman, I probably would have.'

'Was Montague Grenfell there?'

'No.'

'What happened after you refused?'

'He became drunk, accused me of being a prick teaser. In the end, the party ended early, and Albert led him away.'

'His wife came as well?'

'She didn't take part.'

'And Albert?'

'I slept with him the one time. Gertrude, on another.'

'Where can I find George Sullivan?' Wendy asked.

'I've no idea. He may be dead, same as all of us. I am the only one still alive. You do realise that?'

'We found Malcolm.'

'Still living it up with his young tarts?'

'You never mentioned that you knew where he was.'

'I never knew. Did Montague?'

'Montague knew everything,' Wendy said. 'And Malcolm is now the incumbent lord.'

'Does he know?'

'I told him.'

'He will destroy the good name of the Grenfells. He is the last of the line. After him, there will be no more Lord Penriths.'

'Is that a bad thing?' Wendy asked.

'I still believe breeding counts for something,' Mavis Richardson said.

Wendy realised that it was not for her to discuss Montague Grenfell's will. That was for a more formal occasion. Wendy assumed that Mavis Richardson knew its contents, but she would only live for a few more years before she died, or became too old and frail to understand what was required of her. Wendy wondered what happened in such circumstances, but assumed there was a procedure.

'Have you nominated another lawyer?' Wendy asked.

'Not yet. I'm not sure who I can trust.'

'Maybe you should.'

'Malcolm will turn the ancestral home into a bordello,' Mavis said.

'Garry Solomon had a son.'

'I am aware of that.'

Mavis Richardson appeared tired. Wendy made her excuses and left, not sure what she had achieved by visiting. The old woman had not provided any more useful information, and judging by her condition, she was not in a fit state to take on the responsibilities as the executor of Montague Grenfell's will.

Lord Penrith's wealth would be a sufficient motive for anyone, and Gertrude was independently wealthy, as was Mavis. What would happen if Mavis died? She had no living relatives, other than an ex-husband, but he was at death's door.

The only person who had anything to gain from Mavis's death would be Kevin Solomon, the son of Garry Solomon.

Wendy phoned Larry. They agreed to meet up with Kevin Solomon to see if he knew any more.

***

Isaac had received an urgent phone call from Katrina Smith, still up at Lord Penrith's house in Leicestershire. 'Malcolm Grenfell is here,' she said.

'What did he have to say for himself?'

'He was drunk; he had a woman in the car. At first, I assumed it was his daughter.'

'She's not his daughter,' Isaac said.

'He thought I was part of the deal.'

'Violent?'

'He could have been.'

'What did you do?'

'Kneed him and punched him in the face.'

'I didn't know you were so tough.'

'You've not checked out my history?'

'No.'

'Five years with the British Army, two of those in Iraq. I received training in unarmed combat and weaponry.'

'Were you on the front line?'

'Baghdad, field hospital.'

'Tell me about Lord Penrith.'

'The new one?'

'Yes.'

'He wanted to move in, spend the night. There wasn't a lot I could do to stop him. I told him his brother was still in the house.'

'They've not taken the body away yet?'

'You would think it was royalty that had died. He is lying in state, and all the staff, local dignitaries, other members of the aristocracy are filing past. It's macabre.'

'Did Malcolm Grenfell want to see his brother?'

'Hell he did. He was more interested in doing an inventory of anything valuable.'

'Is he still there?'

'Yes.'

'Can you leave?'

'Not with his brother lying dead in the other room. Can you come up?'

'It may be an excellent opportunity to meet Lord Penrith.'

Isaac arrived at the Penrith House at six in the evening. Katrina came out of the front door on seeing him arrive. She could not resist and gave him a hug and a kiss.

'He's impossible,' she said.

'What's he done?'

'He found the key to the wine cellar, and he's down there with his woman. I took a look, and it was evident she is not his daughter. Both naked and covered in wine, almost like a bacchanalian orgy.'

'I'll deal with it,' Isaac said. Katrina had phoned the local police, but they were reluctant to intervene as the man was now the lord. Isaac knew what Wendy's comment would have been.

Isaac walked down the stone steps to the basement. The two people at the bottom were unconscious drunk. Katrina came down, and they carried them both upstairs and put them to bed. Isaac assumed one bed would be sufficient for the pair.

'They won't have much to say until tomorrow,' Katrina said.

'No point going back now. Do you have a spare room?' Isaac asked.

'If you don't mind sharing.'

Chapter 21

Kevin Solomon was not initially pleased to see Wendy and Larry. 'What do you want?' he asked.

'A few more questions,' Wendy said.

'You'd better come in.'

'How are you?' Wendy attempted to lighten the sombre tone of the meeting.

'You gave my phone number to my mother.'

'She was concerned.'

'Not concerned enough when she put me in that boarding school.'

'What did you say to her?'

'I was polite.'

'Have you met her?'

'I said I would. She sounded lonely.'

'I think she is,' Wendy said.

'I was angry at the time, but now I'm all right,' Kevin Solomon said. 'Do you want a drink?'

'Coffee for me,' Larry said.

'Make that two,' Wendy added.

'Mavis Richardson, it is assumed, will be the executor of Montague Grenfell's will, and the proxy for his business and legal affairs.'

'What has that to do with me?'

'Your agreement with Montague. Was it watertight?'

'I signed some papers, but I've been so spaced out for the last few years, I don't know. He could have made me sign anything.'

'That's unlikely,' Wendy said.

'Why?'

'We have had qualified people checking his paperwork. The man was meticulous, and there is no trace of his cheating anyone. And besides, you're family.'

'Illegitimate family, wrong side of the bed.'

'It appears to be a minor distinction.'

'Enough to keep my father from the title.'

'Does that concern you?'

'My mother said it upset him.'

'What else did your mother say?'

'Most of the time I was either drunk or injecting myself.'

'Do you intend to stay clean?'

'I spent two years at university studying law, one of my few clean periods. I plan to make sure my mother gets her fair share after my grandmother died. I don't trust anyone.'

Wendy looked around the room. It was clear that Kevin Solomon had tidied the place, a sure sign that his mother was intending to visit. Wendy was pleased as animosity between mother and child is always unpleasant. Her sons had always been there for her except in their troublesome teens and early twenties. Then, it had been too much alcohol and wanting to bring females home. She had relaxed her strict rule on a couple of occasions, and an unknown female face at the breakfast table the next morning had given her a slight tinge of regret that she had agreed, but apart from that, it had been fine. Finally, she had drawn the line when two females and one son had presented themselves at the table one morning looking for bacon and eggs. She had made it clear that she was not a hotel nor a brothel, and if either son wanted to avail themselves of the local talent, they'd better find somewhere else.

Not that she could blame the females, as her sons took after their father with their rugged good looks, but threesomes in her house had been too much.

She had relented when her two boys had matured and settled down with steady girlfriends.

The funeral of her husband was scheduled for later in the week. She had asked Isaac to give a eulogy as he had met her husband several times over the years, and she knew he would say the right words. The sons would speak as well. Wendy knew that she would be incapable.

She had appreciated the opportunity to continue at work, and the case had focussed her mind away from her husband's death. Bridget continued to stay at Wendy's house, although one son or another was always there. Still, Bridget was female and would understand more than the sons what their mother was going through.

'Wendy, Wendy.'

'Yes, Larry. Sorry.'

Wendy, comfortable in Kevin Solomon's flat, had drifted off, probably fallen asleep for a few minutes. Her sleep pattern had been disturbed since her husband had died, and her regular eight hours had been replaced by short periods of one or two hours, sometimes three, sometimes none.

Severely embarrassed, Wendy apologised.

Kevin Solomon said not to worry.

'Do you intend to make a legal claim on the estate?' Wendy asked, pretending to be fully alert, and now sitting forward on the comfortable chair.

'If there is an issue, although, as you say, Montague Grenfell was an honourable man.'

'We believe that to be the case, but…'

'Malcolm Grenfell?' Kevin Solomon said.

'What do you know about him?' Larry asked. Wendy had moved towards the window, aiming to take in the breeze from outside, attempting to wake herself. The toll of the last few weeks was catching up with her, and once everything had settled down, she intended to take a break, sit in the sun somewhere. Hopefully, Bridget would come. If she didn't, she would go on her own.

'My mother told me what she knew once I was old enough to understand.'

'Your mother seems to have no financial problems.'

'My mother is not concerned about the money, only that she, as the widow of Gertrude Richardson's son, and I, the grandson, are treated in the correct manner.'

'And why should Malcolm Grenfell be an issue?' Wendy asked. She had resumed her seat, confident that she would not embarrass herself again. She knew the answer but wanted to hear it from Solomon.

'Somehow, the Grenfells and the Richardsons are inexorably linked.'

'Is there more to the story than we know?' Larry asked.

'From what my mother has told me, the aristocracy, or at least, the Grenfells' version, abide by a different set of values. According to my mother, I should never trust them.'

Wendy could only agree. She had only risen as far as a sergeant in the London Metropolitan Police, but she took pride in that she had benefited society, helped to reunite lost and alienated children with their parents, taken a major part in putting some villains and murderers in jail. Just because someone put 'Lord' before their name meant little to her.

'Your mother is coming?' Wendy asked.

'In about an hour.'

'Are you looking forward to see her?'

'Yes. I would appreciate some time to prepare.'

'Fine,' Wendy said.

Outside in the car, with the heater on, the two police officers evaluated what Kevin Solomon had said.

'He seems to know a lot about the Grenfells,' Larry said.

'At least, his mother does. Did she ever meet any of them?'

'She never met Gertrude Richardson, although she could have met some of the others. Did she meet Montague Grenfell personally? I suppose we will never know.'

As they sat in the car, they saw Emma Hampshire exit a black London taxi. She waved to the two of them but did not come over to speak. She appeared to be in a good mood, and her son had obviously told her about the two police officers sitting outside.

Larry suggested knocking on the door and questioning the woman. Wendy, sentimental and motherly, was firm in her response.

'No. Those two have a lot of talking to do,' she said.

***

Malcolm Grenfell, the newly incumbent Lord Penrith, was up and about by eight in the morning. The lord's young woman was still sleeping off the effects of the drunken excess from the previous night.

Isaac made sure to give the impression that he had just arrived. His lordship was not pleased to see him, although Isaac was not sure whether that was because of Grenfell's throbbing head, or whether he was just an arrogant man, or whether acquiring the title had somehow elevated him above the law and probing questions.

Regardless of what the man wanted or thought, Isaac had questions, Grenfell had the answers.

'Who is going to deal with the reading of the will and the legal and financial matters after your brothers' deaths?'

'Which brother? The former lord, or Montague?' Malcolm Grenfell made the pretence of eating his breakfast, although not in the kitchen with the staff. He was sitting at one end of a large table in a formal dining room. Isaac sat at the other end. He realised that if he had not come with the authority of the London Metropolitan Police, he would be in the kitchen, and would be expected to bow and scrape.

Katrina had forewarned Isaac that Malcolm Grenfell was taking his responsibilities as Lord Penrith very seriously, especially the part where the peasants fawned to their master. She had stated that once the previous lord was in the funeral home, then she was leaving, which was that day.

'Montague gave executor powers to that woman, Mavis Richardson. Not that she can do much, too old,' Malcolm Grenfell said.

'You know her?'

'Not intimately, as Montague obviously did.'

'What are you inferring?'

'I know about Montague and the Richardson sisters.'
'What do you know?'
'Don't be obtuse. The fact that they were screwing each other.'
'Kevin Solomon?'
'What about him?'
'Do you know him?'
'Never met him, although I went to the same school as his father.'
'Garry?'
'If he had only the one father, then Garry. Is there another one?'

The cook came in with a pot of tea. She poured a cup for Isaac, poured another for his lordship. As she left the room, and with Malcolm Grenfell's back to her, she cocked her nose in the air and held a finger underneath. Isaac smiled; he knew the universal gesture for someone with airs and graces and a snob.

'You were about the same age as Garry Solomon,' Isaac said.
'I was three years older.'
'Did you spend time with him?'
'When we were in our teens, we would go out drinking, chasing girls.'
'Later?'
'He met up with Emily. After that, we lost contact. I never saw him again.'
'You knew Emily?'
'She was a good-looking woman. Fancied her myself, but she wanted Garry.'
'Have you seen her since?'
'Around London. We moved in the same social circles. Nothing sinister.'

The young woman who had arrived with Grenfell walked into the room. Isaac thought it was more a crawl than a walk, as she was rubbing her eyes and trying to focus. Her hair was tousled, and she was wearing a dressing gown. It was tied loosely at the waist, her breasts almost exposed.

'Are you going to make me a Lady?' she asked of Grenfell after planting a semi-drunken kiss on him.

'Later maybe. I'm busy for the present.'

The woman, young enough to be Penrith's daughter, sat down on a spare chair. 'I want breakfast,' she slurred.

Judging by Grenfell's facial expression, her chances of him marrying her were slim. Isaac could see that she was going to be dumped within a short period of time. He felt sorry that such a young girl felt the need to hang around with a man in his sixties, instead of finding someone her own age. Not that it concerned him, as in his years of being an active member of the police force, he had seen many unlikely couples, some happy, others not so.

'Go down to the kitchen with the rest,' Grenfell barked, or attempted to, but his voice was still subdued and raspy after the wine of the previous night.

The woman ambled out of the door.

'What did you speak to Emily Solomon about?'

'It's been a few years, but she had moved on from Garry, or he had moved on. Regardless, she was very cosy with Bob Hampshire.'

'You knew Hampshire?'

'Good man. He worshipped Emily, although she called herself Emma with him.'

'And her?'

'She was devoted to him.'

'Tell me about Mavis Richardson. How is she going to deal with Montague's complex legal and financial matters?'

'I've no idea. What is the legal process in such issues? She is clearly not up to the task.'

'And Albert?'

'I will deal with it. There is a lawyer in the town who is reputable. I'll put the matter in his hands.'

'Trustworthy?'

'He will be with me. This is all mine now. I don't intend to let anyone cheat me out of my dues.'

'And the woman you brought up?'

'I was the brother of a lord before.'

'Better class of woman now?' Isaac said contemptuously.

'I hope so.'

Isaac left the man to his breakfast. He needed to see a friendly face; he needed to see Katrina.

Chapter 22

Larry was leaning back in his chair at Challis Street. Wendy had left early, some last-minute arrangements for the funeral. Bridget was busy, collating all the paperwork that a murder enquiry created.

She was still helping Wendy with her reports, or Sergeant Wendy Gladstone, as her promotion had come through. Bridget had managed to get Isaac's paperwork under control, and if she focussed, she could complete it within an hour.

Bridget enjoyed working in the department, even if the hours could be long, but there was not much for her at home. The former live-in lover had been unceremoniously shown the door two weeks earlier. She had come home late and he had been sitting down with a couple of friends in the kitchen, drinking beer.

'We need some food,' he had demanded.

'Get your friends out of here and clear up this mess.' Bridget saw red. The lover lived there rent free. The only requirements on him were that he kept the place clean and showed her the attention she craved.

'Woman, do what you're told or you will feel the back of my hand.'

He had tried it once before, but it had been early in their relationship, and she had forgiven him after he had sobered up, but now…

Coupled with the pressure of work and her friend Wendy's sadness, Bridget reached a decision. A well-built woman and surprisingly strong, she grabbed the man by the scruff of his neck and ejected him through the back door. The other two men sheepishly retreated.

The trio had stood outside the house for thirty minutes before she phoned Wendy, who phoned a contact down at the local police station. The trio spent the night in a prison cell. Bridget ensured that her previous companion's clothes were deposited at the police station. According to Wendy, he was warned by the local police that if he attempted to make contact with Bridget, he would be thrown in the cells for a week.

Bridget had been sad for a few days but soon got over him. Wendy offered her one of her cats for comfort, but she declined. Besides, both of the women were looking to pool their resources and move in together. Bridget's house seemed the best possibility, as Wendy's was cold and damp. They had even discussed buying a small flat somewhere warm, renting it out to holidaymakers when they did not need it.

Larry's phone rang. 'Grant Meston. We met at the Baxters.'

'How are you?'

'Fine.'

'Any update on the grille at the Baxters?'

'It was installed in February 1987.'

'You knew that already.'

'I have the name of the company that installed it.'

'And the name of who paid for it?'

'No such luck. It was a long time ago. I made a quick phone call to save you the trouble, but no one remembered.'

'Send me an email with the address, and I'll get out there,' Larry said.

Isaac arrived back in the office just after midday. Katrina Smith was still up in Leicestershire and would be down in London later that night. Isaac offered to pick her up at the station, but she had declined. Her mother was picking her up, and she should spend some time with her.

Bridget rushed into Isaac's office with a cup of coffee on his arrival. Larry came in soon after.

'Take a seat,' Isaac said. He had been a little weary after the drive down, but Bridget's caffeine-rich coffee soon revived him. Five minutes later, DCS Goddard entered the room. He was in an ebullient mood. Isaac wondered why but assumed he had been pressing the flesh with the movers and shakers again.

DCS Goddard saw a protégé in Isaac; DCI Isaac Cook saw a mentor in DCS Goddard. It did not isolate Isaac from his boss's wrath and frustration; a kick up the arse when it was needed.

Today was not one of those days.

Bridget brought another coffee for their DCS. He thanked her.

'What's the latest, Isaac?'

'Loose ends, sir.'

'DI Hill, what are you up to?' Goddard asked.

'We know where the grille that prevented entry into the murder room was constructed, sir.'

'And when are you going out there?'

'As soon as I leave this meeting.'

'Wendy?' The DCS looked at Isaac.

'The funeral is tomorrow.'

'Who will be going?'

'All of us.'

'Fine. I will be there as well,' Goddard said. 'Bridget, what have you to report?'

It was evident to Isaac that someone was asking Richard Goddard questions, or just winding him up to bring the case to a conclusion. Someone influential, but who and why? Isaac did not see it as important, and besides, it was a murder enquiry, and setting a schedule for murderer apprehended, murderer convicted, case closed did not work. As far as Isaac was concerned everyone was doing their best, even Wendy who should be on compassionate leave. But he had known the DCS longer than anyone else in the department, and when you needed support or advice, his door was always open.

'Montague Grenfell seems to have been an exceptionally precise man, very honourable and decent.'

'He still ends up murdered.'

'We're not sure about that,' Isaac said.

'There is a scuffle. He falls down the stairs, dead at the bottom. That's murder in my book.'

183

Isaac knew that his DCS was baiting him. 'It could have been a disagreement that unfortunately had fatal consequences.'

'Gordon Windsor's report stated clearly that the man had been manhandled through the door of his office. He then attempted to wedge his foot against the wall at the top of the stairs. It looks conclusive to me.'

'As you say, conclusive.' Isaac saw no validity in contradicting his senior's opinion.

'Were Garry Solomon and Montague Grenfell killed by the same person?' DCS Goddard asked.

'It seems unlikely,' Isaac said.

'Why?'

'There is almost thirty years between the two murders. There must be a strong possibility that the murderer of Garry Solomon is dead.'

'How much longer do you need with this case? I'm being asked to keep costs under control.'

'Not at the expense of a murder investigation,' Isaac said.

'The accountants only understand the bottom line. They are out of touch with reality, but unfortunately we all have to contend with them.'

Isaac knew that it was rhetoric and that Richard Goddard would keep the wolves at bay. And besides, the department's key performance indicators were good. The last three cases they had found the murderer and ensured a conviction within an acceptable time period.

'We are conscious of budgetary restraints,' Isaac said.

'Fine. Montague Grenfell seems the easiest case to solve,' DCS Goddard said.

'Yes.'

'I need an arrest within ten days.'

'Why ten days, sir?'

'I am to make a presentation to the prime minister on the modern police force. I intend to use your department as an example.'

'It will not be possible to present the current case, sir.'

'Understood. Unofficially, off the record, I can.'

'We will do our best.'

'Budgetary cuts?' Larry asked after DCS Goddard had left.

'Rhetoric,' Isaac replied. 'I've known the man for many years. If we keep doing our job, he will make sure we are left alone.'

'Our jobs are secure?' Bridget asked.

'Totally. Larry, you'd better chase up on that grille.'

'Five minutes, and I'm out of the door.'

'If we don't meet again, 2 p.m. tomorrow afternoon at St Agnes.'

'We'll all be there,' Larry said. Bridget nodded her head.

***

The sign over the door said 'O'Reilly's Metal Fabricators', although thirty years previously it had said Dennison. Larry was not optimistic.

'No computers back then,' Sean O'Reilly, a big blustery man with a beer belly proudly extending at his front, said. He used braces to keep his trousers up, as his waist and a belt did not provide an adequate restraint against the laws of gravity.

'I appreciate it's a long shot, but I need to try,' Larry explained. He had shown his ID badge on arrival, been afforded a friendly welcome and a quick tour of the facilities.

'Not much has changed in thirty years, apart from the computers. The majority of the work is manual labour, and it's hard to find any of the younger generation interested now.'

'Is it just you?'

'I have one man, but he's part time now. A bit long in the tooth, he's pushing seventy, and he's not much use really.'

'Why keep him on?'

'He's been here forever, even before my time, and I need the help. Once I go, the place will close down.'

'Your offsider, would he be able to remember back to 1987?' Larry asked.

'He'll be here within the hour. You can ask him then.'

Larry took the opportunity to grab a coffee and a sandwich in a small café not far from O'Reilly's.

'Tom's in the office,' Sean O'Reilly told Larry, having found him in the café.

'How did you know I was here?'

'It's the only place nearby. I always come here for my lunch,' O'Reilly said. Larry had assumed that the man always indulged in a pub lunch, but chose not to comment.

The two men walked the short distance back to O'Reilly's premises.

'This is Tom Wellings,' O'Reilly said.

'Please to meet you, Detective Inspector.'

Larry observed a small, sprightly man who had stood up rapidly on his arrival. The face etched with lines showed a healthy tan, no doubt from years of standing outside in the yard where the metal was stored, or leaning over a fabrication with a welding torch in his hand.

'How long have you been here, Tom?'

'Ever since I left school. It must be fifty years at least.'

'Don't you ever feel like retiring?' Larry asked, making general conversation before asking the important questions.

'To do what? Go fishing, play golf?'

'I suppose so.'

'Not for me. I will keep working until they take me out of here in a wooden box. Anyway, Sean pays me enough to pay for my drinks.'

'You don't look like a drinker.'

'Drink me under the table, will our Tom,' Sean O'Reilly said.

'Tom, in 1987 a metal grille was installed at an address on Bellevue Street. Do you remember that job?'

'Business was booming back then. I would not be able to remember that far back, or at least, specific jobs.'

'Is there any way to jog your memory?'

'We used to store the job cards and the accounts up in the roof when they were no longer needed. Fire hazard, I suppose, if the truth is known. They may still be there.'

'Can we look?' Larry asked.

'I suppose so,' Sean O'Reilly said. 'I've not been up there, so it won't be too pleasant.'

'Let's look anyway.'

Tom led the way. At the top of the old building, there was a small door into a roof cavity. Sean O'Reilly fetched a hacksaw to remove the lock that was secured to the door.

'What a mess,' Larry said.

All that could be seen in the light of Larry's phone was a mass of papers. The smell was overpowering. All three men retreated for fresh air.

'Are you certain it is in there?' Larry asked Tom.

'Old man Dennison was a stickler for keeping paperwork. He thought it may be needed someday for another job.'

'Old man?' Larry asked.

'Back then I was only in my twenties. Bill Dennison was in his sixties. I suppose that makes me Old Man Wellings now.'

'You? Old? Never,' Sean O'Reilly said.

'I will need to get some people from Challis Street. Is that okay by you?'

'Sure,' O'Reilly said. 'You're welcome to whatever you can find.'

Larry phoned Gordon Windsor.

Early the next morning two juniors from Gordon Windsor's department arrived at Sean O'Reilly's premises. Larry pitied them the task ahead. He stayed with them until midday and then excused himself. He had a funeral to attend.

The two juniors by that time were cursing, but as Larry had observed, they were diligent in their approach. The paperwork they retrieved was being placed carefully in containers for transportation. It would take five to six hours to complete the retrieval. From there on, it would be a case of sifting through the papers looking for 1987 and Bellevue Street and number 54.

***

The church was only two streets from Wendy's house. She arrived dressed in black, her two sons on either side of her. Bridget walked behind them.

Isaac had arrived early, as had DCS Goddard. Both men wore black suits. Larry came a little later, as he had picked up his wife. She had met Wendy once, instantly liked her, and wanted to be present.

Mavis Richardson, who had come to know Wendy during her visits to her house, sat at the rear of the church on her own. Isaac thought it a decent gesture from a woman who was in mourning herself. Firstly, for Gertrude Richardson, then Montague Grenfell, and lastly, Ger O'Loughlin, her ex-husband. News of his death had been phoned through to Larry by his daughter earlier in the morning.

Everyone was in the church when the coffin arrived. The priest, an elderly, grey-haired man, conducted the service. He was a softly-spoken man, his voice ideal for the solemnity of the occasion, although Isaac thought that at any other time his monotone would put everyone to sleep. Both sons and Bridget rose from their seats to give a bible reading.

Isaac shed a tear, as did the other members of the department. Once the coffin had left with the immediate family following the hearse in their cars, the others filed out of the church.

Isaac noticed that Mavis Richardson had left promptly, her BMW moving down the road.

Wendy's house had not been suitable for the wake. A hall adjoining the church had been hired. Wendy returned from the burial later in the afternoon. Isaac gave her a hug and a kiss on the cheek, as did Larry's wife. Larry gave her a hug, as did DCS Goddard.

She thanked everyone, especially their DCS.

The wake was not a time for mourning, more a time for celebration for the life of Wendy's husband.

Both sons made brief speeches.

Isaac was asked to speak on behalf of the police department, as a special request from Wendy. He was used to public speaking, having been involved in enough press conferences in his time. He had even been on television, met the prime minister on a couple of occasions.

Isaac spoke about Wendy's husband, his achievements in life, his devoted wife, his two sons. He said that her husband had supported his wife, an invaluable member of the London Metropolitan Police. It was a nice touch to the day's proceedings. Wendy thanked him later.

Eventually, the wake concluded, and Isaac left. He had wanted to meet up with Katrina, but it was too late. He would see her the following day, murder enquiry permitting.

Chapter 23

The following morning, Larry visited the two juniors who were busy sifting through the papers in a room at the back of Challis Street Police Station. Their mood was not much better than the day before.

Larry brought two coffees from a local café, hopeful that it would lighten the mood. 'What have you found?' he asked.

'Apart from a total mess?' a young woman in her twenties said. Larry thought she looked too young to be a qualified crime scene investigator, or maybe he was starting to get old. He was in his early forties, and the junior police officers straight out of police college were looking young to him. He did not like the idea of getting old, which explained why he and his wife were into a vegan diet and macrobiotics and anti-oxidants.

He thought their interest in the subject may be helping, but he and his wife were still getting older. He wondered if Tom Wellings, the seventy-year-old employee of Sean O'Reilly, had the right idea.

Here was a man who had led a good life, stress-free, and still had the ability to down the pints of a night time. Nowadays, Larry started to feel woozy after two pints, but apparently Wellings was good for six, and the next day he would be at work early, none the worse for wear.

Larry picked up some old order books, browned and covered in dust, to see if he could help.

'We have a system here,' an obviously well-fed man in his thirties said. Larry had seen him at O'Reilly's, attempting to take control of the retrieval operation. The young lady assisting him had taken little notice of him, and she had been collecting from one side of the roof cavity, he from the other. To Larry, personality counted for a lot, the ability to get on with your fellow worker was vital. It was clear that the man with the expanding waistline, even though he was still young, had very little in the way of personality and little to recommend him.

'Rose, watch what you're doing,' Duncan said, a little too loudly for Larry.

'You mind your side of the room, I'll mind mine,' Rose said. It was clear she had the measure of her colleague.

'What have you found?' Larry asked for the second time. Both Duncan and Rose had stopped work for a few minutes. Duncan took the opportunity to pop outside for a cigarette.

'Don't worry about him,' Rose said to Larry when it was just the two of them in the room.

'Fancy himself, does he?'

'And any loose piece of skirt.'

'Has he hit on you?'

'He's tried. Not a chance.'

'Apart from your colleague, what have you found?'

'There is paperwork dating back to the sixties. It had basically just been thrown in there, collecting dust and spiders' webs, and God knows how many dust mites.'

'1987 is the year we are after,' Larry reminded her.

'Not so easy. We can only sift through in a logical manner. No point diving in here and there.'

'I suppose not,' Larry said. He was enjoying his conversation with the young lady.

'We need a couple of days. Some of the paperwork, especially the work orders, are in very poor condition, eaten through by dust mites, and the rats had made a home in there at some time in the past.'

'Fine. Let me know when you find anything of interest.'

Duncan returned, bringing the smell of stale cigarettes with him. 'That's better,' he said.

Larry left the pair of them to the task, glad to be out of the room with the stuffy old smell. He took a deep breath on exiting, taking in the fresh air. The weather was getting colder, and he knew that Wendy would soon be feeling the aches and pains in her body, the signs of increasingly debilitating arthritis.

She had taken a couple of days off after her husband's funeral, but he knew she would be back in the office the next day. Larry liked the woman a lot. Sure, she smoked terrible cigarettes, her diet was certainly not vegan or macrobiotic, but she was energetic and enthusiastic and determined. He had to admire that in a person.

He was still not sure about his relationship with his DCI. He knew that Isaac was competent and loyal to his staff, Wendy's elevation to sergeant testament to that fact. He also knew that Isaac was ambitious and determined to solve their current case as soon as possible.

***

Isaac was not in a good mood on Larry's arrival at the office. 'Mavis Richardson is dead,' he said.

'Suspicious?' Larry's reply.

'Gordon Windsor is on his way out to her house.'

'The woman was eighty-five.'

'You know what this means?' Isaac said. 'All those who could have killed Garry Solomon or knew the reason for his murder are now dead, every last one of them.'

Larry understood what his DCI was saying. Chasing Garry Solomon's murderer was of less interest than resolving who had pushed Montague Grenfell down the stairs outside his office, and if Mavis Richardson's death was suspicious, then somebody knew something about the past.

'It's all related to the death of Garry Solomon, I'm sure of it.' Isaac, like many an experienced police officer, especially in a murder investigation, had developed a sixth sense that defied logic. Larry knew he did not have it yet.

'Even Montague Grenfell's death is proving difficult,' Larry said.

'It shouldn't be,' Isaac replied. 'We know it was a man he scuffled with, the shoe size found at the top of the stairs proves that. And a woman would not have had the strength, or should I say, any of the women we know of in this case.'

'Anyone else out there that we don't know of, sir?'

'Call me Isaac. At least, when we're alone.'

'Thank you, sir, Isaac.' Larry was pleased that their relationship had developed enough to allow first names to be used.

'I still don't understand why Montague Grenfell was killed,' Isaac said. 'He was the one person who had full knowledge of the Grenfells' and Richardsons' finances and legal matters. Without him, who is going to take over? Is there anyone else capable?'

'You've always suspected that he knew more than he was telling,' Larry reminded Isaac.

'What do you mean?'

'All families have skeletons in the cupboard. Facts they would prefer not known.'

'And we can assume that the Richardsons and Grenfells had more than most.'

'And Montague Grenfell would have had the dirt on everyone, whether he chose to use it or not.'

'Don't you think we would have found out whether he had used it to his own advantage by now?' Isaac said.

'Why? Montague was careful to cover his tracks, keep all details to himself. Maybe the others didn't know they were being manipulated.'

'You believe that he could have been cheating the others, and they didn't know?'

'It's possible. What has Bridget's man come up with?'

'Nothing, other than Montague Grenfell was meticulous. He appears to have acted honourably at all times.'

'Sounds like a nomination for sainthood to me, Isaac,' Larry said. A sceptical man, he did not trust people with no vices, no apparent failings.

'You're right,' Isaac conceded. 'There has to be something about him.'

'Keith Dawson has been helping Bridget with Grenfell's records. We need him here.'

***

Gordon Windsor phoned Isaac. 'Heart attack. I will arrange for the pathologist to confirm, but she was old. I doubt if they will find anything suspicious.'

'Thanks. We are up against a brick wall with this case,' Isaac replied, venting his frustrations with the crime scene examiner.

'Everyone dying or dead?'

'That's about it.'

'Anyone still alive?'

'Only three now. Gertrude Richardson's grandson, the incumbent Lord Penrith and Garry Solomon's wife.'

'Must be one of them,' Windsor said.

'No motives, that's the problem.'

'I'm glad I'm only a crime scene examiner. I'll leave the detective work to you.' Gordon Windsor hung up and waited for an ambulance to remove the body. His team would go over the house in detail, although he was not expecting to find much.

Keith Dawson came into the office. Isaac had seen him around the office over the last few weeks. Apart from regular meetings and the daily pleasantries, they had not spoken much. Dawson, he knew by reputation and their limited communications, was a gruff man. He always wore a dark suit with a brightly coloured tie, out of sync with his less than bright manner.

'DCI, what can I do for you?' Dawson said, his body weight straining the frail chair he was sitting on.

'Montague Grenfell.'

'Excellent records.'

'No sign of fraud?'

'None that I could see. Mind you, I had been asked to check his records to see that they were in order. A man such as Grenfell could fudge the records with little trouble.'

'Is there any way to check?'

'It would help if I had something specific to go on. What are you looking for?'

Wendy came into the office with Bridget. It had only been a few days since the funeral.

'I couldn't stand it anymore,' Wendy said. 'Everyone phoning up or visiting every five minutes asking if I was fine.'

'Are you?' Isaac asked.

'As well as can be expected.'

'Ready for work?'

'Coming here is the best therapy. He is dead and buried. Moping around won't bring him back.'

Isaac was pleased to see her back in the office. Not only for her benefit, which was important to him, but there was work ahead. The case had been going on for too long, and DCS Goddard was starting to annoy him. And besides, Katrina Smith was spending time in London, and he wanted to see her more than he had.

They had managed to snatch a late-night meal together, and she had spent the previous night at his place. He liked her, maybe not as much as he had Jess O'Neill, but that relationship had been doomed due to his brief romantic encounter with Linda Harris. At least with Katrina Smith there were no incidents of misbehaviour that would damn the relationship before it had started.

Isaac still looked to settle down, find a steady woman, but each time there was something, either from the woman or from him. He knew he was a romantic looking for the ideal woman, the ideal starry night.

'You've still not said what I'm meant to be looking for,' Dawson said. Isaac's friendly banter with Wendy had not impressed him.

'*Get on with it,*' Dawson thought.

'Keith, we don't have a motive for the deaths of Garry Solomon and Montague Grenfell.'

'Do you expect me to find a motive for you?' Dawson said sneeringly.

Isaac chose to ignore the inferred criticism of his handling of the case. He knew other men within the police force, men who had been there for a long time, men who were covertly racist.

'Let's focus on Montague Grenfell,' Isaac said. 'Even if his death was unintentional, the evidence of a confrontation at his office is overwhelming.'

'So?' Dawson offered a one-word comment, as if he wanted to say 'get on with it and stop wasting my time'.

'The confrontation would indicate a recent conversation or a recent case. Now, as we know he only dealt with the Richardsons and the Grenfells, it is fair to assume it is related to them.'

'There are a lot of research notes. I haven't looked at them,' Dawson admitted.

'He told me that he spent his days in the office studying and reading. There may be something there,' Isaac said.

'I'm from Fraud.'

'So?' Isaac felt that it was his turn for a one-word comment.

'Looking at his notes is not in my area of expertise.'

'I don't understand.'

'I am an expert in legal and financial. Reading through the man's notes is not my area.'

'Do you have a problem?' Isaac looked Dawson straight in the eye. Keith Dawson, now the focus of attention, drew himself up, sucked in his stomach, although it still left his shirt hanging half out.

'I'm not the best person for the job,' he admitted.

'Bridget can work with you.'

'Okay. I can give you a day of my time. If we see anything, we'll let you know.'

'Wendy, what are your plans?' Isaac asked.

'Emma Hampshire is still around from when Garry Solomon died.'

'Fine. You concentrate on her,' Isaac said. 'Larry, we need to find who ordered the grille.'

'The record is probably there, but it's not a pleasant job sifting through thirty years' worth of papers.'

'When will we have an answer?'

'Today. I'll make myself a nuisance until they find it.'

Isaac wrapped up the meeting, giving them all a pep talk as to how this was a crucial day: a day when the pieces come together.

'How's Katrina Smith?' Wendy asked as she left the office.

'Promotion to sergeant can always be reversed,' Isaac replied with a smile.

Chapter 24

Malcolm Grenfell, the new lord, had brought up some friends from London, and they were partying around the clock. The cook who had been with the previous Lord Penrith for twenty-five years had left one day after Katrina Smith.

The young girl that Grenfell had in tow had been supplemented by another two, and according to the housekeeper, there was enough Viagra in the lord's bedroom to stock a pharmacy.

Isaac still had his reservations about the man. Of all the people in the case, he was the one with the most to gain. If Montague Grenfell had acceded to the title, he might have cut off the younger brother's allowance.

It was clear that Malcolm Grenfell was incapable of earning a salary. His forte appeared to be seducing susceptible young women, no doubt enamoured by his easy spending.

As Isaac sat back in his chair the phone rang. 'Lord Penrith,' the voice said.

The person he had been thinking about was talking to him. 'What can I do for you?'

'How long are you going to take with this bloody case?' His lordship was clearly as drunk as a lord.

'We are hoping to start arresting people in the next few days.' Isaac realised that it was not the truth, but he was looking for a reaction.

'Then bloody well hurry up.'

'Why is it so important?' He should have addressed Lord Penrith as 'My Lord', or 'Sir', but that would have been acknowledging that Malcolm Grenfell deserved respect, when he did not.

'I can't access Montague's bank accounts.'

'His death is regarded as suspicious.'

'The man had one leg. He was bound to fall down those stairs at any time.'

'Have you been to his office?'

'A few times.'

'When was the last time?'

'Two years ago, when he was not paying me regularly.'

'I was under the impression that he always paid on time.'

'Maybe he did, but not then.'

'Any reason?'

There was a pause at the other end of Isaac's phone.

'I upset Albert.'

'How?'

'I called him a miserable old man.'

'Why?'

'I was drunk. That was all.'

'If Montague had not died, you would not have become Lord Penrith.'

'Are you saying that I killed him?'

'It's a good enough motive. In fact, the only motive we have. No one else wanted him dead.'

'Montague had his secrets.'

'What do you mean?'

'I'll let you find out.' The phone line went dead. Isaac tried to ring back, but no answer.

***

Wendy, still not fully recovered from the emotions of the previous days, was glad to be back at work.

Emma Hampshire, as usual, was just about to go out when Wendy knocked on her door. Wendy was not sure if it was true or whether the woman always said it for effect. Regardless, the woman invited her in.

'I am sorry for your loss,' Emma Hampshire said. She was the same age as Wendy, but she had spent her life looking after herself: regular trips to the gym, no cigarettes, no excessive drinking.

'Thank you.'

'What can I do for you?'

'Malcolm Grenfell is now Lord Penrith.'

'Yes, I know.'

'Tell me about him,' Wendy said.

'I used to see him from time to time.'

'What was your opinion of him?'

'He was often drunk and rude.'

'Tell me about Garry?' Wendy asked.

'What's to tell? We've spoken about him before.'

'Garry was murdered for a reason, as was Montague.'

'Are you certain about Montague?' Emma Hampshire asked. She had settled back in her chair, resigned to the fact that she would have to go out later. And besides, Wendy Gladstone was good company, even if she was a policewoman.

'Mavis Richardson has died.'

'I know.'

'How?' Wendy asked.

'Malcolm Grenfell phoned me.'

'He has your number?'

'I'm in the phone book.'

'What did he say?'

'Just that Garry's aunt was dead.'

'Did you know her?'

'Not personally.'

'What else did Malcolm Grenfell say?'

'He was crude.'

'What did he say?'

'He assumed I would have screwed him for a title.'

'Your reply?'

'I was polite. I think he had a woman with him.'

'Was he serious in his offer?' Wendy asked. Everyone in the department assumed Malcolm Grenfell was only interested in women half his age.

'About screwing me or the title?'

'Either, I suppose.'
'He always tried it on when Bob wasn't looking.'
'Did you take him up on the offer?'
'No way. I was devoted to Bob, still am.'
'There are conflicting statements as to why you left Garry Solomon.'
'I realise that.'
'What is the truth?'
'It was a rough patch in our marriage. Garry's business was not going well, and he was becoming abusive.'
'How old were you?'
'I was about twenty-six, Garry was one year older.'
'And?'
'We were friendly with Malcolm Grenfell. They had been to the same school, although Malcolm was three years older.'
Wendy braced herself.
'Kevin was just three, and Garry was sleeping down at his business most nights of the week.'
'You were separated?'
'Not totally, but we were not as husband and wife.'
'Something is coming that is going to shock me, isn't it?' Wendy said.
'Malcolm came over to the house one night. He had a bottle of wine in his hand and two glasses.'
'And you let him in?'
'I wanted to say no for Garry and Kevin's sake, but I was young and lonely.'
'You slept with him?'
'The one time.'
'When he threw you out, was it because he had another woman?'
'Yes, but he treated Kevin and me well until the money ran out.'
'Have you slept with Malcolm Grenfell since?'
'No.'
'Did Bob Hampshire know?'

'No.'

'Garry?'

'I don't know. I never mentioned it, but Malcolm…'

'Indiscreet?'

'He can be after a few drinks.'

It was evident from Emma Hampshire's confession that there was another element in the death of Garry Solomon: the possibility of genuine love from Malcolm Grenfell for Emily Solomon, the possibility that Garry Solomon had found out and had been using it to his advantage.

There were still some missing elements, though. The affair between Malcolm Grenfell and Emily Solomon had occurred in or around 1977, although Garry Solomon had been alive for another ten years before his murder.

Emma Hampshire claimed to have not seen him after 1979 when he had been released from his first prison, and then it had only been a fleeting visit for him to see Kevin.

'So now we have a possible motive for Garry's death,' Wendy said. Emma Hampshire appeared to be relaxed in her chair, but Wendy could see her clutching the armrest.

'I only slept with him the once.'

'Jealousy is a strong enough reason to kill someone.'

'What jealousy? Garry was hardly a saint, and I never gave him reason to suspect me. He was a good man, always a little headstrong, given to criticising his family and the Grenfells.'

'Why the Grenfells?'

'He must have learnt some of the stories from his mother. How his grandfather was illegitimate, and the Richardsons had always been treated as the leper relations. He would surmise what his life would have been if his grandfather had not been illegitimate. If he had been born on the right side of the bed, as Malcolm.'

'Did he envy Malcolm?'

'Only the fact that he was legitimate.'

***

Larry had arrived at the room where Duncan and Rose were working. He brought them both a coffee from the café across the road. Gordon Windsor's juniors were in a more agreeable mood.

'Sorry about yesterday,' Duncan said. 'I was a bit on edge. It's a crap job, only fit for juniors.'

'Breeds character,' Larry humorously replied.

'I'll take your word for it.'

Larry noticed that the majority of the papers were stacked according to year and month. Rose had printed some labels from the printer and had stuck them to the table using tape.

'1987 is over in the far corner,' Rose said.

'You needn't have sorted the other years,' Larry said.

'What if you want another date?' Duncan said. Larry thought it was a fair comment. They had one date when the grille had been installed, but what about the bars on the inside of the windows in the house, and the person who had placed the order may have requested additional work.

It was clear that the firm back in the 80s had been exceptionally busy. There must have been over four hundred individual items: most were single sheets of paper, the rest were order books or job specifications. Larry regretted his enthusiasm. 'I'll leave it to you,' he said.

'It's a junior's job, is that it?' Rose said.

'I suppose so. I was a junior once. I know the pain you are going through. Phone me when you find something.'

'We'll send you a scanned copy,' Duncan said.

***

Isaac had spent the morning in the office dealing with paperwork. Bridget was too busy with Keith Dawson to help him out. Larry, after leaving Rose and Duncan, met Wendy for an early lunch.

'How are you?' he asked.

'That's all I've heard for the last week. Tell me about the case and where we stand,' Wendy said. She knew how she felt: she felt sad and sorry for her deceased husband. Apart from that, she was fine. Kind words and condolences did not help, solving a murder case did.

Wendy had just come from seeing Emma Hampshire. The woman's slender figure had caused some reflection on Wendy's part. She ordered a salad.

Larry, glad to be out of the home and away from the latest diet, fasting for two days a week, ordered steak and chips. He knew he would be in trouble when he got home, but for the moment he would be in heaven.

'Isaac is worried,' Larry said.

'Isaac!' Wendy exclaimed.

'Sorry, DCI.'

'That's fine. I've known him for a long time, but he will still be "sir" to me.'

'What did Emma Hampshire have to say?'

'Apart from the fact that she had an affair, or at least a one-night stand, with Malcolm Grenfell when she was married to Garry Solomon, not much.'

'Have you told DCI Cook yet?'

'Not yet. How important do you think it is?' Wendy asked.

'What do you think? Apparently, Grenfell is keen on her, but she does not reciprocate apart from sleeping with him the one time.'

'It's a motive for Garry Solomon's murder.'

Wendy phoned Isaac, or to her, DCI Cook.

Isaac's reaction was understandable. Another vital piece of information had been uncovered. Not only were the Richardson sisters screwing Montague Grenfell on a regular basis, and Albert on two known occasions, it now appeared that their behaviour had moved to the next generation, in that Gertrude Richardson's daughter-in-law had slept with a Grenfell.

Isaac wondered what sort of morality these people adhered to.

'Remember George Sullivan,' Isaac said. 'He's the one person we've not contacted yet.'

'Do you think he's important, sir?' Wendy asked.

'Maybe, maybe not, but who knows? Emma Hampshire wasn't until she gave you that little nugget.'

'I'll look for him, sir. Leave it to me,' Wendy said, her stomach rumbling. She regretted her poor choice in nourishment. *Fit for rabbits*, she thought. She called over the waitress. 'Give me what my colleague just ordered,' she said. As far as she was concerned, she would rather be overweight and happy than skinny and miserable.

As Wendy dealt with the rumbling in her stomach, Larry continued their conversation. 'George Sullivan? Any ideas?' he asked.

Wendy answered between mouthfuls of food. She was gasping for a cigarette, but that would have to wait until they were outside, and outside was cold and becoming colder due to an Artic wind from the north.

'I've not a clue,' Wendy said. 'The man must be in his eighties by now, and it's a common name.'

Chapter 25

Meanwhile, unbeknownst to them, Emma Hampshire was on the phone. 'I told Sergeant Wendy Gladstone.'

'What the hell did you do that for?'

'It would have come out one day.'

'Why? We were always discreet.'

'Someone may have seen us.'

'It's been thirty years. No one's alive now.'

'That may be true, Malcolm, but I'm tired of living with a lie.'

'You never told Bob, but you end up telling a policewoman. Do you realise where that places me?'

'No. Where does it place you?'

'Right at the top of DCI Isaac Cook's list of murder suspects.'

'And me.'

'Why?'

'If you killed Garry because of me, I may be seen as an accomplice.'

Lord Penrith realised that Emma Hampshire was talking nonsense. They had been lovers in the past, not now. Sure, he had been flirtatious on occasions since when Bob Hampshire had been looking the other way, but it had never been more than an amorous fondle from him, an indignant rebuff from her.

'I never killed him. How many times have I told you? Do you think I waited nearly ten years after our affair to kill him? I would have rid myself of him back in 1976, not waited until 1987.'

Emma Hampshire hung up, unsure whether she had been right in confronting a man who had meant something to her once. She knew him as unpredictable, his actions uncertain, and his morality of little consequence if it came between him and the life he wanted. She realised that Malcolm Grenfell and Emma Hampshire had a lot in common. He had offered her the title of Lady Penrith, half-joking, half-drunk. She had spent too much time on her own since Bob Hampshire's death, too much time pining, too much time waiting for a man to occupy her bed.

Malcolm Grenfell was a lecher, a rogue, a man who partied and whored, but she could control him. A lord needs respectability, she would give it to him.

***

Larry Hill was in the office at Challis Street when Rose phoned from the crime scene examiner's office. 'Detective Inspector, we found something.'

Larry inexplicably found himself excited at the prospect of meeting up with the woman again. 'Twenty minutes,' he replied.

'I'll supply the coffee this time,' Rose said.

'We found this,' she said later as they sat in the café.

'It's what we've been looking for.'

'There's a contact phone number.'

The photocopy that Larry had in his hand was not clear. Age and the rain seeping through the roof where it had been stored had yellowed it badly.

'We've put the original into an evidence bag and labelled it,' Rose said.

'Send it to Forensics and ask if they can pick up the details. In the meantime, can you send me a scanned copy.'

'Once I'm back in the office.'

'Thanks. We have a lady in the office who is great with computers. She may be quicker than Forensics.'

Larry realised on leaving that they had spent forty minutes chatting. It was not as if he was interested in pursuing a relationship with Rose. He was happily married and intended to stay that way. It was just that it was flattering, good for his ego, to have the company of an attractive woman for a short period.

***

'Mavis Richardson died of natural causes,' Gordon Windsor said. Isaac Cook had phoned the senior crime scene examiner for an update.

One less murder to deal with, Isaac thought.

The need to wrap up the case was long past. He had discounted the possibility of a conviction for Garry Solomon's murder. All the people who knew him had since died, except for Malcolm Grenfell and Emma Hampshire. The revelation of their affair had come as a shock.

The reason for Garry Solomon's unwillingness to contact his mother continued to baffle Isaac.

The mother had been at the party that night he had come home unexpectedly and found his aunt on top of his father. He must have known or assumed that his mother was with another man, but that should have evoked anger and hurt, hopefully followed by forgiveness.

There had been several years between that night and when he had left the house at the age of nineteen. Isaac wondered what his relationship had been with his mother in those years. Was it distant, loving, or ambivalent? The only person who may have an inkling was Malcolm Grenfell, as all the others who may have known were dead.

Isaac did not relish the trip up to Leicestershire again as the sight of the ageing Lothario cavorting with young women did not excite him. Before he met Katrina Smith, he would have been curious, as his love life had taken a definite turn from good with Jess to lukewarm, and on to non-existent.

Isaac phoned Lord Penrith, not expecting more than a few moments of his time. If the man was reluctant to speak, he would set up an interview at a police station, bring the man in, formally caution him, and then put him on the spot.

'Lord Penrith, DCI Isaac Cook.'

'Yes, DCI. What can I do for you?' Malcolm Grenfell said. Isaac noticed the man spoke with respect, and he sounded sober. *A good start*, Isaac thought.

'Answers to questions,' Isaac said.

'Let me have your questions.'

'You knew Garry Solomon when he was young.'

'I've already told you this. We were at the same school, although he was three years younger than me.'

'Did you acknowledge each other. Look out for the other?'

'Hell, no. We used to treat his year like shit.'

'What do you mean?'

'You've not been to boarding school?'

'No such luck,' Isaac replied. He had been to the local comprehensive from the age of eleven, and whereas it had served him fine, it had not had a great record of academic achievement.

'Luck! No luck if they send you to the school we went to.'

'What do you mean?' Isaac asked.

'Boarding schools for the offspring of the rich and the influential are only there to satisfy the egos of the parents, and as a dumping ground for their children.'

'Bad?'

'Sadistic teachers. They ruled with an iron rod as well as a wooden cane, split at the end to increase the pain for the unfortunate student who received ten of the best across his arse.'

'I thought that wasn't allowed.'

'Corporal punishment, the last vestige of privilege for exclusive boarding schools.'

'It sounds sadistic.'

'It was, but any student dumped there was invariably angry with their parents.'

'Did you receive any discipline?'

'More than most.'

'And Garry?'

'After he seduced the headmaster's daughter?'

'Yes.'

'They beat the shit out of him. I had left by then, but I heard about it soon after.'

'What did you think?'

'He went up in my estimation.'

'It didn't stop you sleeping with his wife.'

'Garry changed. He was treating her badly.'

'Were the two of you serious?'

'I suppose we were. She was, still is, a good-looking woman, and back then, the idea of marriage appealed.'

'And now?'

'Marriage? I don't think so. I'm still young enough, and you know what the title gets me?'

'A better class of woman.' Isaac pre-empted Malcolm Grenfell's expected crass reply.

'That's right. Is that what you phoned me for?'

'Garry Solomon never contacted his mother after the age of nineteen.'

'That's probably correct.'

'Do you know the reason why?'

'He never spoke about it. I know about the party.'

'Which party?'

'Where his aunt was screwing his father.'

'That was seven years before he walked out on his mother. And then he sends her a postcard from India two years later.'

'Montague would have known.'

Every time the answer is Montague, and he is not available, Isaac thought. Montague Grenfell's burial, after the body had been released, was due to be conducted in three days' time. Isaac planned to attend the service, the body then to be interred in the family plot in the churchyard adjoining Penrith House.

'Anyone else?'

'Emma, maybe, but no one else. It's a long time ago.'

'You mentioned that Montague had secrets. Can you elaborate?'

'Nothing concrete, but he had too many fingers in too many pies. Impossible to resist fudging the numbers.'

'Would you?'

'If I had his acumen, probably.'

Isaac terminated the phone call. In three days' time, he would be in Leicestershire. It would be a good time to conduct a formal interview. While Malcolm Grenfell had been polite on the phone, Isaac had little time for the man who, without the benefit of money and now a title, would have been out on the street scrounging for food and money.

***

Wendy was on the phone in the office following up on all the George Sullivans that Bridget had managed to identify. Bridget had used a set of criteria to narrow the field: age, wealth, reference in *Burke's Peerage*, school attended.

She had looked for a correlation between Albert Grenfell, who was known to be a snob, and George Sullivan, the criteria reflecting the fact that Albert was hardly likely to be friendly with someone who was not of an equal social standing.

Regardless, George Sullivan was a common name, and *Burke's Peerage* had not helped, as the only George Sullivan had gone to school in Scotland, whereas Albert had gone to Eton.

Wendy, as usual, was diligent in her pursuit of Sullivan. Her mood had improved after the funeral, and one night of the week she would stay with Bridget, and another night Bridget would stay with her. Bridget, she had found out, was allergic to cats, and had come up in a rash on her arms.

Larry had the paperwork with Bridget and Forensics. The phone number on the work order was indecipherable. He could see a four and an eight and a couple of other numbers, but there should be more. As for the name alongside the phone number, the rats had eaten that many years previously.

DCS Goddard was keeping his distance and had not been in the murder room for seven days. Isaac expected to hear from him at any time.

Keith Dawson continued to wade through Montague Grenfell's papers. He said little, only grumbled occasionally. Bridget ignored his protestations. He had even complained to his boss, who had complained to Isaac, who told him that there were two murders, maybe more, and if DCS Goddard needed to ensure Dawson stayed in the office with them, he would call him up.

The last comment from Dawson's boss. 'He's a miserable sod. Keep him for as long as you want.'

Isaac had met up with Katrina Smith on a couple of occasions, although not as many as he would have liked. She had found herself a job in London and was already working long hours.

She had spent a few nights at his flat, but it was early days for both of them, and no decision had been made for her to move in on a more permanent basis. Besides, her mother was prudish, and Katrina would not want to upset her without giving her fair warning.

As Albert's and his brother Montague's bodies had been released at the same time, there was to be a joint funeral. Katrina would travel up with Isaac for the funeral. They planned to spend the night in a hotel.

Wendy was going as well, mainly to take note of who attended and whether there were some unknown faces, maybe the elusive George Sullivan or maybe someone they had not taken into account.

Wendy and funerals were happening too often for her liking. There had been Gertrude Richardson's, and then her husband's. Now she had Albert and Montague Grenfell's to attend, and then two days after, Mavis Richardson. Both Larry and Wendy planned to attend her funeral, as both had come to know her well. Her death and their attendance at her funeral did not excuse her from any crime that may have been committed, but she was dead. Her guilt or otherwise would be decided at a later date.

Larry thought they were drawing blanks and there would never be a resolution for a thirty-year-old murder. Isaac, more optimistic, refused to accept his view.

Bridget's attempts to clean up the scanned copy of the work order to read the phone number for Bellevue Street had not worked. She had tried Photoshop: reduce the hue, increase the saturation, lighten, darken.

The most she had ascertained was that the number was probably in London and that it began with a five and ended with an eight. She had made a guess of what the missing numbers may have been, made a few phone calls, but only received the sound of a disconnected line.

'Phone numbers have changed since then,' Bridget had said. Regardless, she knew that a full phone number, no matter how old, could be traced, and an address and a name attached to it.

Isaac moved over to the white board in the corner. On it was listed the victims, their relationship to the suspects, possible motives, current addresses, their backgrounds and histories. He was certain that somewhere on that jumbled board was the solution to both of the murders. Instinct told him that Garry Solomon's and Montague Grenfell's murders were related; although it may not be the same murderer, the same basic motivator remained, but what?

Montague Grenfell had been pushed down a flight of stairs. Even if a culprit was found, they could easily claim self-defence, an argument, an unfortunate accident. A murder conviction seemed unlikely, more likely manslaughter unless a full confession was received. Garry Solomon was murder, no one would dispute that, but why hide his body in that fireplace? Isaac had had restless nights thinking over that.

To put the man's body in a house owned by his mother and his sister seemed callous. The condition of the body had made it impossible to ascertain whether he had been murdered in the house or elsewhere.

Michael Solomon had been friendly with his son on a casual basis but hadn't told the boy's mother, and had not attempted to look for him after his disappearance.

Isaac knew that somebody knew something, but who and what.

'Larry, let's go and see Michael Solomon's widow,' Isaac said. It was more an act of frustration on his part than a reasoned action.

'What are you thinking, Isaac?' Larry asked.

'Too many unknowns. Michael Solomon may have said something to his second wife.'

'He only had the one wife,' Wendy said.

'As you say,' Isaac acknowledged.

Chapter 26

Larry and Isaac could hear the sound of babies crying when they arrived at the house. Larry knocked on the door. A woman came to the door, her hair not brushed, her face showing anger. 'What do you want?'

'DI Larry Hill. This is Detective Chief Inspector Cook.' Both men showed their ID badges.

'Come in. Find a seat if you can.'

In the hallway of the house was a pushchair which they had to push to one side to get through. Once past, there were the remains of a child's dinner. They stepped over it and went into the only room that appeared to show any semblance of homeliness.

Five minutes later the woman came in. Isaac noticed that she had changed her dress and brushed her hair.

'Mrs Solomon,' Isaac said. 'Sorry to arrive unannounced.'

'Call me Mary.'

'Mary, you met his son.'

'Solly?'

'We refer to him as Garry Solomon.'

'Still the same man.' The voice of a crying baby echoed through the walls. Isaac found the noise irritating; Larry appeared ambivalent.

'When was the last time you saw him?'

'How would I know?' Mary said. 'Sometime in the eighties. I only knew him as my husband's friend.'

The cry of another child and Mary Solomon rushed out of the door. The sound of a smack, more crying, and Mary's harsh voice: 'Shut up, shut up. You'll be the death of me.'

Isaac could see the need for a visit from Child Welfare.

'Her children have dumped their offspring on her,' Larry said.

'No right to hit children, is it?'

'No. She needs assistance, not our criticism.'

Mary Solomon returned. 'Sorry about that. DI Hill knows the situation. If the house were not in my name, I would walk out and leave my son and daughter to it. As it is, I've taken a court order against my daughter for maintenance.'

'You don't see her?' Larry asked.

'Not often, but I'm not surprised,' the woman said. More crying from the other room. She continued speaking, determined to ignore it. 'DCI Cook, my daughter is a whore, selling herself up in the city. She is either flat on her back with her legs open, or in a ditch drugged out of her mind. My apologies for talking about my daughter like that, but that's the reality.'

'You need help,' Isaac said.

'If someone wants to help, they can take the children. My daughter's are mongrels anyway.'

Isaac could see the frustration in the woman. He could even sympathise, but a child was a child, even if it had no redeeming features and bad blood, the result of a prostitute and her client. He wanted to dislike the woman but found he could not.

'We know that Garry Solomon, Solly, disappeared in 1987. Did your husband ever mention him after that?'

'Not that I remember. Mind you, he was only my husband's friend to me, and not a good friend at that. Does it matter?'

'Probably not, but we are still not sure what happened the night Garry Solomon died.'

'Long time ago. Most are dead, I suppose.'

'Would your daughter know?'

'Unlikely. She was only nine years old back in 1987. A pretty little thing then, not the tattooed tart she is now.'

Mary Solomon rushed off back to the other room at the sound of breaking plates. Larry and Isaac excused themselves and left.

'Wasted trip, Isaac,' Larry said.

'I suppose so.'

'Must be tough when your children turn out bad.'

'Yes,' Isaac said, his mind distracted as he considered the case. 'What I don't get is why no one missed Garry Solomon. He was visible, and then he disappears.'

'And his mother Gertrude never went looking for him.'

'Precisely,' Isaac said. 'He was never more than ten to fifteen miles from her, apart from his time in India. What are the chances of not inadvertently bumping into each other?'

'It's always possible.'

'Garry Solomon was killed for a reason, yet there is no reason. His mother never finds him, and he never contacts her, apart from a postcard from India.'

'Something happened on his return to sever the relationship, and it was not when he was nineteen.'

'It's possible.'

'Who do we ask?'

'Emma Hampshire and Barbara Bishop.'

Isaac and Larry took the opportunity of an early lunch. Larry, feeling guilty and remembering the ear-bashing he had received after eating a steak on a previous occasion, kept to an orange juice and a Greek Salad. He eyed Isaac's plate, wished he had ordered pasta as well.

***

Wendy, drawing blanks on finding George Sullivan and aware of Isaac's wish to visit Emma Hampshire, suggested that she go with him instead of Larry. Isaac agreed with her recommendation.

Larry returned to the office. Wendy joined Isaac outside Emma Hampshire's house. She was pleased to see Kevin Solomon's car parked across the road.

'Emma, this is DCI Cook,' Wendy said. She had phoned ahead to tell Emma Hampshire that they were coming.

'Pleased to meet you,' Isaac said. Wendy noticed that Emma Hampshire, although thirty years older than her boss, visibly blushed as he took her hand firmly and shook it.

The Isaac Cook charm, how can any woman resist it? Wendy thought.

Kevin Solomon came to the door and introduced himself. Wendy could see that mother and son were getting along fine.

'Come in please,' Emma Hampshire said.

Wendy knew that she would have to make a point of forewarning the woman if they visited again. On the table in the dining room there were sandwiches, some cakes, and a pot of freshly-brewed coffee.

'Coffee, DCI?' Emma Hampshire asked.

'Thank you.'

It was clear that Kevin Solomon was moving back in with his mother; the suitcases in the hallway testament to the fact.

According to Keith Dawson, Emma Hampshire and her son would be well provided for once Gertrude Richardson's assets had been dealt with.

Kevin, as the only legitimate descendant of Gertrude, was to be given the responsibility of handling probate, but as he was not a qualified lawyer, he intended to re-engage with his studies.

A fellow student when he had been studying, now qualified, would deal with Gertrude. Mavis presented another problem. She had no descendants, and Kevin's father had not been on good terms with her. Kevin believed that her wealth should go to his mother as well, but Mavis's will had been ambiguous. She had placed sole responsibility in the case of her death with Montague Grenfell, and he was dead. Failing that, she had named her sister, although her sister may not have known, and she was dead too.

According to Kevin's understanding, a decision about her assets would require legal advice.

The death of Montague Grenfell was apparently causing other difficulties. The incumbent Lord Penrith may have had access to the stately home, and sufficient funds to maintain his singularly self-indulgent lifestyle, but the bulk of the wealth remained out of reach.

'What can I help you with?' Emma Hampshire asked, directing her gaze at Isaac.

'We have not been able to find out the reason for the animosity of your first husband towards his mother,' Isaac said.

'I never knew.'

'We are aware of an incident when he was twelve, although he remained in the family home until he was nineteen, barring time at boarding school, so we do not believe that the incident was the catalyst.'

'I believe it was.'

'Did he tell you the details?'

'Yes.'

'When?'

'When we were in India.'

'And then there is the postcard he sent when he was there,' Isaac said.

'We were at a retreat in the hills, puffing hash, attempting to come closer to nirvana.'

'And?'

'Have you tried it?'

'No,' Isaac replied. There had been some uppers and downers sold around the schoolyard when he was in his teens. He had tried one once, made him sick and sad. He never tried them again. Even the drunken nights with his mates, he had largely avoided; the alcohol put him to sleep and affected his ability to chat up the young women.

'Garry was melancholy, at peace with the world. He wrote the postcard, put a stamp on it, and put it in the mail. The next day he tried to get the postcard back. Even offered a bribe, but it was too late. The postcard was on its way, and there was nothing he could do about it.'

'His mother treasured it. Did you contact her?' Isaac asked.

'I phoned her once after Garry had left me.'

'Why?' Wendy asked.

'Curious, I suppose. If Garry could treat me the way he did, and he hated his mother so much, then what was she like?'

'And what was she like?'

'She knew who I was. Accused me of turning her son against her. It was not a pleasant conversation. In the end, I slammed the phone down.'

'Did Gertrude Richardson ever mention this to you?' Isaac asked Wendy.

'Never, but my time with her was limited. She was friendly that last night when she had seen Garry, but she died soon after.'

'She saw him after thirty years!' Emma Hampshire looked astonished.

'Yes,' Wendy replied.

'What did he look like?'

'Do you really want to know?'

'I suppose not.'

'Mrs Hampshire,' Isaac said.

'Please call me Emma.'

'At any time did you have reason to believe that someone would want your husband dead?'

'After he left me, he fell in with a bad crowd. They may have.'

'He was found in a house belonging to Gertrude and Mavis Richardson. Did you ever visit that house?'

'Bellevue Street? I never visited, although I knew about the mansion.'

'How?'

'Garry pointed it out once.'

'He never thought to go in?'

'He said he used to visit there as a child, nothing more.'

Isaac turned his focus to Kevin, the son. 'What do you know about your family history?'

'Mum's told me about Malcolm Grenfell. Is that what you are asking?'

'Yes.'

'People make mistakes, and I can believe what she tells me about my dad. I can remember him vaguely, but I never saw any presents or Christmas cards from him after he left. As if he didn't care.'

'Bob Hampshire did,' Isaac said.

'He was a good man.'

'Why the drugs?'

'Susceptible to them. My father's generation became alcoholic, my generation took drugs.'

Isaac felt that the interview was going nowhere. If Emma Hampshire knew anything, she was keeping it close to her chest. As for Kevin, he may have been too young.

Wendy thought that Emma Hampshire and her son were good people. Isaac tended to agree, but experience had taught him that the most unlikely people were often closer to the action than appeared at first glance. He was not ready to discount either of them yet.

***

Isaac and Wendy drove over to Barbara Bishop's house in Knightsbridge. There appeared to be no one at home on their arrival. Wendy phoned the woman's mobile. Barbara Bishop appeared five minutes later.

'Yoga class,' she said.

'This is Detective Chief Inspector Cook,' Wendy said.

The woman, wearing yoga pants and a tee shirt, looked up at Isaac. 'I need a shower. Give me five minutes. Help yourself to coffee, the cups are in the cupboard to the right of the sink,' she said.

Wendy took up the offer, found some biscuits as well. Ten minutes later the woman returned, dressed in a white blouse and a short skirt.

'Mrs Bishop, by your own admission you were the last person to see Garry Solomon alive.'

'I told Constable Gladstone this last time.'

'I am aware that you spoke to Sergeant Gladstone, and that you were very cooperative. Sometimes it pays for a different police officer to ask the same questions. Garry Solomon's death is highly suspicious, but we have no reason for it.'

'He was a good man with me,' Barbara Bishop said. 'I would have married him if he had been available.'

'What did he feel about you?' Isaac asked.

'He loved me. I'm certain of that.'

'Did he say so?'

'A woman knows, it doesn't need words.'

'What mood was he in when he left that day?'

'Cheerful.'

'And where was he heading?'

'I don't know.'

'You asked him?'

'He said he would be only forty minutes and then he was going to take me out to the movies.'

'Did you see anyone suspiciously loitering in the street?'

'No.'

Chapter 27

Forensics had come back. 'We managed to get you the phone number off the work order you sent us,' a deep woman's voice said. Larry recognised the tell-tale sign of a heavy smoker.

'Can you email it to me?' Larry asked.

'It will be in your inbox within ten seconds,' the woman replied, a rasping cough interrupting her speech.

Larry had been back in the office when the woman had phoned. He had not had much to do that morning other than to tidy his desk, always a bit of a mess due to his habit of not tidying the night before. He could not understand how Isaac managed to keep his so tidy, and then there was DCS Goddard. Their DCS's penchant for a clean desk was legendary. 'Clean desk, clean mind,' he would say if pressed.

Larry sipped his coffee, pressed the key repeatedly to refresh the inbox on his laptop. Bridget had said that it was not necessary, but he was impatient. In forty seconds, not the ten promised, he saw that he had received a new email. It was what he wanted. Bridget was working hard in her corner of the office. Larry had mentioned before to Isaac that she needed help, but Bridget, when asked, had resisted any assistance. 'It's the way I work best. If I am not under pressure, I lose focus,' she had said.

Isaac had not pursued the matter any further, and besides, he had not had a lot of time. If he was not in the office, he was worrying about the case. If he was not worrying, he was with Katrina Smith.

Once in the office, fully involved in the deliberating, the discussing, the attempts to find a solution, the time would pass unnoticed. Almost as if the hands of the clock on the wall had stopped rotating.

He knew that was why Jess O'Neill had moved out, and probably why Katrina Smith would not be in his life for too long.

He sometimes wondered, not often, as he had little time for daydreaming and idle speculation, if it would be different with Katrina, although he assumed it probably wouldn't be.

He was a man who looked for a long-term companion, the patter of little feet rushing to him when he walked in the door at night after a hard day's work, the embrace of a loving woman, but he could see himself as a life-long bachelor whose life was interspersed with a succession of women. He had seen Malcolm Grenfell in his sixties playing around with women young enough to be his daughter. Isaac did not want that for himself. He resolved to find someone to share his life with, but would it be Jess O'Neill or Katrina Smith, maybe even Linda Harris, although he did not know where she was.

'Isaac, Isaac.'

'Sorry, deep in thought,' Isaac replied, rubbing his eyes, pretending to put pen to paper.

'Fast asleep more likely,' Larry said. 'Don't worry. We're all feeling that way.' He had news, vital news, for his DCI.

'Too many hours here,' Isaac replied.

'We have a phone number for the grille.'

'And?'

'It's an old number. I tried dialling, but it came up blank. Just a hollow ring on the other end.'

'But traceable?'

'Bridget is working on it.'

'Great. Keep me posted.'

Wendy came into Isaac's office. 'Sir, I'm drawing a blank on George Sullivan.'

'How many likely candidates?'

'In Berkshire and surrounding counties, over thirty.'

'Have you contacted them all?'

'We've tried to be selective. No point phoning a George Sullivan unless he's in his late seventies to eighties, is there?'

Isaac leant back in his chair. Wendy was looking for a measured response when he could not think of one. She was the best there was at finding people, whether they wanted to be found or not. Isaac knew that she would find George Sullivan, even if he was buried in a churchyard somewhere or his remains were ash.

'You're right.' The only useful comment that Isaac could offer.

'He could have moved around the country, but collating that amount of information will take some time,' Wendy said.

'Bridget is weighed down,' Isaac replied. 'And now she is working on the phone number that Larry has found. What will this number tell us, Larry?' Isaac asked.

'Who ordered the grille to be installed.'

'So, someone gave them the key to enter the house, but not to enter the room. On the one hand, someone is trying to conceal a body, and on the other, they give a third party access to the murder scene. It all sounds bizarre to me,'

'What do you mean, sir?' Larry asked. Wendy was in the room, so the familiarity of addressing his boss by his first name was not appropriate.

'Did they install the bars on the windows.'

'It appears that way, sir.'

'If they entered the room, were they alone?'

'After thirty years? Who would know?'

'What about the old man that is still working there?'

'It's a thought. I could take him to the house. It may jog his memory.'

'You'd better do it today,' Isaac said. Larry cursed under his breath. He was an experienced police officer, and he had not thought of it. He had been slowly gaining the confidence of his DCI, and here he was, making the most basic of errors. Thirty years was a long time, but Tom Wellings came from an age before computers and smart phones.

Larry remembered that his father in his seventies could remember phone numbers and car registrations from his youth, but had no idea as to his own phone number. If anyone asked, he would open his wallet and take out a piece of paper with it typed on.

***

Bridget hurried into the office. Usually she shuffled along maintaining a predictable pace. Encountering her in the corridor was always a chore. Isaac moved fast, as did Larry, but with Bridget, it was the same lumbering forward momentum, and it was impossible to get by. But this time, she was moving fast, even knocking off some papers precariously perched on the top of Larry's filing cabinet.

'I've found an address,' she said.

'George Sullivan?' Isaac asked.

'It looks possible.'

'Wendy, fancy a trip to the country,' Isaac asked.

'Ready and willing.'

'Go easy on expenses,' Larry reminded her. He knew she would still have a slap-up meal in a quality restaurant. 'Necessary to maintain cover,' she would say afterwards.

Besides, if she came back with a result, he would sign the expense form.

Wendy took the printout from Bridget and left the office. Five minutes later, just long enough for her to collect her handbag with the police issue credit card, grab the keys to the police car, and she was gone. She always carried a small bag with her in case there was an overnight stay involved. Berkshire was not far, only thirty-five miles down the M4, no more than an hour, sometimes less if the traffic was flowing, although it could take longer at peak times. It was eleven in the morning before she turned the key in her car. She turned left as she exited the Challis Street car park. The traffic was relatively light for the time of day, apart from a truck blocking the road two miles away. She knew the area well, and she diverted down a few side streets. Soon she was heading through Chiswick and onto the M4.

The address was 81 Charter Street, Reading. Wendy found it with little difficulty. It was an attractive house, indicative of the area. A neat garden out the front, some flowers; the season was unfavourable for them to bloom, although they looked ready to once the coldness in the air had been replaced with the rays of the sun. A small dog yapped inside the house as Wendy pushed open the gate at the front. The yapping was quickly accompanied by a woman's shrill voice. 'Stop the barking, or I'll have the neighbours complaining,' it said.

Wendy noticed that the dog took no notice. She had had a dog when she first married. A spritely Yorkshire terrier who would jump up when she came in, but not for her husband, who was more disciplined with the animal. Still, her husband had shed more tears than her when it had died at the age of thirteen.

After that, both of them vowed no more dogs, although their two sons had had a collection of rabbits, guinea pigs, even salamanders, but none ever lived for long, and no one ever formed an emotional attachment. Wendy could not say that about the two cats she now owned. She realised that she had become fond of them, and she would be sad when they departed.

After two attempts at ringing the bell on the house, a two-storey terrace built in the 1950s, the door opened.

'Sergeant Wendy Gladstone, Challis Street Police Station. I'm with Homicide,' Wendy said.

'No bodies here,' the woman replied. She was attempting to hold back the dog which wanted to surge forward and welcome the visitor.

Wendy could see that making friends with the dog would gain the confidence of the woman. She bent down and patted it, even though it was old and scruffy, a mongrel of indeterminate parentage.

'He doesn't take to strangers,' the woman said.

The dog barked at Wendy's touch but stopped soon after. It was clear that the dog did not go out often, and it was in need of a good bath.

'You'd better come in. No point standing out there in the cold. Cup of tea?'

'Yes, please.'

Wendy noted that the house had seen better years; the wallpaper was fading, and the carpet was threadbare in certain areas. It was a good house in a good street, but the inside showed neglect, whereas the gardens, front and rear, showed love and affection. It seemed incongruous, but probably not related to Wendy's current line of enquiry.

The woman came back with two mugs of tea. 'Sorry, there's no sugar, although I have sweetener if you prefer.'

'Sweetener is fine,' Wendy answered. The dog had taken his place next to her. The smell of it was distracting.

'May I ask your name?'

'Victoria Sullivan.'

'And your husband is George?'

'Yes.'

'May I ask where he is?'

'He will be back soon,' the woman replied. 'Why are you interested in George?'

'You are aware of a body that was found in a fireplace?'

'It was on the news.'

'We believe that your husband visited that house at some time.'

'You don't believe he killed the man?' The woman looked alarmed at the prospect, not sure what to say, other than the inevitable defence of her husband.

'Not at all,' Wendy replied, although George Sullivan could have been as guilty as any of the others.

'Does the name Solomon mean anything to you?'

'Other than it was the name of the body.'

'And Grenfell?'

'My maiden name.' Wendy sat up, disturbing the dog, at Victoria Sullivan's reply.

'Lord Penrith?'

'He was my second cousin. We shared the same grandfather, that's all.'

As the old woman hobbled over to make them another cup, Wendy took the opportunity to SMS Isaac. 'Found him.'

Isaac's reply. 'Good.'

'What was your relationship with Albert Grenfell?'

'We exchanged Christmas cards, attended weddings, but apart from that, not a lot.'

228

'Any reason?'

'The title and the wealth followed Albert's line of the family. I'm from the poor side.'

'But you kept in touch.'

'Yes. He was a good man.'

The dog jumped up and ran to the front door. Its tail was wagging, but it was not yapping. 'My husband's home,' Victoria Sullivan said. A key in the lock and the door swung open.

'Down, boy, down,' the man said.

Even though he was in his eighties, George Sullivan looked to be a fit person. Wendy noticed that he stood firm, although he carried a wooden cane in one hand. He took off his coat and came into the room.

'We have a guest,' his wife said.

Wendy stood and introduced herself.

'Not often we have a visitor from the police.'

George Sullivan beckoned Wendy to sit down again. He walked over to the electric fire, the fake flames trying to create the look of a real fire but missing the effect entirely. He stood with his back to it, enjoying the heat.

'What can I do for you? I see that Victoria's provided you with a cup of tea.' He looked over at his wife. 'Any chance of one for me, love?'

Once his wife had left the room, George Sullivan whispered, 'Is this about Garry Solomon?'

'Yes.'

'I never met him, but I knew the name.'

'You're a material witness, but you never came forward?'

'I thought about it, but my wife doesn't know.'

'The parties.' Wendy ventured a guess.

'I'm embarrassed to tell you now.'

'We need to talk in detail,' Wendy said.

'Not with my wife around.' The man appeared concerned not to upset his wife. According to Mavis Richardson, he had been an obnoxious bore the night of the party.

'We either talk here or down the local police station. Which do you prefer?'

'Do you like walking?' he asked.

'Before arthritis,' Wendy replied.

'It's the same with my leg. There's a park not far from here. We could go there, grab a coffee, and you can ask me what you want.'

'And you will tell me all I need to know?'

'Yes.'

Victoria Sullivan returned and took a seat. All three drank their tea and spoke about the weather and the dog. It was evident that both were fond of the animal, even though it preferred to lie across Wendy's feet.

'We're just going out for a while,' George Sullivan said.

'Wrap up warm. You don't want to catch a cold.' The reply from the dutiful wife.

'Will you stay for tea, sergeant?' Victoria Sullivan asked.

'Thanks for the offer, but I need to get back to London.'

Chapter 28

Wendy pulled up the collar of her coat as she stepped from the heat of the Sullivans' house into the bracing wind outside.

'Global warming. Makes no sense to me,' George Sullivan said. Wendy noticed he moved with a slight limp.

The park was well looked after. Apart from the ducks in the pond, close to where they had entered, there was little movement: a few hardy souls jogging, someone doing yoga, although Wendy did not understand why or how, and a few dog owners throwing Frisbees repeatedly.

George Sullivan seemed not to concern himself with the cold. Wendy realised that she could not conduct a comprehensive interview while her feet were cold and her hands were shaking.

'There's a nice café around the corner. We'll go there,' Sullivan said.

Wendy appreciated the gesture.

The café prided itself on home-made cakes. Wendy chose two for herself. Both of them ordered lattes.

'What do you want to know?'

Wendy went through the procedure, gave him the caution about whatever you say…

'I know the rigmarole. I worked with Army Intelligence back in the 50s. During the cold war, stationed in Berlin, listening in on Russian military communications.'

'Do you understand the language?'

'I did. My mother was Russian. Nowadays, I can just about understand the Russian news on the television. Anyway, you want to know about Bellevue Street.'

'Yes. Do you mind if I record our conversation?'

'I only hope my wife never finds out what I'm going to tell you.'

'That's not a guarantee I can give,' Wendy said.

'Whatever happens, I will tell you all I know.'

'Thanks.' Wendy ordered another latte. She still had the expense account, but it appeared likely that she would not be able to give it much exercise.

'I was friends with Albert Grenfell. We had worked together in Berlin. He was a snob. I suppose you know that already.'

'It's been mentioned.'

'We started meeting on a social basis. Not often, but whenever he was in London, he would call, and we would go out to a bar or a club.'

'Disreputable?'

'Albert knew with me that I would be discreet, and I was young, not yet married, although I was courting Victoria. Sowing a few wild oats seemed fine at the time.'

'You said he was a snob.'

'What was he doing with me, is that it?'

'I suppose so.'

'Colonel in Army Intelligence counted for something. It was the cold war, spies and espionage were always in the news. My rank and my job gave me a certain allure. Today, they would say shades of James Bond, but to be honest, I spent most of my time in a room with another ten men listening to boring Russians speaking, and then writing endless reports which would have been filed within ten minutes of someone reading them.'

'Albert Grenfell liked the ideas of spies and espionage?'

'He portrayed this staid, conservative man, but underneath it, he wanted to be daring and dashing and naughty. With me, he could.'

'You started going out to bawdy clubs?'

'Not often. He was married, and his wife watched him like a hawk.'

'You met her?'

'With Victoria?'

'Yes.'

'We have been told that she was at the Richardsons' party.'

'She thought it was going to be a family gathering.'

'It must have come as a shock.'

'It came as a shock to me as well.'

'Did Albert know beforehand?'

'No, but with the Richardson sisters anything was possible.'

'Are you saying that a family gathering turned into an orgy?'

'Yes.'

Wendy, feeling hungry, ordered pasta; Sullivan ordered the same. The weather had turned bleaker outside, and it was raining heavily. George Sullivan phoned his wife to tell her he would be delayed. 'She's a terrible worrier,' he said.

'Does your wife know any of this?'

'Nothing, and that's the way I would prefer it to stay.'

'You realise the importance of what you're saying?'

'Yes.'

'And that withholding information could be seen as an offence?'

'You had difficulty finding me?' he said in reply.

'Yes.'

'Even after all these years, I am afforded some protection, some secrecy, some leniency as to my civic responsibilities.'

'What does that mean?' Wendy asked.

'Once a spy, even if not James Bond or anything glamorous, always a spy.'

'Does that mean if there was a court case, the truth could be suppressed?'

'Not in the case of Garry Solomon, but otherwise it could be.'

Wendy realised that it was not a threat, merely a statement of fact. She pressed on, only stopping to eat some more pasta.

'What changed with the family gathering?' Wendy asked.

'The younger sister.'

'Mavis?'

'Yes, that was her name. I can't remember the other sister's name.'

'Gertrude.'

'Yes, that's it. We are all sitting there. I am engaged to Victoria, but she could not come. After so many years, I can't remember why. Albert's wife is knocking back straight gin. Apparently, she became semi-alcoholic in later years. I'm drinking heavily, beer mainly, as is Albert. Gertrude is knocking back vodka and lime at a fast rate, and Mavis is drinking wine and something else.'

'Something else?'

'A drug of some sort, although I don't know what it was.'

'What happened?'

'Albert's wife becomes unconscious, and they put her in the other room. Mavis, now free of the woman, sits on Michael Solomon's lap. It doesn't seem to be the first time, either. She is kissing him full on the mouth, even though he is family. Albert sits there like a stunned mullet, unable to look, unable to look away.'

'Why?'

'I told you. Albert loved the dirty and the downright sleazy. I took him to some very discreet places where no one knew him, and he was straight into it.'

'Women?'

'Yes.'

'What happened with Mavis?'

'She moves over to Albert. Starts teasing him, tells him to loosen up. She grabs hold and kisses him. Everyone is urging him to go upstairs with her. She grabs hold of him and drags him out of the door.'

'Once they've gone?'

'Gertrude comes on to me. Back then, I was a good-looking young man, plenty of energy, always ready for a woman.'

Wendy could see that he was still good-looking, although no longer young.

'What did you do?'

'I took advantage, and took her upstairs.'

'We are aware of an incident.'

'That was me, I'm afraid.'

'Tell me about it?'

'I came back downstairs after about forty minutes. Albert reappears five minutes later, a sheepish look on his face and a big smile. His wife is still out for the count in the other room, oblivious to what has transpired.

'Gertrude moves over to Albert, Mavis makes for Michael Solomon. The younger sister was more beautiful, and I was drunk and as horny as hell. I made a scene, attempted to grab Mavis. She got angry, and I was evicted from the party. I'm ashamed of my actions, but that's the truth.'

The weather had eased outside, as had the conversation. There seemed little more to learn from George Sullivan. Wendy shook his hand and paid the bill.

As they left the café, feeling yet again the biting cold, George Sullivan turned to Wendy. 'Mavis and Gertrude Richardson?'

'Both dead, I'm afraid.'

George Sullivan shrugged his shoulders and moved on, his cane tapping the ground as he walked.

***

Isaac listened as Wendy recounted her meeting with George Sullivan. Wendy felt the man was an innocent bystander, an instinctive reaction on her part. Isaac was more sceptical: too many murders, too many innocent bystanders, but with two murders so far, and another two people dead, he hoped there would be no more.

A drunken, drug-induced impromptu orgy was hardly the reason for Garry Solomon's death, and Montague's death seemed illogical.

Larry still waited on an update from Bridget. Tracing a thirty-year-old phone number was proving time-consuming. Wendy had managed to find a phone book from the period. The only problem: it listed addresses and then phone numbers. There was no way to look for a phone number and then the address.

The only advantage was that the number was in Kingston upon Thames, but even back thirty years, there had been a sizable population. It was only thirty minutes away by car, less by train, but it was a needle in a haystack without an address. Larry pestered Bridget a few too many times before she reacted: 'I'm going as fast as I can.'

Larry, realising that he had overstepped the mark, retreated and pretended to tidy his desk. He gave up after ten minutes, and went and made himself a cup of coffee.

Isaac busied himself waiting for the next development. He did not have to wait for long.

Keith Dawson, in better humour than on previous occasions, burst into his office. 'I've found something,' he said. Larry and Wendy, seeing him enter Isaac's office with Bridget in hot pursuit, moved quickly to find out what was the latest development.

All five were in Isaac's office now, a space that was full with three. Isaac suggested they move to a larger room.

'Keith, what is it?' Isaac asked.

'The man was brilliant, I'll give him that.' It was the first time that anyone had seen Dawson with anything approaching a smile on his face, but now…

'Spill it,' Larry said. 'What have you found?'

'According to Albert Grenfell, and according to the law, the wealth of the Grenfells, or at least the stately home, the real estate holdings, and the substantive majority of the money, should be inherited by the incumbent lord.'

'Seems fair enough,' Isaac said. He had resumed his seat, aware that a prolonged speech by Dawson was to ensue. Although he had to admit that Dawson's usual monotone had been replaced by an excitable speech pattern that was almost pleasant to listen to.

'Are you saying that Malcolm Grenfell is not entitled to his inheritance?'

'He's entitled if he can find it, but I've discovered what Montague did. It's brilliant.'

'Can you give it to us in language that we can understand?' Larry asked. He had little time for Dawson and his less than cheery disposition, his usually dull manner of speaking, his ability to walk by you in the office and somehow not see you.

'The wealth of the Grenfells is held in a number of trusts, offshore banks around the world.'

'Illegal?' Isaac asked.

'Dubious, more like. The wealthy are always looking for a way to hide their wealth, avoid tax, avoid death duties.'

'I thought that no longer applied,' Isaac said.

'Inheritance Tax does.'

'You'd better detail this.'

Keith Dawson stood up and positioned himself by the whiteboard. 'To most people, Inheritance Tax is purely an inconvenience. As long as your wealth is below a certain level, then it just means some additional paperwork.'

'Am I liable?' Wendy asked. She had been contemplating selling her house now that her husband had died.

'As long as it is valued lower than three hundred and twenty-five thousand and you don't have a few million pounds in an account at your local building society, then you're all right.'

'Nothing to worry about there,' Wendy said.

'Mind you, a lot of people don't realise that they could be liable. If your house is worth a million pounds, for instance, then nearly six hundred thousand pounds of it could be liable for a forty per cent tax on your death.'

'Hell,' Larry exclaimed.

'Don't worry too much. There are ways to reduce the liability, give some of your wealth to your children, your wife, and so on. And besides, it only applies at death.'

'What has Grenfell done?'

'He's taken more than fifty per cent of the Grenfells' money and put it into overseas accounts. Not strictly illegal, but I can almost certainly guarantee that he was the only person with the knowledge of how to access it.'

'And now he is dead,' Isaac said. 'What does this mean?'

237

'Someone knows how to access it.' Keith Dawson stood proudly as he announced the first of his great works of deduction.

'What do you mean?' Isaac asked.

'Someone has been accessing the money since his death.'

'But how?'

'Someone has found out the details and the password.'

'You have?'

'No. I have found out how to access the account and download a statement. There is another more complex password for withdrawing the money.'

'Are you inferring that Montague Grenfell gave it to someone else?' Isaac said, momentarily not annoyed with Dawson and his manner.

'Given, taken or forced!' Dawson emphasised.

'A motive,' Wendy said.

'It looks good,' Isaac said.

Keith Dawson returned to his seat. Isaac reasserted his seniority and stood where Dawson had previously. Wendy was confused about some aspects of Dawson's presentation. She would ask for his opinion on her financial status later.

'Let me get this right,' Isaac said. 'Without the password, it would not be possible for anyone to access the money?'

'The account is listed in Grenfell's records, although it is cryptic.'

'Cryptic?' Isaac asked.

'What was he like?' Dawson asked.

Isaac, the only person who had met him when he was alive, answered. 'Pedantic, probably obsessive. His handwriting was extremely small.'

'Some paranoias there,' Dawson replied.

'You never answered my previous question.'

'He often reversed the words and the numbers. For instance, "word" became "drow", and "12658" became "85621".'

'What the hell for?' Larry asked. His passwords were his wife's birthday.

'The hard part was knowing when he was using a cryptic variance and when he was not. And then he would vary which variation to use. Sometimes, it would be the reverse, at other times transpose one letter to the right, one to the left. It's easy once you know what to look for.'

'A nightmare,' Isaac said.

'The password to withdraw from the offshore account was not there. He must have memorised it.'

'The money would have been lost if he had not given it to someone?' Larry asked.

'Not entirely. It may have taken some time to access, years maybe, but it was not completely lost. Let me rephrase. As long as someone knew about the account.'

'His executor was Mavis Richardson,' Isaac said.

'She may know the password. You'd better ask her,' Dawson, who had taken little interest in the department, said.

'She's dead,' Wendy said.

'Murdered?' Dawson asked.

'Natural causes.'

'It's very convenient.' Dawson's usual morose style of speech had returned.

'I'll give Gordon Windsor a call,' Isaac said.

'I attended her funeral,' Wendy said. 'You know that.'

'I know,' Isaac replied, aware that the woman's body may need to come up again, a lengthy process with endless paperwork.

Chapter 29

'I don't give a damn what Dawson said. The woman died of natural causes,' Gordon Windsor said when Isaac phoned him up. Isaac had known the man for many years, and this was the first time he had known him to be angry. With the London Met, Isaac realised that Gordon Windsor had a flawless record, and Dawson's aspersions, purely based on Montague Grenfell's records, were reflecting on his professional judgement, and that of the pathologist who had conducted the autopsy of Mavis Richardson.

'It's only an idea.' Isaac tried to calm the man down.

'You'll never get the permission anyway, and if you did, what tests do you want us to conduct?' Windsor said, his previous outburst slightly mellowed.

'Toxicology?' Isaac suggested. Even he had to admit that the possibility of Mavis Richardson dying of anything other than old age seemed remote, but he had to sound out Gordon Windsor.

'The woman was eighty-five. She had led an active life and drank a little too much at times. There were signs of smoking, although minor. Clearly, her blood pressure was a little high.'

'How do you know that?'

'Tablets in her bathroom. We checked with her doctor, standard procedure, and he confirmed.'

'Until we have further reason Mavis Richardson stays where she is.'

'Messy business digging up the dead, although she's not been buried long,' Gordon Windsor said. Isaac could only agree.

Gordon Windsor hung up the phone. Isaac regretted calling him, regretted reminding him that he had made a mistake once in the past, where he had confirmed that the man had died of self-inflicted wounds but it was later found out to be murder.

Isaac was well aware that he had made mistakes over the years, pursued one person believing him to be guilty only to find that the unattractive and ill-mannered man was innocent, whereas the attractive and agreeable person turned out to have personal issues and a desire to kill.

Isaac knew that a police officer was fallible, the same as everyone else. He understood the need for procedures and paperwork as they maintained a detachment that allowed the focus to be directed to facts and evidence, not to assumptions and instincts.

It was only when he was confronted with endless paperwork that he became downhearted. DCS Richard Goddard could only sympathise, but as he had said, 'what the new commissioner wants, he gets.'

Goddard and Cook regarded each other as friends. Isaac had been over to the DCS's house on a few occasions, had even been invited to the wedding of his eldest daughter. On that occasion, he had taken Jess. That was the time when their romance was full on. She had enjoyed the ceremony and the reception immensely; even hinted to Isaac to make an honest woman of her. It was also before their first argument over Linda Harris.

Isaac realised that he kept reflecting back to Jess. Linda Harris had been attractive and briefly available, Sophie White had always been there, and Katrina Smith, his current girlfriend, was certainly attractive and he liked her a lot, but always there was Jess O'Neill in the back of his mind.

It concerned him sometimes, wondered if it was love. He just did not know. He considered whether he should phone Jess up, take her out, but he was aware that Linda Harris would reappear, not as a physical incarnation but as a mental barrier. He could forget that he had been foolish and lustful that night, but Jess never would.

He collected his thoughts and refocussed on the paperwork.

No point regretting the past, he thought.

Isaac managed another twenty-five minutes at his desk, completed a couple of reports, but it was long enough for him. Keith Dawson had caused everyone in the department to analyse the investigation.

Larry Hill, untidy desk aside, was going through his notes. A clear motive for Montague Grenfell's death had been given, and it could only mean one thing: the murderer was alive, and he had the password.

Wendy was talking to Keith Dawson, the majority of the conversation spent on the case, the rest spent on her financial status and Inheritance Tax. Dawson's constant reiteration that there was nothing to worry about was not helping.

She knew she was numerically dyslexic, and his analysis on a piece of paper showing what she owned and what she owed meant little to her. 'If I take your assets, here in the left column, and your liabilities in the right column and subtract, you are below the threshold.'

Bridget sat to one side. It seemed clear to her, but for Wendy it was not.

'Don't worry, I'll be there with you,' Bridget said.

'You understand what Keith is saying?' Wendy asked.

'It's all quite simple.'

'Not to me,' Wendy replied, feeling a little stupid that the simplest mathematics left her confused.

***

Isaac could see that he needed to give his people direction. He called them into his office. 'Gordon Windsor is adamant that Mavis Richardson died of natural causes,' he said.

Wendy was pleased to hear Windsor's comment. Bridget, who professed a belief in the Almighty and the afterlife, thanked God. Both women had not liked the idea of digging the old woman up just after she had been buried. To them it was disrespectful.

Larry, who had no such concerns, had said after Dawson's statement, 'Dig her up.'

Isaac had been brought up by Jamaican parents to believe in God and the Almighty, but also to be fearful of evil spirits. His English education had discounted the evil spirits, but he maintained an abiding respect for God, even if his visits to church were relegated to Christmas and Easter.

'I suggest we focus on Montague Grenfell's death,' Isaac said.

'I thought we were,' Larry said.

Isaac thought Larry's comment was condescending, but let it pass.

'Do we have a list of suspects, sir?' Wendy asked.

'There are two issues to consider: firstly, who would have known about the secret account, and secondly, who would have had the strength to manhandle Grenfell to the top of the stairs.'

'Malcolm Grenfell,' Larry said.

'He's the most likely suspect, but can we prove it?' Isaac asked.

'Does he have an alibi?' Wendy asked.

'We know that Grenfell died between the hours of 11 p.m. and 2 a.m. on the night of the twenty-fifth.'

'Malcolm Grenfell will not have an alibi.'

'Other than he was at home with his woman,' Isaac said.

"Judging by the condition of the girl we met, she would not be reliable,' Larry said.

'What do you mean?' Bridget asked.

'Drunk, spaced out. She was there with Malcolm Grenfell for a good time and money, nothing more. Besides, he has dumped her now. May be hard to find.'

'Who else would have known?' Wendy asked.

'Mavis Richardson, obviously. Possibly Albert.'

'They are both dead.' Larry stated the obvious.

'Agreed, but who else would have known?'

'Montague Grenfell was not the sort of man to tell anyone,' Wendy said.

'Agreed, so let's look at the more unlikely.'

'Emma Hampshire, Kevin Solomon, and the other children of Michael Solomon,' Larry said.

'What about George Sullivan?' Wendy added.

'You said he was an old man,' Isaac reminded her.

'He is, but he's still agile.'

'We are not aware of any contact between Michael Solomon's other children and Montague Grenfell. According to their mother, neither of them are of any consequence. The son follows after his half-brother Garry.'

'What do you mean?' Bridget asked.

'Petty criminal.'

'Apparently, the daughter, a heroin addict, is selling herself up in the city,' Isaac said.

'Hardly great recommendations for the offspring of Michael Solomon,' Larry said.

'As you say.'

'Should we check them out?' Wendy asked.

'We only have their mother's opinion on her children. She's probably correct, but we need to check.'

'Bridget, compile a dossier on Michael and Mary Solomon's two children. Aim to have it prepared for our 5 p.m. meeting,' Isaac said. 'In the meantime, Larry, follow up on who ordered the grille to be installed at Bellevue Street. Wendy, what are your plans?'

'I will see if I can get the contact details from Mary Solomon for her two children.'

'And you, DCI?' Larry asked.

'Gordon Windsor. I will go and visit him, have a chat. I upset him earlier, and Montague Grenfell's death is still not conclusive. It could have just been an accident.'

'There were two sets of footprints,' Larry said. 'Both men's shoes.'

'I'm aware of that, but if we are about to place pressure on our suspects, then we need our facts to be double-checked.'

'Don't forget about Emma Hampshire and Kevin Solomon,' Wendy said.

'Kevin Solomon has some legal training, and Emma Hampshire knows more than she says,' Isaac replied. 'Both of them are highly suspect.'

'I hope it's not Emma Hampshire,' Wendy said.

'Personally, I would agree, but professionally we charge the guilty person, not choose on whether we like them or not.'

'I understand,' Wendy replied.

***

Mary Solomon was not pleased to see Wendy on her doorstep again. 'What the hell do you want?' she screamed, attempting to make her voice heard over the crying of the baby that she held in one arm. Wendy could see that the woman had no idea with babies, and was holding it too tight. It was clear from the smell that it was in need of changing.

'Let me have it,' Wendy said. The baby quietened as she felt Wendy's warm body against it. Wendy, ever practical, took the baby into the bathroom up the stairs and cleaned it. Afterwards, she found a baby's bottle and filled it with milk. Soon, the baby was resting quietly.

'That's Deidre's,' Mary Solomon said. Wendy remembered that on a previous visit Mary Solomon had said that the baby had been affected by its mother's drug addiction. Wendy could see neglect by its grandmother more than the afflictions of its birth mother.

'I need to talk to your children.'

'Why do you want to speak to them?'

Wendy had noticed that the woman's hands were shaking slightly. Wendy recognised that this could be the early signs of Parkinson's, although it could just be nerves, but why? Was it because Wendy wanted to talk to her son and daughter, or because she was incapable of looking after three young children?

'Standard procedure in a murder enquiry.'

'But they don't know the people murdered.'

'I agree that is probably true, but we still need to interview them.'

'They come here to pick up the children.'

'When?'

'Deidre sometimes once a week, sometimes it's as long as three weeks.'

'It's not for you to look after them. What do you use for money?'

'She gives me the money that a drunk has given her after he has screwed her.'

'Not a very pleasant thing to say about a daughter,' Wendy said.

'Do you want me to say "for favours given". Does that sound more palatable to you? She is a prostitute who opens her legs for any man who has the price. No other way to put it.'

Wendy could see that the woman was embittered and under strain, but her estimation of her daughter seemed inappropriate.

'Your son?'

'He comes here every night, picks up his child and leaves.'

'Does he give you money?'

'Half what the child care facility up the road would charge. I'm not even on the minimum wage.'

'But they're your grandchildren.'

'Maybe they are, but they are mongrels.'

'Who?'

'My children and their children. I should never have married that lecherous bastard, and then it was not legitimate. They are all bastards, legally or otherwise.'

Wendy could see no reason to prolong the conversation. 'I need their contact details.'

'They're on my phone.'

Wendy took the details and left. She was certain the woman had serious issues, and the children should not be in her care. She had resolved once before to contact the appropriate authorities. This time, she would do so after she had contacted the woman's two children.

Chapter 30

'Nothing to do with me,' Daniel Solomon said when Wendy contacted him.

'So far, I've only given you my police rank and told you I was from Homicide.'

'Has my mother implicated me?'

'In what?'

'Montague Grenfell's death.'

'Did you know him?'

'He was friendly with my father when I was younger.'

'I can come and see you now, or you can present yourself at Challis Street Police Station.'

'It's best if you can come and see me. I will send you the details. Give me an hour.'

Wendy, with time to spare, went into a café not far from Mary Solomon's house. She was upset at the condition of the woman, and the neglect that the children in her care were showing. A latte calmed her down.

She phoned Larry. 'I'm meeting with Daniel Solomon, Garry Solomon's half-brother.'

'Do you want me there?'

'I'm not sure what to expect.'

'Give me fifteen minutes.' Larry was pleased at the opportunity to get out of the office.

Wendy had expected to find Daniel Solomon in a rundown office down a back alley, not a street-front location. The office was modern and well equipped, with three desks, a person sitting at each one.

'Daniel Solomon, pleased to meet you.' Wendy saw in front of her a relatively short man with good features and a pleasant smile. He was dressed smartly and wearing a suit jacket, but no tie. He was not what she expected.

'This is Detective Inspector Hill,' Wendy said.

'Coffee?' Solomon asked.

'Yes, please. Two sugars for me, none for DI Hill.'

'Business is good,' Solomon said once they were sitting in his office at the rear. He had closed the door securely after they entered.

'The sign outside says industrial cleaning,' Wendy said.

'I set it up five years ago,' Solomon said. 'I managed to pick up some government cleaning contracts. Never looked back.'

'We are aware that you have a record,' Larry said.

'I was wild in my youth. You won't find anything on me, apart from the occasional parking fine, maybe speeding, for the last eight years.'

'That is correct,' Larry said. He had seen Bridget's preliminary dossier on Daniel Solomon and his sister. The man had told the truth.

Wendy saw the Solomon charm in the way he spoke. He was thirty-six, the same age as his half-brother when he had died. The similarity between the two men was astonishing. Comparing them, Wendy had to wonder if breeding counted. Garry had firm features, was a rugged, handsome man, whereas Daniel was rugged but not as attractive.

'You're not what I expected,' Wendy said.

'My mother?'

'Yes.'

'Life's not been good for her.'

'She cannot handle the children.'

'Did you see mine?'

'Yes.'

'He's okay, and she looks after him well enough.'

'Your sister's children?'

'They have problems.'

'Would you care to elucidate?' Larry asked.

'Not unless it's relevant.'

Wendy noticed that they had touched a raw nerve. She changed the subject.

'When Montague Grenfell died, what did you think?'

'Nothing really. He was someone from my childhood.'

'Why is your child with your mother?'

'My wife went back home to look after her dying mother.'

'She did not take the child?'

'She knew he would be all right with me.'

Wendy thought the story strange; Bridget could check it out. The man had become edgy, irritable, as though he wanted them to go away. Neither Larry nor Wendy intended to leave until they had answers. One of the women came in from the outside office. Daniel Solomon gave her what she wanted, and she left.

'Sorry about that. Pressure of work,' Solomon said. Wendy wondered if it was pre-arranged to hurry them out. She decided to give him the benefit of the doubt.

'When was the last time you saw Montague Grenfell?' Larry asked.

Solomon looked into the air, searching for an answer. 'Over twenty years.'

'Can you be more specific?'

'I was young. People come, people go. I was not keeping a diary.' The man's reply was curt.

Larry wanted the man down the station, formally cautioned, and then he would prise the truth from him. Wendy could see Solomon's charm dissipating, a characteristic apparently all too familiar in his half-brother.

'Did you know Garry Solomon or Solly Michaels?' Wendy asked.

'My mother mentioned that you had been asking about him. I would have been six or seven when he disappeared. If I had seen him, you could not expect me to remember him.'

'Tell us about your sister?'

'Not much to tell.'

'Humour us,' Larry said. He knew when someone was avoiding direct answers to direct questions.

'She's made some bad decisions in her life.'

'Men?'

'Men, drugs, yes.'

249

'Have you seen her recently?'

'Once a week.'

'Why?'

'Brotherly love. It is important to some of us, you know,' Daniel Solomon said bitingly. It touched a raw nerve with Larry, who had a brother that he never saw as a result of a family dispute. It silenced him for a moment.

'I'm busy. Is there any more that you want?' Solomon asked.

'I think that's about all for now,' Wendy said.

There was one more call that day, the sister. Wendy made the phone call, a female voice answered. She noticed no great enthusiasm from the woman to meet until Wendy firmly told her that it was now, or else down at Challis Street Police Station. If she wanted, she would organise a marked police car to pick her up.

'King's Road, Chelsea. I'll meet you in front of the Saatchi Gallery.'

Wendy knew there were good restaurants in the area. Interviewing a suspect in one of them would not be inappropriate.

Larry phoned Bridget. 'Check out Daniel Solomon's business. I'll send you the details.'

***

Larry had to look twice when a woman in a smart blue dress introduced herself.

'Hi, I'm Deidre Solomon.'

Larry realised that this was no ordinary prostitute. The woman, an air of assuredness about her, oozed class and quality. He noticed other men looking her way, other women too.

'Pleased to meet you,' Wendy said.

'I can give you one hour of my time,' Deidre Solomon said.

'Lunch?' Wendy asked.

'I'm a light eater. Why not?'

The three relocated to the restaurant inside the Saatchi Gallery. Larry noted the prices were high. Wendy never looked.

'What business are you involved in?' Larry asked.

'My mother told you I'm a drug-addicted prostitute selling myself to any man with the money.'

'Something like that,' Wendy replied.

'I'm clean now.'

'And the other part?'

'I'm not ashamed. I'm still for hire at a price.'

'You are still a prostitute?' Larry asked.

'I prefer gentleman's companion, but if you want to use a cruder term, then I am.'

'We met your brother.'

'Good man. Did you like him?' Deidre looked over at Wendy.

Larry knew the woman was thirty-seven, though she looked younger. Her breasts were firm, the result of surgery he assumed. The colour of her skin, a light brown, was either a result of cream or a tanning salon. She wore red high-heeled shoes with a stiletto point. If he did not know her history or what she had just admitted, he would have assumed that she was one of the idle rich who strolled up and down King's Road, flaunting themselves and their credit cards. He could not tell if she had money or made the pretence to induce wealthy men to part with their cash for a few hours of her time.

'Yes,' Wendy replied, although his criminal record showed a litany of crimes when he had been younger.

Wendy scanned Bridget's updates on Deidre Solomon while Larry continued the interview: *Deidre Solomon, prostituting, shoplifting.*

Nothing major there, Wendy thought.

The brother had been in court on a charge of grievous bodily harm, but it had been dropped on a technicality, and he walked out of the court a free man. Still, to Wendy, it was interesting that the man was capable of violence.

'Do you know Montague Grenfell?' Larry asked.

251

'Daniel said you would ask.' Deidre Solomon ate a salad, and even then, very slowly. Wendy assumed she had a problem keeping the weight off, and semi-starvation was a necessity.

'And?'

'Yes. I knew him.'

'How?'

'With my father when I was a child.'

'And?' Larry persisted, the hesitancy in the woman's reply concerning him.

'He came to see me occasionally.'

The woman's statement caused Wendy to put down her fork. 'You knew him?' she asked.

'He was a nice old man.'

Wendy realised that they had uncovered something very relevant. She pushed her plate to one side, even though a small amount of food remained. Larry had chosen a salad, the same as Deidre Solomon, daughter of Michael Solomon, the paid lover of Montague Grenfell, if what she had told them turned out to be true. The woman had no reason to lie, and by her own admission she had placed herself and her brother at the top of the list of prime suspects.

Larry spoke to the gallery staff, showed his ID. They organised a private room. The two police officers and Deidre relocated there. One of the waitresses brought in three coffees.

Larry formally cautioned Deidre, told her that evidence given could be used in a court of law. Neither he nor Wendy had expected any more from her other than a denial of any knowledge, and a vague recollection of Montague Grenfell.

'Could you please elaborate on your relationship with Montague Grenfell?' Larry asked. He was the more senior of the two police officers. He would take the lead role in the interview.

'He contacted my agency and arranged a booking.'

'He knew your name?'

'Not my professional name. He had chosen me from a website.'

'Did he at any time know who you were?'

'Never.'

'But you knew who he was?'

'The family history. I knew.'

'Did that concern you?'

'Why? He was not related, other than my father had been married to one of his cousins.'

'The man was in his seventies,' Wendy said.

'He was no great stud, but he was good for his age.'

'Why did you tell us?' Larry asked.

'My brother said that it's always best to be open with the police. If they find out later, it's more incriminating.'

'Wise man, your brother,' Larry admitted.

'Did Montague Grenfell tell you anything we should know about? Wendy asked.

'Such as?'

'Family secrets.'

'I was not there receiving his confession. His visits to me were not religious.'

'Carnal?' Larry asked.

'That's what I do. He was lonely; his wife had died, and he wanted company.'

'And screwing?' Wendy said.

'Say it for what it was, a fuck. And why not?'

'Are most of your clients lonely old men?' Larry asked.

'No doubt some are married, but I don't ask.'

'You asked Grenfell?'

'Never. Sometimes he talked, but then I knew who he was and some of what he was saying.'

'Did he discuss his brother?'

'No, but I know there are two. My father told me that before he died.'

'There's only one now.'

'Okay, one.'

'Are you interested as to which one?' Wendy asked.

'Why should I be?'

'We ask the questions, you answer.'

'For the record,' Deidre Solomon said, 'I knew very little about the Grenfells, other than they were upper class and I was not. Satisfied?'

'Satisfied.'

Wendy had another question. 'Your mother is looking after two children of yours. What is the situation?'

'You've seen my criminal record?'

'Yes.'

'Then you know that I sold myself on the street for years until I kicked heroin, or it kicked me.'

'What do you mean?'

'I overdosed, woke up restrained in a drug rehabilitation centre.'

'Who paid?'

'I assume it was my father.'

'Private hospital?' Wendy asked.

'Expensive. I saw a few celebrities in there. Some of them so pure, butter wouldn't melt in their mouths.'

Larry looked at Wendy. They both understood what Deidre's statement meant.

'And after you left?'

'I tried making an income standing up, but the money was lousy. In the end, I went back to what I know best.'

'Screwing for money?' Wendy asked.

'Why not? I still had the looks even after years of abuse. I sold myself from a hotel room for a few months, and when I had enough money, I fixed up the boobs, then the arse. The rest is courtesy of good makeup.'

'You've done a good job,' Wendy said.

'Thanks.'

'After you had sorted yourself out?'

'I found an agency, went on their books. They phone me and either I take the job or I don't.'

'You refuse?' Larry asked.

'I'm not into bondage.'

'Your children?'

'The unfortunate offspring of my earlier years.'

'You don't care for them?' Wendy asked.

'I try, but they bring back unpleasant memories. You've seen them?'

'Yes.'

'Reflection of the men I screwed.'

'Is that why you leave them with your mother?'

'I offered to put them up for adoption, but she wants to keep them.'

'Not what she says.'

'My mother is not well. You do realise that?'

'Yes. She needs help.'

'I've offered, but she only screams at me, calls me a dirty whore.'

'Are you?' Wendy asked.

'I was, not now.'

Chapter 31

Gordon Windsor was still a little miffed when Isaac met up with him. 'You've no right to question my competency,' he said. He had just returned from another murder. Isaac was aware of the details, and if he had been free, he would have been assigned as the senior investigating officer. As it was, he was still involved in two murders. One appeared to be reaching a resolution, although in this case, as with so many others, there was always an unforeseen piece of evidence or a statement that took them off in another direction.

Isaac had formed his opinion as to who was responsible for both murders, but the evidence, at best, was flimsy and would not hold up. A confession was necessary, and for that pressure would need to be applied.

He was not willing to apply that pressure until he was confident of a conviction.

'I apologise, but I have every right,' Isaac said.

'I'll accept your apology, but for the record: Mavis Richardson was old, her health was indicative of her age, she suffered a heart attack, and last, but by no means least, the pathologist knew of her importance. Full tests were carried out, looking for the slightest hint of an induced death. Nothing was found.'

'Exhuming her would be pointless?' Isaac asked.

'Pointless, unless you like paperwork.'

'Are you certain that Gertrude Richardson died of natural causes?'

'DCI, you're clutching at straws. Did you see her son?'

'Not closely.'

'Well, I did, as did Gertrude Richardson. It almost turned my stomach, but the woman stood there and looked. Wendy Gladstone could not take it either. What do you think a mother would feel after being confronted with the thirty-year-old corpse of her long-lost son?'

'And her dying?'

'The woman was eighty-seven and reclusive. She barely ate and was very frail. It was a good job Wendy Gladstone was with her when she died. Otherwise, she may have become a thirty-year-old corpse herself.'

'Montague Grenfell?'

'He fell down the stairs and broke his neck.'

'Is it possible to ascertain whether he slipped or was pushed?'

'You've read my report?'

'Yes.'

'I don't believe there is any ambiguity, do you?'

'Not as to the cause of death, but you did not specify that he had been pushed.'

'It's in the report. The footprints at the top indicated a scuffle. Whether he had been pushed or not is not clear. I left the report open-ended.'

***

Isaac, realising that he may have just been wasting Gordon Windsor's time, returned to the office. He knew what the issue was: it was that as the senior investigating officer he was increasingly confined to Challis Street. He enjoyed the cut and thrust out in the field, probing, asking questions when they were not welcomed, receiving answers, sometimes truthfully given, sometimes not. And in this case, a lot of the answers were just that, not truthful.

The children of Michael and Mary Solomon had brought in a hitherto unknown element. Bridget was checking out the son, while Wendy conducted some more investigations into Deidre.

Larry had enjoyed the photo gallery of Deidre on the agency's website – draped across a bed, showing what the lucky client was to receive. Wendy just saw it as lewd, but it was not for her to comment, and she was certainly not a prude. The prices for a half-hour, two hours, a full day seemed excessive to her, but the woman they had met said that she catered to the well-heeled, and in the case of Montague Grenfell, well-aged.

Wendy had submitted her expenses for the meal at the Saatchi Gallery on her return. Isaac had duly signed his approval, but he knew his DCS would hit the roof. The economy drive throughout the force was gaining momentum, and Isaac knew that once their current murder case, cases, were concluded, he would be asked to make cuts.

Isaac wanted more people for his department, not fewer. He saw it as ironic that there were financial cuts to be made, yet the consultants brought in from outside to oversee the exercise were paid excessively.

Isaac had studied economics at university, and the amount of money allocated for the purpose of saving money would have been better spent elsewhere: an extra person to ease the burden carried by Wendy and Larry, someone to deal with his paperwork.

His relationship with Katrina Smith was going well. He knew that it was a momentary passion, as did she, but neither felt any great disappointment. Both of them were still young, especially Katrina.

They met when they could, spent nights at his flat, but she was busy working in London, discussing her future, and Isaac was burning the midnight oil on the current murder investigation. He only hoped that there were to be no more deaths.

He had put forward a cogent case to his DCS for more staff, only to receive a terse reply.

'Economy drive. There's not much I can do about it. Wrap up this case, and I'll see what I can do.'

Which to Isaac meant one thing: no additional help now, and when the heat is off, then why do you want more.

Not that he could blame his DCS. He had had a rough time when Commissioner Shaw, a man who had guided his career, accepted a peerage. His replacement, a cheerless man, had not taken a shine to the DCS.

Isaac, down at New Scotland Yard the day of his first speech to the people in the building, had listened intently to the new commissioner, Alwyn Davies, had said: '…open-door policy, always open to suggestions. If you want to come and see me, be direct. I have no time for the inept and the ingratiating. Results are what I want.'

It had been meant to inspire the assembled personnel, and although they had clapped, few believed what they had heard. Clichéd comments were all very well, but that was what they were, clichéd.

In the six months since taking over, Commissioner Davies had become disliked by most in the Met. He had proven himself to be a singularly unfriendly man, and those who had taken up the offer to knock on his door had invariably been met with a rebuff. Most of them had retreated, tails between their legs.

It had been the same for DCS Goddard until he had got the measure of the man, and the former commissioner Charles Shaw had found him a place on a government committee looking into crime.

Sensing that DCS Goddard had friends in high places, as well as his known association with MacTavish, the chief government whip, had ensured that Alwyn Davies now treated Goddard with kid gloves.

***

Larry had checked with Dawson. Deidre Solomon's drug rehabilitation had been paid for by Montague Grenfell. Michael Solomon had not been a Richardson or a Grenfell, but by default he had come under their umbrella. Larry could not see how Gertrude Richardson would not have known of her husband's whereabouts, but it was a moot point, as there was no one to confirm it.

Daniel and Deidre Solomon had been seen as irrelevancies, minor players out on the periphery of the investigation, but now they were front and centre.

Deidre's acknowledgement that she had known Montague Grenfell had come as a shock. She must have known the reaction it would have caused with Larry and Wendy.

Bridget had managed to obtain her school records, and it was clear that Deidre was of moderate intelligence, whereas her brother was always top of his class, especially in mathematics.

A subsequent visit to the school, a charmless red-brick building, had been made by Wendy.

'Deidre Solomon. Yes, I remember her,' Brenda Hopwood, a dowdily dressed woman, said. Wendy imagined her shrouded in a nun's habit which would have seemed appropriate. Around her neck, she wore a large cross, which she constantly touched.

'What can you tell me about her?'

'More interested in boys than books. Always had her skirt hitched up around her waist.'

Wendy thought it a crude comment from a woman who looked as if she visited the church every day to pray for forgiveness, although Wendy could not see the prune of a woman sinning, or even breathing.

'Sexually active?' A more clinical term from Wendy.

'Yes.'

'Her brother, Daniel?' Wendy asked.

'Clever boy. I remember him well. Always with one girl or another.'

'He's a good-looking man,' Wendy said.

'I suppose he was back then.'

'You said clever?'

'He was always top of the class.'

'Anything else?'

'Not really. I caught him gambling once outside.'

'What did you do?'

'Nothing. What became of him?'

'He's doing fine now.'

'And his sister?'

'She's fine too.'

Wendy did not see the need to elaborate on the fact that Daniel Solomon had a criminal record, although no trouble for a few years, and that he was running his own business and in financial difficulty. Nor did she intend to tell the woman that Deidre had found herself a good career with what she had learnt at the school, namely the ability to hitch up her skirt and screw for money, a lot of money from what she could see.

Wendy had done the calculations. Deidre Solomon, assuming she spent twenty hours a week flat on her back, could make more money in one week than she did in three months.

***

DCS Goddard was pushing for an arrest. Isaac called in the team. Keith Dawson came, now a valued member, even if his ability to interface with the rest of the team was suspect.

Wendy had tried to relate to him, but he had been cold and dull. Larry had invited him down the pub one night after work, which Dawson had readily accepted. The man had sat at the bar, said little, nothing about his life, and had drunk his five pints and gone home. Larry realised after he had gone that Dawson had landed him with the bill.

Wendy's house sale was going ahead. There had been an offer, too low, but the estate agent was hassling her to accept. Keith Dawson had been firm when he had told her not to accept.

She was anxious to get out of the house as, due to its dampness, her arthritis was causing her lots of pain.

She could only reflect that when a case was in full swing, and when her husband had been dying, she had not had time to think about the pain. She had read a book on positive thinking, heal yourself with the power of the mind. It made some sense, but she had soon tired of it. To her, the pain was real, the house was damp, and no amount of mumbo jumbo was going to change that.

'Larry, what do we have?' Isaac asked.

'Daniel Solomon's in financial trouble. His sister is prostituting herself.'

'Apart from that.'

'That's it for the present moment. Keith is accessing Daniel Solomon's bank accounts, tax returns. Are they under suspicion?'

'We're not discounting them.'

'Wendy?' Isaac looked in her direction. She held a cup of coffee in her hand, as usual.

'I've checked Daniel and Deidre Solomon's school. Deidre has taken the only career path open to her. Her brother was a smart person then, still is by all accounts.'

'Criminal records?'

'None from either for a few years.'

'Keith, what have you found out?'

'Daniel Solomon's bank accounts appear to be in order, although I've only started checking. His tax returns have been filed on time. Nothing to report there, other than he had overpaid last year, and he received a payment back.'

'Is his company viable?'

'He has a serious cash flow problem.'

'Deidre Solomon. Have you accessed her bank accounts?'

'Not yet, although she would probably deal in cash mainly.'

'Why?' Isaac asked.

'The men who use her services don't want a credit card transaction being traced back to her, or, as is often used, a hairdressing salon. They would not want their wives to know.'

'Explanation accepted.'

'If they are implicated, it would be Daniel who would be coordinating,' Larry said.

'And Deidre who had the lever,' Wendy added.

'One screws, the other fleeces,' Larry said.

'Apart from your wording, is that what we think happened?' Isaac asked.

'No proof.'

'Keith, we need you to dig deep. Let us know when you find something,' Isaac said.

Chapter 32

'Tom will be here soon. I've got a rush job. Come in two hours, and you can borrow him for an hour,' Sean O'Reilly said.

Larry arrived at O'Reilly's on time. Tom Wellings was just finishing the rush order, although his speed was anything but a rush. The man moved calmly and with purpose. Larry noted that once he had completed one task, he would tidy before moving on to the next.

'Five minutes,' Wellings said.

'That's fine.'

Sue Baxter had been forewarned that they would be coming. She worked only five minutes from the house, and their visit would coincide with her lunch break. It had been some time since she had seen a policeman at her house, and she had hoped no more would be coming. The uniformed police outside on the street maintaining vigilance over the crime scene had long gone, as had the tape across the door into the murder room.

The Baxters had been given access to the room and had set to work to bring it up to the standard of the rest of the house.

Larry had been impressed when he walked through the front door. 'You've done a great job,' he said.

'Thank you, DI Hill,' Sue Baxter said proudly. Ted Hunter, the handyman who had made the grim discovery, had shown himself to be a competent man, although, as Sue Baxter's husband would have said, 'He still overcharged us.'

Not that the complaint would have been too forceful, as Sue Baxter, ever anxious, had phoned a local estate agent for a valuation. With booming prices in the area and the agent's determination to put it on the market, he had given them a good price, one hundred thousand pounds over what they had paid for the house and its renovation.

Sue enthusiastically had wanted to list the house immediately. It had been her husband who had said no. A renovation of a small house in Manchester, and a larger one in London, was enough for him, and besides, the house was still a crime scene.

'I doubt if we are allowed to sell it yet,' he had said. He knew it was probably not correct, but it sufficed.

'Okay,' his wife had said, and besides, she loved the house and the neighbourhood.

Larry preceded Tom into the house. 'This is Tom Wellings,' Larry said, introducing him to Sue Baxter.

'You've done a great job here, Mrs Baxter,' Wellings said.

'Thank you.'

Larry noticed the photos lining the hallway that showed the transformation from neglected and unwanted to loved and homely.

All three entered the murder room. The walls had been painted, the floorboards had been sanded and varnished. The centrepiece of the room, the fireplace, was resplendent in its glory.

'It gives the room character,' Sue Baxter said.

It gave Larry a chill down his back thinking about what had lain there for thirty years. Sue Baxter, despite her initial aversion when the body had been found, made no reference to the death and the mummified corpse. Larry assumed that if she could, she would have a photo of the body up on the wall in the hallway.

'Tom has worked for the company that installed the grille over the door for over thirty years,' Larry said.

'Closer to fifty,' Tom Wellings replied. He was a man with an uncluttered mind. He did not fill his mind with considering the world situation, politics, and the state of the economy. He had gone through life ensuring he had enough money in his pocket to keep a roof over his head, clothe, and feed himself, nothing more. It had given him the ability to remember trivial details that others had forgotten.

'We fitted the bars on the window,' he said.

'We took them down,' Sue Baxter said. 'Aesthetically they were not right.'

'Oversize. We used what we had in stock.'

'You remember, Tom?' Larry asked.

'Business was quiet. Old man Dennison had laid off a couple of people, so I helped out here.'

Larry had to take a seat. Here, encompassed within this man, was the first positive lead into the murder of Garry Solomon for some time.

'What do you remember?' Larry asked.

'It was a long time ago. It may need a cup of tea for me to remember.'

'I'll get you one,' Sue said. 'No more speaking until I come back.'

Larry wanted to continue with Tom, but the man was adamant. 'When she comes back,' he said.

Larry only hoped he could prevent her from talking to the media again.

'I'm all ears,' Sue Baxter said on her return. She should have been back at the school where she taught, but there was no way she was going to be prised out of the chair she was sitting in.

Tom sat, content with his cup of tea.

'Would you like to continue?' Larry asked. 'I'll record this if it's okay.'

'Fine by me,' Tom said. He appeared to appreciate the attention.

Larry placed his iPhone on the coffee table and hit record.

'We fitted the bars first. We had made a miscalculation, and I had to cut a little off one side.'

'Who let you into the house?' Larry asked.

'I'm coming to that,' Tom said.

'Please, carry on,' Sue Baxter said. She was excited, almost wetting herself from what Larry could see.

'It took us a couple of hours to install the bars. I used Ramset bolts to hold them in place.'

'We had trouble taking some out, so we just plastered over them.' Sue Baxter said.

'The grille?' Larry asked.

'It was awkward to carry, and we had trouble manhandling it into place.'

'Why were you installing the grille?' Larry asked.

'We received an order and the man paid up front.'

'It was a man?'

'I remember him. A tall man. He spoke well.'

'His name?'

'I don't remember him ever giving it to us, although he gave us all a tip at the end of the job.'

'I'll need to show you some photos later, see if you can identify him.'

'Fine by me,' Wellings said.

'What was the house like?' Sue Baxter asked.

'Not much to say. It was empty, although it appeared to be in good condition. There was a toilet down the hallway which we used, and I noticed a woman's touch.'

'What do you mean?' Larry asked.

'There were some small towels.'

'What did that mean to you?'

'I suppose it had only recently been vacated, nothing more.'

'Was an explanation given as to why you were installing a grille?'

'Never asked. It wasn't any of my business.'

Larry realised that in this one man was the possible solution to a case that had baffled them for so long.

Sue Baxter pried for more information, but there was no more available.

Wellings thanked her for her hospitality, complimented her one more time on how good the house looked.

Larry's car was outside. The two men drove a mile down the street, away from Sue Baxter's eagle eyes.

Balancing the laptop on his knees, angling the screen, Larry showed Tom Wellings the photos he had: some old, some new.

'That's him.'

'One hundred per cent?'

'I'd say ninety-nine.'

'Good enough for me,' Larry said.

Larry dropped Tom Wellings back at O'Reilly's and headed straight back to Challis Street. He was in a hurry, and the traffic was not helping. He almost ran a red light on one occasion; the fine for doing so, his responsibility.

Isaac was excited on his return. 'Well done,' he said.

***

Albert Grenfell's funeral, conducted in the church next to Penrith House, was a sombre affair. Isaac could see Malcolm Grenfell suitably dressed in a black suit leading the mourners. Wendy had come up as well. Isaac thought it may be a good idea to have two police officers present.

Isaac had brought Katrina Smith, who was in a black dress. Wendy had driven up on her own after Isaac had mentioned that he was taking someone.

Wendy, not wishing to be a wallflower, had organised a police issue car. She noticed the furtive glances from Isaac to Katrina during the ceremony.

Both the police officers noted who was present: Emma Hampshire was with Malcolm Grenfell. Also present was George Sullivan, the previously hidden man, now very visible. His wife sat at his side.

There were some other people there, some distinguished, others dressed in plain business suits. A later investigation identified them as other aristocrats or local dignitaries from the area. They did not concern Isaac.

Ger O'Loughlin's daughter, the woman that Wendy had met in Ireland, was present. It did not seem suspicious, although Wendy would check later.

Apart from those clearly visible, there were no other family members. In light of recent developments with Montague Grenfell's murder, his body had not been released.

Malcolm Grenfell read one prayer during the service, his tone mellow and humble. Isaac thought that he handled it well, considering that he had not been fond of his brother, and he was an idle fornicating man of little worth. Perhaps the title of Lord Penrith had caused a change in him, though Isaac saw that as unlikely. Malcolm Grenfell would always be the same. There was no frivolous woman around, although Emma Hampshire looked to be very friendly with him. Maybe he preferred older women after all, or at least, Emma Hampshire.

Kevin Solomon, Emma's son, was nowhere to be seen, which was not suspicious as he had not known the Grenfells, apart from Montague briefly.

Katrina was very emotional during the service and held onto Isaac's arm. After the funeral Isaac and Wendy intended to do some probing. It would be inappropriate to conduct formal interviews, but a conversation would be fine.

Isaac thought the friendship of Lord Penrith and Emma Hampshire unusual. Their one-night stand many years ago was well known, but now they looked as if they were about to rekindle it.

Wendy needed to know why O'Loughlin's daughter had attended. There had never been any information indicating that Ger O'Loughlin and Albert Grenfell's relationship justified his daughter attending the funeral.

Intrigue within intrigue, Isaac thought. He was certain they had Montague Grenfell's murderer in the bag, apart from the proof to hammer home a confession.

Even Garry Solomon's case was close to conclusion, although the case against the one person now clearly identified thanks to Tom Wellings was inconclusive.

After the ceremony, the mourners moved back to Penrith House, a ten-minute walk or a five-minute drive. Isaac and Katrina chose to walk, Wendy drove. As usual, the weather was cold, and she needed to warm up with the car heater. She imagined that Penrith House would be cold and draughty; enough weekend trips when her sons had been younger to the homes of the aristocracy reminded her of that fact. She had wondered then, with all their titles and their wealth, why they didn't keep themselves warm. Lord Penrith's finances, courtesy of Keith Dawson, had shown that it was horrendously expensive, and although the Grenfells had plenty of money, it was finite.

Isaac surmised with Malcolm Grenfell as the incumbent lord, the move from finite to infinitesimal would not take long.

At the house, everyone was ushered into the main sitting room. A log fire burned at one end. Wendy made straight for it.

Malcolm Grenfell made a speech as to how his brother, a pillar of society, had served the community well and had enhanced the good name of the Penriths. He pledged that he would attempt to live up to his good name. Emma Hampshire stood close by, smiling as he spoke.

The leader of the local council spoke. He thanked the former lord for his generosity in restoring the local library, helping in the cost of repairing the clock tower at the council offices. Others, lords mainly, offered their condolences.

The speeches concluded within ten minutes, and the food and alcohol were brought out. Wendy eyed them with glee. She helped herself to a plate and a glass of wine, a good vintage according to the label.

'I'm surprised to see you here,' she said to Ger O'Loughlin's daughter.

'Why?'

'I was not aware of any contact between your father and Albert Grenfell,' Wendy said.

'You never asked.' Wendy realised that was true. Then, they had been interested in why O'Loughlin had left Mavis Richardson, not in his friendship with the Grenfells.

'They were friendly?'

'They maintained contact, conducted business together. I don't think there was any more to it than that.'

'Did you meet him when he was alive?'

'A few times. My father liked him.'

'Malcolm Grenfell?' Wendy asked.

'Today is the first time that I have met him. He's not what I expected.'

'His reputation was not good.'

'According to my father, he was idle and useless.'

'That was how we knew him, but today...'

'The woman he is with, who is she?' O'Loughlin's daughter asked. 'She's very attractive.'

'Emma Hampshire,' Wendy replied. 'Does the name mean anything to you?'

'No.'

'Emily Solomon?'

'The body in the fireplace?'

'One and the same.'

'My father told me about him just before he died. He told me a lot of things, some I would have preferred not to hear.'

'Why did he do that?'

'He didn't tell my mother, only me. A last-minute confessional, I suppose.'

'You know about the parties?'

'My father was always faithful to my mother. Always available for my sister and me. I could not believe it.'

'It was true,' Wendy said. 'Did he tell you anything else?'

'He told me that his first wife did not want children, whereas he did. It was the reason they broke up, but he was obviously still fond of her.'

'Anything else?'

'Her sister was eccentric, and her son was wild. Garry Solomon, am I correct?'

'That's right.'

'And his wife is standing over there.'

'Yes.'

'There was a reason Garry Solomon never contacted his mother. Do you know what it was?'

'He caught her with another man.'

'When?'

'The day he left.'

'Your father knew this?'

'He was dying. Sometimes he was coherent, at other times he was rambling.'

'This other man, did he have a name?'

'He never mentioned it, but he was talking nonsense by them. He was alert when he told me about Mavis and the parties, but a lot of what he said I couldn't understand.'

Chapter 33

Katrina had gone to talk with the staff at Penrith House. All apart from the gardener had resigned and left. All of them had come back for the funeral.

Isaac had taken the opportunity to talk to Lord Penrith. 'Good ceremony,' Isaac said. 'My condolences.'

'The old boy got a good send-off,' Malcolm Grenfell said.

'You've changed.'

'Still the same rogue underneath.'

'You're more serious. Is that permanent?' Isaac asked, although the person he really wanted to speak to was standing on the other side of the room.

'I hope not.'

'We're holding Montague's body for a few more days,' Isaac said.

'The man has left me seriously short of funds.'

'You can manage?'

'Manage yes, but until probate is dealt with, I cannot access the majority.'

'And the Richardsons?'

'Up to them.'

'Montague had their proxy.'

'Gertrude has a grandson?' Malcolm Grenfell posed a rhetorical question.

Isaac thought the man looked smug.

'You know the answer to the question,' Isaac replied.

'Emma's son. He can deal with the Richardsons' probate.'

'Your relationship with Emma Hampshire?'

'Friends, nothing more.'

'You have a history of friendship with her.'

'It's no secret that we were involved at one time.'

'While she was married to Garry Solomon.'

'He was treating her badly. I was there as a shoulder to cry on.'

'A man to bed.' Isaac waited for the reaction.

Malcolm Grenfell stood still for a moment, his face reddening in anger.

'As you say, a man to bed.' Grenfell kept his emotions in check. He knew that seducing Garry Solomon's wife was a motive. He had come so far; he was not going to destroy it by an inappropriate comment.

I will not let that working-class policeman rile me, Grenfell thought.

Isaac, a glass of wine in his hand, observed the man. It was clear he was holding something back. Before he inherited the title he had been an easy book to read, but now he had changed.

Isaac pondered whether the change was permanent, but as his mother would say, 'a leopard never changes its spots'.

Grenfell was not a changed man, only a man who pretended to change. His elevation to the title had been too swift, too suspicious, for Isaac to discount skulduggery.

In a matter of days, the previous incumbent had died, and his successor had met with an unfortunate accident. Too many coincidences for Isaac, no proof.

Isaac looked down at the floor at Lord Penrith's shoes. He judged them to be size 7. Gordon Windsor had stated that the unknown footprints at the top of Montague Grenfell's stairs had been size 10. *Scratch one murderer*, Isaac thought.

Grenfell left Isaac and started to circulate the room. Isaac had to agree that he played the part of the lord with great skill. Isaac could hear him discussing plans for a new gym at the local youth centre with a large beefy man with a flushed complexion. Isaac knew the look of a leading councillor in the area. No doubt, an estate agent or local lawyer discussing council business, seeing what was in it for him.

'It's good to see you here, Chief Inspector Cook.' Isaac was no longer alone. Emma Hampshire had come over to talk to him.

'I did not expect to see you here,' Isaac said. He had to admit that she was an attractive woman. She wore a dark dress, obviously expensive, for the occasion.

'Why?'

'Did you know Albert Grenfell?'

'I met him once.'

'When?'

'Malcolm introduced me to him in London once.'

'Yet you decided to come to his funeral.'

'He was Malcolm's brother. Besides, Malcolm asked me to come.'

'I was not aware that you were still friendly with him.'

'I told you, or Wendy Gladstone, your sergeant, that we used to see each other from time to time when I was with Bob Hampshire. We moved in the same social circle, nothing more. There is nothing sinister with my being here.'

'Malcolm Grenfell was responsible for your marriage breaking up.'

'The marriage was broken anyway.'

'Did Garry Solomon know about your affair?'

'Probably.'

'You're not sure?'

'Not totally. It was not discussed. He had found himself someone else, and that was it.'

'You were upset?'

'I had grown up to believe that marriage was forever, and my husband was dumping me for a younger version. What do you think?'

'Your plans with Malcolm?'

'I'll wait and see.'

'Does that mean more than you are saying?'

'Not really. I am an affectionate woman. Malcolm for all his faults is a good man.'

'And the other women?'

'He won't need them,' Emma Hampshire said before walking away, a smile on her face. Isaac knew what she meant. He felt the need to see Katrina; he found her with the staff.

'Hi,' he said.

'Very friendly with his lordship's friend,' she said. To Isaac, it sounded as if she was jealous.

'She's a key witness, you know that.'

'I do.'

'And now close in with the new lord,' Isaac said.

'She spent last night here.'

'With Grenfell?'

'Same bed,' Katrina said. Isaac could see no issue with that revelation, and it was clear that Malcolm Grenfell was not his brother's murderer. Salacious gossip in the kitchen did not help to solve the murders. Katrina took Isaac by the arm, first to kiss him, and then to take him back into the main room to enjoy himself.

'Stop being a policeman for once,' she said.

Isaac and Katrina had booked into a local hotel for the night. Both were anxious to be there. Isaac thought about what he and Wendy had achieved by attending the funeral. They had not come up with any new leads, other than the knowledge that Emma Hampshire and Malcolm Grenfell were continuing their affair where it had broken off thirty years previously.

Ger O'Loughlin's relationship with Albert Grenfell had no relevance. Both men had died of old age, and neither were directly implicated in the murder of Garry Solomon or indirectly in the case of Montague Grenfell.

The wake at Penrith House concluded at eight in the evening. Lord Penrith bid all the attendees farewell as they left through the front door and down the steps outside to their cars. Isaac observed Emma Hampshire at his side as if she was already the lady of the house.

Isaac had to admit that he liked her, but for a woman who had come from a lower middle-class background, she had certainly led a charmed life. There had been Garry Solomon who had turned out to be a disappointment. Then there was Bob

Hampshire who had worshipped her, as she had him. And now Malcolm Grenfell who made a good pretence of being a changed man. Isaac wondered how long before Grenfell took a wife.

Back at the hotel, a timeworn building in the village, Wendy along with Isaac and Katrina had a late supper. Wendy enjoyed herself with a spread of cheese and cake. Isaac and Katrina ate sparingly.

At 11 p.m. Isaac and Katrina went upstairs together, arm in arm. Wendy smiled as they climbed the carpeted stairs. *Lucky woman*, Wendy thought.

Wendy realised that she was the same age as Emma Hampshire and that she was lonely. She felt tears in her eyes. She wiped them away with a tissue. It was her first night away from her home since her husband had died, and she did not want to be there in the hotel.

She sobered up with a strong black coffee and returned to London and the bed she had shared with her husband, the bed where her two sons had been conceived.

Isaac knew the next morning that Wendy had left: a message on his phone, a note at the reception. He could only sympathise.

***

At eight in the morning, Isaac and Katrina drove back to London. He dropped her off at the hospital where she worked. Isaac then drove to Challis Street. He was in the office by eleven.

'Sorry about last night, sir,' Wendy said as he entered.

'Nothing to be sorry about,' Isaac's reply.

Bridget came over with a cup of coffee. Isaac thanked her.

Isaac called an impromptu meeting. 'What do we have?' he asked.

'The name of who ordered the grille,' Larry said.

'It doesn't prove that he is the murderer,' Isaac said.

'An accomplice, at least.'

277

'Can we make it stick?'

'Unlikely,' Larry had to admit.

'We could bring him in, put him under pressure.'

'He would bring a smart lawyer with him.'

'If the person who installed the grille and the murderer are one and the same, how do we prove it?' Isaac asked.

'His motive is flimsy,' Larry said.

'Then make it stronger.'

It was evident to everyone in the room that Wendy was not in good spirits. Isaac knew that a heavy workload was the best medicine.

'Wendy,' Isaac said, 'we need to tie up Montague Grenfell's murder.'

'Do we call them in?'

'What has Keith found out?'

Bridget answered. 'He'll be here in five minutes. You can ask him then.'

Five minutes later Dawson entered Isaac's office. There was a better meeting room down the corridor, but everyone preferred Isaac's office as it was homelier. Not because of Isaac's efforts, but Bridget and Wendy, tired of their DCI's Spartan décor, had put a plant in a pot in one corner. Isaac had come to appreciate it, and each day since, he made sure to water it.

The office was full before Keith Dawson entered; it was overflowing on his entry. Larry stood up and squeezed himself into a corner.

'The money taken out of Montague Grenfell's offshore account has been transferred to an offshore bank account in Jersey.'

'Traceable?' Isaac asked.

'Subject to a warrant, yes.'

'Do you have a name for the account?'

'A company name. It doesn't help.'

'Company register?' Larry suggested.

'Offshore company, difficult to trace. Whoever took the money is smart. Not as smart as Montague Grenfell, though.'

'Why do you say that?' Isaac asked.

'The Channel Islands may be an offshore banking haven, but they still come under British law. There will be little difficulty in ascertaining who is drawing on that account.'

'How long do you need?'

'Two hours.'

'Okay,' Isaac said. 'We reconvene at three in the afternoon. Keith, you've got three.'

'Thanks.' Dawson left the office a happy man. For once he was in his element, finding a felon.

Keith worked solidly, making phone calls, sending emails, pulling in favours. Bridget brought him a sandwich for lunch, and Wendy kept him supplied with coffee.

At two in the afternoon, he moved from his seat. 'I've got it,' he said.

***

The first arrest was made at five that afternoon. Wendy and Larry accompanied by a uniform cautioned the person, applied the handcuffs.

At seven in the evening, the interview room at Challis Street was occupied. Isaac took the lead role, with Larry to his left. On the other side sat the accused and her lawyer.

Isaac dealt with the formalities as required. He gave the names of those present, and the fact that the proceedings would be videoed and a transcript would be available at completion.

All parties acknowledged, including the accused's lawyer, an imperious little man who looked as though he was going to be trouble.

'My client has committed no crime.'

'We have good reason to believe that she is an accessory to murder,' Isaac said.

'There is no evidence,' Leonard Smithers said. Larry knew him, did not like him, but he was smart. Larry had forewarned Isaac to be careful with him.

Isaac chose not to reply and turned his focus to the accused. 'Miss Solomon, you have been charged as an accessory to murder. Would you like to comment?'

Deidre Solomon sat quietly across from Isaac. Her record of prostitution was well known, and there had been a few arrests over the years. It was apparent that she had been preparing to visit a client when she had been picked up. Wendy and Larry had made a point after meeting her in Chelsea to find out where she worked, and the haunts she frequented.

'I am not guilty,' she said. Isaac had to admit she was a fine-looking woman. Her skin was clear with the slightest trace of makeup, her hair was lustrous, and the dress she was wearing looked as if it had been moulded onto her.

'You are charged with being an accessory to the murder of Montague Grenfell. We have proof.'

'What proof?' Smithers asked.

'You have been withdrawing substantial amounts of cash from a bank account in the Channel Islands.'

'What has that to do with the murder?' Deidre Solomon asked.

'That account had been dormant for some time with only a small amount of money in it.'

'I would not know that.'

'In recent weeks, you have been transferring to it from another account at least one thousand pounds a day.'

'It was my money.'

'Are you saying that you earn that every day?'

'Yes.'

'Who set up the account?'

'I asked someone to do it for me,' Deidre Solomon said. Leonard Smithers said nothing. His client was handling herself well.

'Who?'

'A friend.'

'Miss Solomon,' Isaac said. 'An offshore account is not easy to open. A friend would not have been able to open it in your name, or that of a company, without the appropriate paperwork. I am putting it to you that your brother opened the account. Is that correct?'

'Daniel is good at organising. I'm not.'

'We are arresting your brother for Montague Grenfell's murder.'

'He did not kill him.'

'Did he tell you this?'

'My client does not need to answer,' Smithers said.

'He would not harm anyone,' Deidre Solomon said, ignoring her legal advice.

'He has a history of violence,' Larry said.

'When he was younger.'

'We have documented proof that you have withdrawn substantial sums of money from this account. We also have proof that the money in that account came from an account that Montague Grenfell used. The evidence is indisputable.'

'I would not know that.'

'Who would?' Isaac asked.

'My client does not need to answer that question.'

This time, Deidre Solomon heeded his advice.

Isaac continued, aiming to break through the woman's defences, aware that as long as she kept mute, there was not a lot to hold her on.

'We have proof that the withdrawals of the money occurred after Montague Grenfell's death.'

'I don't understand.'

'Miss Solomon. Montague Grenfell was killed for a password to an account that you knew about.'

'How?'

'He visited you on a regular basis. A lonely old man in need of company, the need to talk. I am putting it to you that in a moment of weakness, he opened up about his life and ultimately the account.'

'This is pure conjecture,' Smithers said. Isaac ignored him.

281

'Miss Solomon, you became aware of this account, and possibly while the man was asleep, you managed to check his phone and find the account details.'

Deidre Solomon said little, other than to lower her head. 'I did not,' she whispered.

'And once you were in possession, your brother tried to withdraw money. Do you do this with other clients? Get them heady with love and sex and cheap perfume, and then fleece them.'

'This is harassment,' Smithers said.

Isaac was on a roll; he was not about to stop.

'And then when they are vulnerable or asleep, you look for bank accounts on their phones.'

'No. Sometimes,' the woman admitted, almost screaming the truth out.

Isaac moderated his tone, spoke calmly. 'Your brother found out that Montague Grenfell was smarter than most men, and that he needed another password to withdraw money. He visited Grenfell, obtained the password by force, and then hurled the man down the stairs to his death.'

'It did not happen that way.'

'How do you know?'

'Don't answer,' the lawyer said.

'It doesn't matter,' Isaac said. 'We will discuss this later.'

Chapter 34

Daniel Solomon had attempted to run when the two police cars had drawn up outside his office. He had been arrested before Deidre and was down at Challis Street in the holding cells.

Once the interview had been concluded with his sister, and careful to ensure the siblings did not see each other, he was brought up to the same interview room.

'My sister has been here.' Daniel Solomon sniffed the air, smelling her perfume.

Leonard Smithers, his lawyer as well as Deidre's, sat to his right. Isaac thought they had chosen their lawyer poorly. There had been times during the previous interview when Smithers could have advised Deidre Solomon better. Not that it concerned Isaac. He knew he had his man in the interview room and he was not going to let him get off the hook.

Isaac went through the formal procedure, advised the client of his rights and cautioned him.

'Mr Solomon, you have been charged with the murder of Montague Grenfell. Do you wish to make a written confession?' Isaac asked.

'I have killed no one,' Solomon replied. Isaac had assumed that would be the man's initial response.

'We have proof that monies belonging to Montague Grenfell were deposited in an account controlled by you.'

'What account?'

'An account at the HSBC in the Channel Islands.'

'I don't have an account there,' Solomon said.

'The bank maintains a copy of all applications. Your name and your signature will be there. Do you deny that you have an account in the Channel Islands?' Isaac's voice had risen in volume for emphasis.

'I have a lot of bank accounts.'

'Your sister had the ability to withdraw funds from one of those accounts.'

'What account?'

'The account where you deposited monies obtained fraudulently from Montague Grenfell.'

'I did not.'

'Where did your sister get the money from?'

'You'd better ask her.'

'We have.'

'My client has no more to say,' Smithers said.

'This is a murder enquiry. Mr Solomon doesn't get off that lightly.'

'Mr Solomon, your sister obtained the details of an account that Montague Grenfell had stored on his phone. She gave them to you. You attempted to withdraw money. When you realised that the account needed another password, you visited Grenfell and threatened him.'

'This is all lies.'

'We will conduct checks with other clients of your sister. This may be a scam that you have perpetrated on other men.'

'I deny all of this. This is a fabrication, attempting to make me give you a false confession.'

'Your sister screws them, and then you take their money. What do you do? Wait outside the door while she exhausts them, or do you watch? Maybe you are a pervert who enjoys watching his sister screw other men, or maybe you are jealous because it is them and not you? Have you screwed your sister, Mr Solomon?' Isaac knew he had overstepped the mark, but he wanted the man angry, as angry as hell.

Daniel Solomon was up on his feet and around to Isaac's side of the desk. Two uniforms came in and restrained him.

'After watching your sister screw Grenfell, you make a plan. You visit his office and use violence to threaten him. He resists, you grab him. You force him outside of his office. Cornered, the man gives you the password. Montague Grenfell is a smart man; he knows he can change the password once you are gone.

'You know he's correct, and if he lives you will be charged with grievous bodily harm, and you will go to prison. The money can only be yours if you avoid prison and Grenfell doesn't change the password.'

'This is harassment,' Smithers bellows.

'This is murder,' Isaac answers. 'And Daniel Solomon is guilty.'

'It was an accident. I swear it,' Solomon relaxed and started to sob. 'He fell, that's the truth.'

'Too convenient,' Isaac said. 'If he had not died, you would have killed him anyway. You had no option. It was fortunate that the fall killed him. The murder charge sticks.'

'I did not mean to kill him.'

'Okay. Montague Grenfell's death was not premeditated, but he still died. I want your confession.'

'I will not admit to murder.'

'Then admit to the rest. A judge and jury will decide at your trial as to the truth.'

'You were tough in there, Isaac,' Larry said after Solomon had been remanded pending trial.

'He'll still get off with manslaughter.'

'Deidre?'

'Accessory to manslaughter, fraud. A few years in jail, no more. Ask Wendy to visit their mother and let her know.'

***

The mood in Challis Street changed after the arrests had been made for the death of Montague Grenfell. DCS Goddard had visited the office to thank the team.

Garry Solomon's murder still remained on the books, but the team were confident they had their man, although there seemed to be no logic to it.

The man responsible for installing the grille at Bellevue Street had been identified by Tom Wellings, but there was no tie-in to the body in the fireplace. It was not believed that they had known each other, and it had been a few years since the man's last visit to Bellevue Street.

Due to the man's age, Larry phoned a friend of his at a police station closer to the man's home. A police car, no markings, transported him to the station.

Isaac and Larry followed the same procedure as they had with Daniel and Deidre Solomon.

'Mr Sullivan, we are aware that you installed a metal grille on a door at 54 Bellevue Street, Holland Park in 1987.' Isaac asked.

'After thirty years, do you expect me to remember?'

Isaac could only see a kindly old man who had shaken his hand with no sign of malice. 'What's this all about?' he had asked. 'Always happy to help the police.'

Isaac had to remind himself that thirty years previously, George Sullivan would have been a man in his early fifties, and probably fit and strong. His story and the problem with Mavis Richardson were well known, but that was some time before Garry Solomon had been murdered.

'I appreciate that it may be difficult, but it is important.'

'Assuming it is, what does it mean?'

'The grille isolated Garry Solomon's body from the rest of the house.'

'Gertrude's son,' Sullivan said.

'You were at Albert Grenfell's funeral,' Isaac said.

'As were you, Chief Inspector. And very friendly with Albert's nurse.'

Isaac could see that a forceful interview would serve no purpose. He still struggled to believe that George Sullivan had murdered Garry Solomon. No connection had been found between the two men.

'Let us assume that you installed the grille,' Isaac said. He leant back on his chair to appear less intimidating. George Sullivan had declined his right to legal representation.

'If that is what you want.'

'We are aware that you attended one of their parties.'

'I was younger. Not much use to me now.'

'Would you have installed the grille on someone else's behalf?'

'It's possible.'

'For who?'

'I am not at liberty to say. Your sergeant told you that I was with Army Intelligence?'

'Yes, and so was Albert Grenfell,' Isaac said.

'And he's dead.'

'Did he ask you?'

'It's possible, but I do not know why.'

'Were you in the habit of helping him?'

'Ex-Army Intelligence. Yes, we looked after our own. It was the time of the Cold War, still top secret. I told your sergeant that I was a pen-pusher, not a field operative. Unfortunately, it was a lie on my part. We risked our lives to help each other. Albert saved mine once. If Albert wanted something, he could rely on me.'

'And you could rely on him?' Isaac asked.

'Totally. People today do not understand the concept. They have never experienced war, being behind the enemy line, death only one bullet away.'

'Is that what you and Albert were involved with?'

'It's still classified, although I don't know why after so many years.'

***

Isaac saw no reason to hold George Sullivan any longer. The man was too old to stand trial, and there was no case against him. A metal grille on a door leading to a room with a body was not an admission of guilt, although Albert Grenfell's friendship with Sullivan might be.

Protecting the family name at all costs had been mentioned by Mavis Richardson in the past. *Would that include covering up a murder as well?* Isaac thought.

Once back at the office, he surfed the internet hoping to understand what it all meant. Five hundred years, even more recently, maintaining the family name allowed a multitude of sins, but this was the twenty-first century. Surely such behaviour would not be condoned today.

The day was drawing to a close, and he took the opportunity of an early night. He had planned to meet up with Katrina and to go out to a restaurant near Tower Bridge. There was a sense of relief in Homicide now that the Solomons were in custody.

Wendy had visited their mother. She was visibly distraught, but not surprised. She still loved them as the children she had given birth to, but according to her, they had both turned out bad, just like their father. Wendy had phoned social services to ease the burden on the woman caused by the babies. She also made an appointment to take the woman to see the doctor. She would pick her up, wait for her, and take her back. Mary Solomon appeared to have no friends, no relatives, and now no children.

Wendy knew that although life had taken a turn for the worse for her, she still had two loving sons, a friend in Bridget, and colleagues she admired and cherished. Sadness for Mary Solomon's life was temporarily replaced by contentment with hers.

Larry had an appointment with a paint brush. His wife had finally got him on home renovations, and an early break from work meant only one thing to him: purgatory.

Bridget and Keith stayed back late in the office.

***

With the most recent murder resolved, apart from the paperwork involved and the subsequent trial, the intensity of the Murder Investigation Team lessened. As DCS Goddard had said on one of his visits, 'It's a great result. Everyone should be proud of themselves.'

Wendy had taken the opportunity to have a couple of days off, as had Larry. Bridget stayed in the office as the paperwork showed no sign of abating. The prosecution case files still needed completing, and besides, the office was more agreeable than her home.

She had kicked out the malingering lover, but she missed him. He may have had his faults, but he had been there when she had arrived home at the end of the day. Now all she had was a cold house and four walls to look at, apart from the television in the corner.

Isaac continued as usual, his workload supplanted by assisting on another case. Katrina Smith was still very much in his life, but the intensity of the relationship was starting to wither, as he always knew it would. That was how his life operated, and whereas he wished Katrina well, he could see it as only a matter of time.

Keith Dawson continued to work through Montague Grenfell's records. Isaac had to admit that he had done a good job, and even though he lacked the natural camaraderie of the other people in his team, he still fitted in well. Larry's opinion of the man had changed after Dawson had even paid for a round of drinks one Friday night.

It was three weeks after the arrest of Daniel and Deidre Solomon when the department came back together. Events had moved on, and the murder of Garry Solomon had taken precedence again.

After thirty years, it would have been possible to put it to one side and declare it as unsolved. As Isaac said to the team, 'If we had arrested the murderer then, he would by now have been released from jail.'

Finding a killer after so long seemed like finding a needle in a haystack, but it had been Keith who had found it, hidden deep inside a file on Montague Grenfell's laptop. Bridget had checked, found it to be correct. It was damning evidence, and its repercussions could still be felt today after thirty years. It was a clear motive.

Katrina had told Isaac two days earlier that Malcolm Grenfell had married Emma Hampshire in a registry office in

Leicestershire. Her son, Kevin, had given her away. Katrina thought that Malcolm Grenfell had changed; Isaac was not sure.

Nuptials aside, Isaac knew that he needed to question the bride and groom again. He made plans to drive up to see them, but first he needed to interview George Sullivan again.

***

It was Wendy who picked up George Sullivan from his house. It had only been three weeks since she had last seen him, but his health had deteriorated.

Not long now, Wendy thought.

George Sullivan was as always polite and amenable, although he needed Wendy's assistance into the police car.

Interview Room A at his nearest police station. Isaac was already there.

'Mr Sullivan, thank you for coming.'

'Always willing to help the police.'

Isaac went through the cautioning process, informed him of his rights. Sullivan waved them away. Isaac continued to a conclusion. It was always difficult interviewing old people, and whether Sullivan was guilty of any crime or not, it was clear that the man would not stand up in any court in front of a judge.

'We need to go over why you installed the grille on Albert Grenfell's behalf,' Isaac asked.

'It was a favour. Albert asked me.'

'He could have dealt with it.'

'Dealing with tradesmen? Not Albert's style.'

'Beneath him?' Wendy asked. She was sitting to the left of Isaac.

'If he could avoid it. I told you before that Albert was a terrible snob. Admirable in many ways, but he saw himself as above the common man. It may be an outdated attitude, but he was firm in his beliefs.'

'But you are not from his class,' Isaac said.

'The son of a butcher, and not even a gentleman's butcher.'

'Then why the friendship?' Isaac asked.

'Please. I am an old man.'

'I'm sorry, but we owe it to Garry Solomon to solve his murder.'

'I suppose so.'

Wendy organised some tea to be brought in. She also took the opportunity to ask Isaac to ease his interrogating style.

'The friendship?' Isaac asked. His manner was less forthright.

'Albert was behind enemy lines. The Stasi, the East German secret police, had captured him and were holding him on the outskirts of East Berlin. I went in and rescued him.'

'Dangerous?' Wendy asked.

'I killed two men to get him out. We were both lucky to get out alive.'

Isaac had to admire the man, even if his involvement with the death of Garry Solomon was suspected.

'You said before that you installed the grille as a favour.'

'Yes.'

'If you had known that it was being installed to cover up a criminal act?'

'If Albert Grenfell had told me, I would have still installed the grille.'

'And been an accessory to murder?'

'You both belong to a different generation,' Sullivan said. 'Albert and I had a long history. What we did all those years ago formed a bond that cannot be broken. Whether Albert knew what was in that room or not, is not important to me. I did my duty, as he would have done for me.'

'Including murder?'

'We killed in Germany, although it was called political assassination. Over there we received medals for our actions, not prison cells.'

'Let me get this clear,' Isaac said. 'You installed the grille, but you had no part in the placement of the body in the fireplace or his murder.'

'That is correct. My conscience is clear. I did my duty, and God will be my judge.'

'Thank you, Mr Sullivan. There are no more questions.'

Isaac concluded the interview. Wendy organised a policewoman to take George Sullivan home.

'What do you think?' Wendy asked Isaac outside the police station as they prepared to drive back to Challis Street.

'Albert could have killed Solomon. He had the motive.'

'How do we prove it?'

'We can't. The truth, if he knows it, lies with Sullivan.'

'Do you intend to question him again?' Wendy asked.

'No. That is the last time we will see George Sullivan,' Isaac said. 'As long as he denies any involvement in the murder, there is nothing we can do.'

Chapter 35

Isaac made the trip up to Penrith House to meet Lord and Lady Penrith. He took Wendy with him. They were met at the front entrance to the house by Lady Penrith.

'Pleased to see you,' the former Emma Hampshire said.

'It came as a surprise,' Isaac said. He had to admit she looked resplendent. Around her neck she wore an emerald necklace.

'Family heirloom,' she said, after noticing Wendy admiring it.

'I did not see his lordship as the marrying kind,' Isaac said.

'Neither did I,' Lady Penrith said.

'Then why?'

'We are both older, and neither of us wants to be on their own.'

'Malcolm Grenfell was never on his own,' Isaac said, unsure of her Ladyship's reaction.

'The women who kept him entertained were there for a good time, not him. He will never have reason to doubt my motives.'

'What are your motives?'

'To be with Malcolm, of course.'

'And the title?'

'I appreciate it, but it is not the prime motivation.'

'In the thirty years since you first slept with Malcolm Grenfell, were you ever unfaithful to Bob Hampshire?' Wendy asked.

'No. I loved Bob.'

'And Malcolm?'

'I loved him as well.'

'Complicated.'

'I don't see why. It is possible to love more than one person, difficult to live with them both. I chose Bob because he was reliable and able to provide for Kevin. Malcolm was Malcolm, and he was not reliable or the father figure that I wanted. Malcolm always knew that. We both knew that one day we would be together.'

'We need to talk to you separately,' Isaac said.

'Malcolm is waiting for you.'

***

Isaac and Wendy were ushered into a room at the back of the house.

'It used to be the smoking room. In the past, the men would retire here to smoke cigars and talk about business. The women would stay in the other room discussing needlecraft,' Lord Penrith said. He stood erect and was wearing a suit.

'Thank you for seeing us, your Lordship?' Isaac did not know why he had respected the man's title. Grenfell had self-indulgently wasted his life, yet now he looked worthy of the title; almost too good to be true.

'It's Emma. She's changed me.'

'She told us that you and she always had a belief that you would be together one day.'

'More hope, although I don't regret my past life. It was full of fun and no responsibility. Now I am involved in God knows how many charities. They even want me to judge the best vegetable of the year at the local agricultural show.'

'What do you know about vegetables?' Wendy asked.

'Not a lot. What do you want, by the way?' Lord Penrith asked. 'You've arrested the people who killed Montague.'

'We have reason to believe that Albert murdered Garry Solomon,' Isaac said.

'Preposterous. Poor old Albert wouldn't hurt a fly,' Penrith said.

'Are you aware of his time in the army?'

'Pushing a pen for Queen and country.'

'He never told you?'

'He was older than me. We had different mothers. Our conversations were few and far between.'

'Your brother was not in an office. He was undercover.'

'A spy?'

'Yes.'

'Are you saying that Albert was behind enemy lines, spying?'

'Our source is good.'

Malcolm Grenfell sat down and let out a sigh. 'Albert, a regular James Bond, licensed to kill.'

'That is correct.'

'Hard to imagine Albert with a bevy of women.'

'I don't believe that is the reality, do you?' Isaac said.

'Not really, but I have to give him credit. All those years pretending to be a stuffy aristocrat, and there he was with a story worth telling. And you believe he killed Garry?'

'Our evidence points to that conclusion.'

'Are you saying that because he killed in the army, he could have killed Garry?'

'Yes.'

'Murder! What is so significant that would justify that course of action? Unless it was maintaining the family name.'

***

Isaac could not fault Malcolm Grenfell. His brother Albert had been in his twenties when he had been born, so it was very possible that there was little communication between the two men.

Emma Hampshire's reason for marrying Malcolm Grenfell appeared relevant. Isaac and Wendy found her in a conservatory at the back of the house.

'We have reason to believe that your first husband was murdered by Albert Grenfell,' Isaac said. He waited to see the reaction.

'My brother-in-law, Malcolm's brother?'
'Yes.'
'Can you prove it?' Lady Penrith asked.
'The witnesses are all dead, as is the accused,' Isaac replied.
'And the motive?'
'I am not at liberty to discuss that.'
'Why not? Is it a big secret?'
'It may become relevant at a later date.'
Isaac thought that the former Emma Hampshire was on edge.
Wendy had questions of a more personal nature.
'Why did you marry so quickly?' she asked.
Lady Penrith took one step back, unsure of what to say. 'I told you before that I loved him.'
'You have been able to marry him since Bob Hampshire died,' Isaac reminded her.
'I was not ready.'
'Not ready or was it because Malcolm Grenfell had no money and no title.'
'That's an outrageous statement, Chief Inspector.' Isaac had his reaction. He had the measure of the woman.
'I put it to you that you were glad to be rid of Garry Solomon because he had no money. And then Bob Hampshire comes along.'
'You are accusing me of prostituting myself to the nearest rich man.' Lady Penrith was on her feet and shouting.
'And as long as Bob Hampshire kept you and your son in luxury, you stayed with him. Did you sleep with Malcolm Grenfell while you were with Bob Hampshire?'
'How dare you accuse me of this. I was faithful to Bob.'
'And once he died, did you resume your relationship with your current husband?'
'No, yes, sometimes.'
'What's the answer?' Isaac persisted.
Wendy looked at Isaac, uncertain where he was heading.
'We sometimes went away together for a few days.'

'While he was seducing young women?'

'Yes.'

'Did you agree with his behaviour?'

'I was not willing to marry him until he stopped.'

'Are you saying that you did not marry him for his title?'

'Yes.'

'But you were sleeping with him before. Why?'

'I'm a woman. I need a man in my bed.'

'Lady Penrith, did you know that Albert Grenfell had murdered your husband?'

'No, why would I? What was there for me to gain?'

'Protection for Malcolm Grenfell.'

'Protection from what?' Lady Penrith asked. Isaac declined to answer.

***

'You were rough on Lady Penrith,' Wendy said on the drive back to London.

'I'll apologise later,' Isaac said as he focussed on the road ahead.

'What did you hope to find out?' Wendy liked Emma Hampshire. The woman had been through a lot, and now she sat in the stately home with a title. Wendy had noticed the female touch in the house. In the hallway, there were flowers, as in the other rooms. The curtains had been flung open, the light streaming in. Upon their arrival, Wendy had noticed a van belonging to a company of professional cleaners, although not Daniel Solomon's, as the doors to his business had closed after his arrest for murder.

'I wanted her to be angry and confused. Only then would I know the truth.'

'Do you?'

'Yes.'

'What do you know?'

'Emma Hampshire is not guilty of any crime.'

Upon their return to Challis Street, Isaac called the team together, even though it was late. 'Keith, what do you have?'

'A scanned copy on Montague's Grenfell's laptop. There was a password that I had to crack first.'

'Genuine?'

'I've checked, sir,' Bridget said.

'There's only one issue,' Larry said. He was glad of the late night, a chance to get away from home renovations.

'What's that?'

'Albert Grenfell could not have murdered Garry Solomon.'

'What?' Isaac was sure they had their man, even if they could not prove it.

'He was out of the country for two months during that period.'

'Proven?'

'Conclusively.'

'George Sullivan as a favour to Albert Grenfell?' Wendy asked.

'He was not in the country either.'

'Montague?'

'It's possible,' Larry said.

Isaac, unsure how to proceed, phoned DCS Goddard. 'We are at a dead end.'

'What do you mean?'

'We can prove that Albert Grenfell did not murder Garry Solomon.'

'Other suspects?'

'Montague Grenfell, but it's not provable. And besides, he's dead.'

'What do you want to do? Shelve the investigation?'

'Not yet, sir.'

'One week maximum,' DCS Goddard said.

Isaac could see only one approach. He needed to take all those involved and push them to the limit.

Wendy would go and talk to George Sullivan, although the man was too old for intense questioning, and he would probably say very little.

Larry could talk to Kevin Solomon, now the stepson of Malcolm Grenfell, Lord Penrith.

Isaac knew that Malcolm Grenfell had been obtuse with him. This time his interview would be formal and direct. He hoped the man had good legal representation, as his legal rights were going to be severely challenged.

***

Larry found Kevin Solomon at his flat in Hampstead. The man was in a good mood and invited him in.

'Coffee?' Solomon asked.

'Yes please.'

'I assume your visit is not purely social.'

'Your mother married Lord Penrith.'

'Why not?'

'You have no problems with it?'

'Why should I? She is still young, and Malcolm is, at least, good fun. Bob Hampshire was a good man, but he was not always the most entertaining.'

'You knew Malcolm Grenfell from before?'

'He was a friend of Bob's, and my mother knew him.'

'You were aware of their past relationship?'

'I believe I told you that already.'

***

Wendy met George Sullivan. They sat in the front room of his house. His wife continued to fuss, always bringing drinks and snacks. Wendy asked if they could have fifteen minutes without interruption. Victoria Sullivan acquiesced.

'Albert Grenfell did not murder Garry Solomon,' Wendy said.

'I never thought he did,' Sullivan said.

'Why?'

'Albert was a man of honour. Killing for your country, protecting the good name of the family is honourable, but murdering a civilian for no good reason made no sense.'

'There is a motive,' Wendy said.

'Sufficient to murder?'

'Yes.'

'Even so, I cannot think badly of Albert.'

Wendy phoned Isaac. 'George Sullivan can tell us nothing more. Albert Grenfell asked him to install the grille, that is all.'

Larry updated Isaac. 'No more to tell. The trail has run cold.'

'No, it hasn't,' Isaac said. 'All three of us are going to Penrith House.'

***

Lord and Lady Penrith were not pleased to see Isaac and his team. Kevin Solomon was there, as were several prominent locals.

'This is an intrusion, Chief Inspector,' Lord Penrith said. Isaac had ensured a marked police car was outside with two uniformed officers. Isaac realised he was taking a risk here, but he could see no alternative. The only hope for a resolution to the murder of Garry Solomon lay with Lord Penrith. Lady Penrith echoed her husband's criticism.

Isaac chose to ignore them both. 'This is a murder enquiry, and I intend to resolve it today. Lord Penrith, if you will please accompany me into the other room.'

'This is my house. How dare you order me around.'

'It's either here or down the station. I have two officers outside. Any obstruction on your part and I will have you in handcuffs. Do you understand?' Isaac knew if he were wrong, his DCS would not be able to protect him.

'Emma, make my apologies to the others. Tell them we will meet again tomorrow,' Penrith said. 'Chief Inspector, I have no option.'

'Correct.'

A dining room table was in the centre of the room: Larry and Isaac on one side, Lord Penrith on the other. Isaac gave the customary caution. Penrith asked for Kevin Solomon to be present. 'He's had some legal training.'

'You murdered Garry Solomon,' Isaac directed his gaze at Malcolm Grenfell.

Emma Hampshire, who had been listening at the door, burst in. 'How dare you accuse my husband,' she said.

Wendy followed soon after. 'I couldn't stop her.'

'Very well,' Isaac said. 'Lady Penrith, you can stay, as long as I have your word that you will not interrupt. Otherwise, we will reconvene at the local police station.'

'Malcolm Grenfell, I put it to you again. You murdered Garry Solomon,' Isaac said.

Lady Penrith rose from her chair, her face ablaze with anger. Wendy took a firm hold of her and sat her down. 'You must remain calm,' she said.

'Why would I do that?' Lord Penrith replied.

'Because he came between you and the title.'

Penrith let out a nervous laugh. 'Thirty years ago, are you joking? Do you think I was interested in the title of Lord Penrith? I had two older brothers and my chance of ever claiming the title was remote. And why? What has Garry Solomon got to do with my title?'

'We have found proof that Archibald Grenfell, your grandfather, was married two times, not one as previously thought.'

'Rubbish,' Penrith said.

'He was married to your grandmother, as well as the mother of Frederick Richardson, the father of Gertrude and Mavis. Frederick Richardson was legitimate, and as such, had a claim on the title.'

'What proof?'

'I am putting it to you that you murdered Garry Solomon to hide the truth. To conceal the fact that Garry Solomon may have had a claim on this house, and possibly the title.'

'Even if that was true, he was younger than me.'

'He threatened you. Told you that he would ensure you never gained the title. Both Albert and Montague were in their fifties, so they were unlikely to have any male heirs. The title was yours if you waited long enough, and suddenly there was another person who could threaten your succession.'

'Is this true, Malcolm?' Emma Hampshire screamed.

'It's rubbish. He can't prove a word of it.'

'Garry Solomon was involved with ruthless men. He could have had you killed and then waited for Albert and Montague to die. Even assisted their deaths as well. The title may be contentious, but the Grenfell wealth never was. As the oldest surviving male relative he would have had a clear right to it.'

'He suspected the truth, but he never had any proof.'

'Suspected what? That your grandfather had married a maid, Bronwyn Richardson. That is why Frederick, Gertrude and Mavis's father, was given the surname of Richardson. To hide the truth, the shame that Archibald Grenfell had married for love, and outside of his class.'

'Albert told me.'

'Bronwyn Richardson?' Isaac asked.

'She died in childbirth. Albert knew the full story.'

'Why did Albert tell you?'

'We had an argument. I told him that I wanted to marry Emma, or Emily as she was known then. He said I could not.'

'Why?'

'Bad form taking the wife of a relative. That was Albert, always worried about the family name, even when nobody knew.'

'Is that when you decided to murder your wife's first husband?'

Kevin Solomon and Lady Penrith sat mute, unable to comprehend.

'Why would I kill Garry and then hide his body where it might be found?'

'There are two motives for the death of Garry Solomon,' Isaac continued. 'The first is so you would be able to claim Emily for yourself, but I am not sure that is the most important reason.'

'Why?' Lady Penrith asked.

'He wanted you, that is clear,' Isaac said, 'but why did he hide the body?'

'You have an answer?' Lord Penrith said, almost sneeringly.

'You killed Garry Solomon and placed him in the fireplace. You concealed the fireplace and admitted it to Albert.'

'Why would I tell Albert?'

'You needed him to protect you. If your plan went wrong and the body was found, the blame would have come back to you. Albert was crucial. You knew that Albert would not allow the good name of Grenfell and the title of Lord Penrith to be sullied by something as common as murder, especially one committed by his half-brother.'

'It's a good story, but there is no substance,' Penrith said.

'George Sullivan installed the grille at Bellevue Street, oblivious to what was inside the room. He even admitted that if he had known, he would still have installed the grille based on the bond between him and Albert.'

'You're talking in riddles, Chief Inspector.'

'You knew that in time it would be found. You planned for such an eventuality.'

'But why?'

'You did not think it would be thirty years, maybe just a few. You were aware that after Mavis Richardson found her husband in bed with Gertrude, there was a plan to sell the house. Montague Grenfell had documents attesting to the fact.'

'Why didn't they sell it?' Penrith asked.

'Montague talked them out of it.'

'Why?'

'I believe you said it yourself. Montague knew everything. He was aware of what you had done and what was in the fireplace. Albert had told him.'

'Then why after thirty years did he agree to sell it?'

'Montague had been fiddling the books. We found proof of it, and it cost him his life. The cash was running short. He must have thought that after thirty years nothing would have remained in the fireplace. He had discounted the accumulated coal dust and pigeon droppings, and they had mummified the remains.'

'If the body had been found sooner?' Penrith asked.

'There was proof of George Sullivan installing the grille, and his relationship with your brother was well known. The blame for the murder would have pointed to Albert.'

'There was no proof.'

'Montague knew that if Albert was in jail, even condemned to hang, he could still lay claim to the title and the wealth. You had confided in him, knowing full well that he would be complicit. Documents from Garry Solomon to Albert threatening to reveal the fact that his grandfather should have been entitled to the title were with Montague. At the appropriate time, Montague would have ensured that they were found in Albert's possession. The motive was there, George Sullivan was there, and Albert's military expertise in assassination would have been revealed.'

'None of this connects back to me, it is unprovable,' Lord Penrith said.

'We have found this much. We will find more. Malcolm Grenfell, Lord Penrith, you will be going to jail for the murder of Garry Solomon. It is only a matter of time. I do not believe that you will enjoy the time until your formal arrest. You have murdered your wife's first husband and the father of your legal representative. I do not believe they will be here for very long.'

Wendy consoled Emma Hampshire who was in tears. Kevin Solomon moved away from Lord Penrith and over to his mother.

'Very clever, Chief Inspector. Garry's attempt at blackmail was amateurish. He had stumbled on the truth, and he was threatening Albert,' Penrith said.

'Are you saying Albert killed him?'

'He had no problems when Garry died.'

'You killed him?'

Malcolm Grenfell looked over at his wife. 'I did it for you, only you. Why do you think I never married?'

Lady Penrith stared at him blankly.

'Please excuse me,' Lord Penrith said. He walked over to a desk in the corner of the room and pulled open a drawer. He took out a loaded gun, Albert's old gun. He pointed it at his temple and pulled the trigger.

The End

ALSO BY THE AUTHOR

Murder is a Tricky Business – A DCI Cook Thriller

A television actress is missing, and DCI Isaac Cook, the Senior Investigation Officer of the Murder Investigation Team at Challis Street Police Station in London, is searching for her.

Why has he been taken away from more important crimes to search for the woman? It's not the first time she's gone missing, and why does everyone assume she's been murdered?

There's a secret, that much is certain, but who knows? The missing woman? The executive producer, his eavesdropping assistant? Or the actor who portrayed her fictional brother on the Soap Opera?

Murder Without Reason – A DCI Cook Thriller

DCI Cook, now a Senior Member of London's Anti-Terrorism Command, faces his Greatest Challenge. The Islamic State is waging war in England, and they are winning.

Not only does Isaac Cook have to contend with finding the perpetrators, but he is being forced to commit to actions contrary to his mandate as a police officer.

And then, there is Anne Argento, the Prime Minister's Deputy. The man has proven himself to be a pacifist and is not up to the task. She needs to take his job if the country is to fight back against the Islamists.

Vane and Martin have provided the solution. Will DCI Cook and Anne Argento be willing to follow through? Are they able to act for the good of England, knowing that a criminal and murderous activity is about to take place? Do they have any option?

Hostage of Islam

Kate McDonald's fate hangs in the balance. The Slave Trader has the money for her, so does her father and he wants her back. Can Steve Case's team rescue her and her friend, Helen in time?

Three Americans are to die at the Baptist Mission in Nigeria - the Pastor and his wife in a blazing chapel. Another, gunned down while trying to defend them from the Islamists.

Kate is offered to a slave trader who intends to sell her virginity to an Arab Prince. Helen, to ensure their survival, gives herself to the leader of the raid at the mission and the murderer of her friends.

The Haberman Virus

A remote and isolated village in the Hindu Kush mountain range in North Eastern Afghanistan is wiped out by a virus unlike any seen before.

A mysterious visitor checks his handiwork clad in a space suit, and American female doctor succumbs to the disease, and the woman sent to trap the person responsible, falls in love with the man who would be responsible for the death of millions.

Malika's Revenge

Malika, a drug-addicted prostitute waits in a smugglers' village for the next Afghan tribesman or Tajik gangster to pay her price, a few scraps of heroin.

Yusup Baroyev, a drug lord enjoys a lifestyle many would envy. An Afghan warlord sees the resurgence of the Taliban. A Russian white-collar criminal portrays himself as a good and honest citizen in Moscow.

They are entwined in an audacious plan to raise the quantity of heroin shipped out of Afghanistan and into Russia and ultimately the West.

Some will succeed, some will die, some will be resurrected from their plight and others will rue the day they became involved.

ABOUT THE AUTHOR

Phillip Strang was born in the late forties, the post-war baby boom in England; his childhood years, a comfortable middle-class upbringing in a small town to the west of London.

His childhood and the formative years were a time of innocence. Relatively few rules, and as a teenager, complete mobility, due to a bicycle – a three-speed Raleigh – and a more trusting community. It was the days before mobile phones, the internet, terrorism and wanton violence. An avid reader of Science Fiction in his teenage years: Isaac Asimov, Frank Herbert, the masters of the genre. How many of what they and others mentioned have now become reality? Science Fiction has now become Science Fact. Still an avid reader, the author now mainly reads thrillers.

In his early twenties, the author, with a degree in electronics engineering, and an unabated wanderlust to see the world left the cold and damp climes of England for Sydney, Australia – the first semi-circulation of the globe, complete. Now, forty years later, he still resides in Australia, although many intervening years spent in a myriad of countries, some calm and safe – others, no more than war zones.

Printed in Great Britain
by Amazon